To Donna,
with love
and appreciation,
Bonnie Dodge

WAITING

BY
BONNIE DODGE

Booktrope Editions
Seattle WA 2014

Cover Design by Greg Simanson

Edited by Ally Bishop

This is a work of fiction. Names, characters, places, brands, media, and incidents are either the product of the author's imagination or are used fictitiously. Any resemblance to similarly named places or to persons living or deceased is unintentional.

Print ISBN 978-1-62015-500-4

EPUB ISBN 978-1-62015-516-5

DISCOUNTS OR CUSTOMIZED EDITIONS MAY BE AVAILABLE FOR EDUCATIONAL AND OTHER GROUPS BASED ON BULK PURCHASE.

For further information please contact info@booktrope.com

Library of Congress Control Number: 2014912584

"WE MUST BE WILLING TO GET RID OF THE LIFE WE PLANNED,
SO AS TO HAVE THE LIFE THAT IS WAITING FOR US."

— *JOSEPH CAMPBELL*

for Loretta, and everyone who ever asked,
"What am I waiting for?"

CHAPTER ONE

RESIDENTS OF ASPEN GROVE don't talk about the unrest they experience each November as they watch snowflakes accumulate, marking time until there is enough snow for the local ski resort to open. They don't discuss the discontent they encounter each Idaho spring as they wait for the cherry trees to bud and the daffodils to bloom. They've grown up with this sense of unrest. Something in the water, retired postman Mr. Peters said one day, grumbling about how annoyed he was waiting for his grass to turn green. Like birds fluffing feathers against the frigid winter breeze, it's a feeling every resident of Aspen Grove acknowledges whenever the sun shines, or the wind turns the leaves of the trees into shimmering, silver medallions.

It's a feeling Maxine Foster gets every morning as she drags out of bed to fix Herb's lunch, a lunch she knows he'll throw away because he's done that for at least three years now, ever since he took that job at Andy's Auto Supply. She knows this because Herb's favorites—steak sandwiches and chocolate cake—that she used to pack for him dwindled to leftover lasagna or tomato soup and other foods Herb hated. If he *had* been eating his lunch, he would have complained that the food she packed wasn't fit for a pig.

Instead, he often came home whistling that irritating tune he had developed over the last year, which meant he was headed to the kitchen where he would drop his lunchbox, open the refrigerator and down a can of beer before even saying hello. By the time he flopped on the sofa and flipped the TV channel away from Maxine's favorite show "Jeopardy!" to the local news he never watched let alone listened to, he'd be well into his second beer.

Each morning Maxine yelled, "Eat your lunch," as Herb slid into his red Ford Ranger and backed out of the driveway headed for work.

"At least feed it to Andy's cat," Maxine mumbled as she watched him turn the corner. "You don't make enough money to throw away good food."

Truth was they didn't have much of anything to throw away. Herb was their primary source of income. When he worked. Just last year, three weeks before Maxine turned sixty-two, they'd had a lengthy discussion about money. She had planned to file for Social Security until she discovered she didn't have enough credits. Sure, she made a few bucks cleaning houses for a couple of doctors' wives, but that wasn't a *real job* with deductions and benefits. If she was going to draw Social Security, she needed a real job and who would hire her now, an old woman with osteoporosis and arthritis in her hips? Besides, she knew the minute she had a steady paycheck, Herb would quit his job, stay home and drink all day. Sure as summer, she would come home tired to find him passed out in front of the television. She knew this because that was how he spent Saturdays and Sundays. Instead of fixing the fence or mowing the lawn, every weekend Herb drank himself into a stupor.

With a weary sigh, Maxine turned from the window and launched into her morning ritual. Every day before she started her chores, she opened the old Zenith cabinet and flicked the record player lever. While she tidied the kitchen and dusted the living room, she'd croon along with Elvis and wish that she were sixteen again and still dating Larry Fisher.

When she was in high school, Larry lived down the street from Maxine. He couldn't carry a tune, but every day after school, he would carry her books like boys used to do. When he tipped his head and crooked his eyebrow, he looked just like Elvis Presley. At sixteen, Maxine had fallen in love with Larry. Hard. She would have married him, too, if he hadn't gone and gotten himself killed.

"Ah, Larry." Maxine blotted the tears in her eyes. She turned the record over, flipped the lever and sang, "I will love you longer than for eh-everrrrr."

If dusting wasn't bad enough, singing along with Elvis and dreaming of Larry put Maxine in an awful mood. By ten o'clock she was too depressed to clean her own home. She turned off the record, filled her coffee cup, lit a cigarette and burrowed into the sofa while she waited for her favorite soap operas to begin. She especially liked Lucinda Walsh, past president and CEO of WorldWide Enterprises on *As The World Turns*. Maxine didn't believe in reincarnation, but if she had, her wish would be to die and be reborn as the beautiful Lucinda Walsh, stronger than metal with a backbone of ice. Too restless to sit still, Maxine picked up her knitting. *Something's got to change*, she thought as she watched Lucinda yell at Dr. Dixon. There was a new president in the White House, proof that there was still hope for the future.

*   *   *

Across town, in a two-story house of brick and cedar, Maxine's daughter Grace was just stepping out of the shower. Her husband Rob had left hours ago, promising to drop their daughter off at school. Earlier that morning there had been another fight. They'd argued about his scheduling work on a night he had promised to take Grace to dinner. In the last week alone she had had to cancel two dinner engagements and a movie because he was unavailable. "Tell them I'm busy," he had said when she asked, almost begged him to go a friend's house for cocktails. And since she wouldn't be caught dead without an escort, Grace sat home alone, looked at *Vogue* and *Glamour*, and pouted.

Brushing her auburn hair until it curled under in a neat bob emphasizing her sleek neck, Grace paused in front of the mirror and gazed at her naked body. She turned left, then right and assessed her stomach, still flat and smooth. For a woman in her early forties she looked good, even if she said so herself. The morning runs and Atkins diet paid off. She had never been this thin, not even the day she married Rob. She'd also never been so unhappy or so sexually aware. Something was wrong with her hormones.

Grace laid her brush on the dresser and picked up their wedding picture, encircled perfectly in its golden frame. College sweethearts, they'd been so much in love. But love could make you do stupid things, like drop out of college and get married. Once married, Rob abandoned his dream to be a college professor and took a job selling cars, a job he was quite good at. Good enough to buy a nice house and support his wife so she didn't have to work. Grace, on the other hand, got just what she wanted, until she didn't want it anymore.

She put the picture back and sighed. Forty-three was too young to stay home and host dinner parties. Her sixteen-year-old daughter Abbie no longer needed supervision. "Tomorrow," Grace told her husband while he showered, "I'm going to work for Aspen Grove Realty." It wasn't that she needed to work; Rob was a good provider. But she was bored and she liked to look at houses, redecorating them in her head. Every year, she volunteered at the annual tour of homes. What could be better than a job where they sold houses? Maybe they'd even let her stage a few.

But that wasn't the only reason she took the job. She hoped it would force Rob to pay more attention to his conflicting schedules, and maybe even to her.

For sixteen years, Grace had vied for his attention, and she was tired of competing. "Abigail," he said when the baby was born, naming her after some heroine in one of those books he still kept in his office. The minute Grace delivered the child, she was sorry, because everything changed. Rob no longer saw his wife as sleek and pretty. In fact, he no longer saw Grace at all. From the minute Abbie arrived, all Rob saw was his precious, darling daughter.

Well, she'd show him. Grace turned from the mirror and flipped on the light in her large walk-in closet. As she moved along the rows of blouses, many still bearing price tags, she decided to go shopping. After all, she had a new job and needed something nice to wear.

She was on her way to the mall when she turned off Main Street and headed for Cedar Lane. Ever since viewing a certain house—her dream house—on the tour of homes, she was fixated. It might have been hers, too, if Rob had secured the loan like he promised. But he wasn't quick enough and someone with more money closed the sale before they could even make an offer.

Grace turned onto Cedar Lane and slowed the car, coveting the manicured lawns and maple trees just starting to turn colors. The subdivision, less than a year old, was evolving into a comfortable section of town. The for-sale signs were gone, replaced with new cars in driveways and hanging baskets near front doors. Grace let the car idle in front of the house at 2122 Cedar Lane. The great entryway was made of brick with columns extending at least twenty feet high. Below a large picture window on the second floor, a double oak door with etched glass panes opened into the house. White and gray, the house had a clean, fresh look, a design that would always be attractive. Grace liked the bay window, but the part of the house she liked the most couldn't be seen from the street. The large sunken living room just three steps down from the kitchen was her favorite. In her mind, she had already filled the room with a big, comfy sofa where she could relax and read fashion magazines. She startled when a car beeped behind her, causing her foot to hit the gas pedal and accelerate. Reluctantly Grace left Cedar Lane and turned toward the mall. She couldn't have the house, but she'd have a nice afternoon trying on dresses.

* * *

While Grace contemplated new items to add to her wardrobe, Abbie waited for the buzzer to dismiss her sophomore English class. As soon as it did, she rushed to her locker, grabbed a notebook and met her best friend Heather in the auditorium. Seats filled fast. Who knew a fine arts meeting after school would generate so much interest?

Abbie and Heather settled as close to the front of the stage as possible, ending up behind Jessica Anderson and her tagalong friends.

"This is awesome!" Heather's voice raised an octave.

"Grow up." Jessica turned in her seat. "It's just a stupid meeting."

Heather and Jessica glared death at each other before Jessica sneered, "Loser." Jessica's friends echoed her and burst into laughter.

"It's just a stupid meeting," Heather mimicked. "Bitch."

"Ignore them." Abbie knew how it felt to suffer Jessica's contempt. Having clear skin, eyes the color of a winter sky, and hair so blond it looked white in the sun didn't make Jessica a nice person. Pretty, popular and selfish, it was no secret: whatever Jessica wanted, she got, one way or another.

But Heather didn't leave it alone. She kicked the seat in front of her until Jessica turned and said, "Stop it, Bitch."

"Hear you and Lane broke up again," Heather taunted.

"Shows what you know." Jessica glanced at the boys seated two rows away.

Abbie shot Heather a warning. *Leave it alone.* But Heather bragged. "I know I have a date to Sadie Hawkins, and you don't."

"With who? The janitor?" Jessica and her friends laughed.

"With Tyler Frazier, that's who," Heather said.

"Poor Tyler. You know he's a lousy kisser, don't you?" Jessica puckered her lips, and her friends laughed.

"Stop it." Abbie held out her hand just in time to keep Heather from taking a swing at Jessica.

"Missed." Jessica adjusted her turquoise sweater over her ample breasts and fluffed her long hair. "I suppose you have a date, too, Abbie, with someone just as charming. Like Tyler's little brother. You're both so yesterday." Jessica's friends tittered.

Abbie didn't have a date, but that didn't stop Heather. "Abbie's going with Jeremy Blackburn."

"I am not." Abbie glared at Heather.

Jessica and her friends laughed so hard, students sitting nearby turned to see what was so funny.

"Right," Jessica said when she stopped laughing. "Like that will ever happen."

Abbie glanced in Jeremy's direction. Super talented and more than cute with that wavy dark hair, he sat three chairs from her in art class. Like most of the girls in her sophomore class, Abbie harbored a secret crush on him, had since fall classes began. She'd had lots of crushes before, but they never amounted to anything. Maybe a walk home from school. A few passed notes in class. None of them held her interest for long, not like Jeremy. There was something different about him. Something that made her heart beat fast every time she said his name. It was all she could do to keep her eyes pointed straight ahead; all she could do to keep from turning in his direction.

She kicked Heather for almost spilling her secret and then leaned forward as her art teacher approached the podium.

"Well." Mr. Young smiled at the audience. "Nice to see so many faces."

Abbie had been looking forward to this meeting all week. Her summer—in fact, her future—depended on it.

"I'm delighted to inform you Aspen Grove High has agreed to sponsor two students to the Oakland Bay art internship in San Francisco." He held up two fingers. "This is a great opportunity for some of our students to advance their studies and perhaps develop a promising career."

That's what she wanted: a promising career and someday, her own art gallery.

He stepped aside to accommodate the large screen dropping from the ceiling. The auditorium filled with hoots and smack-like kisses as the lights dimmed and the room grew dark. Jessica tittered and whispered to her friends.

"Shhh," Abbie said. "Shut up and listen."

The film ran approximately twenty minutes. In addition to information on the art college, the picture highlighted Coit Tower, Fisherman's Wharf and Golden Gate Bridge, all places Abbie hoped one day to see.

When the lights came on, Mr. Young said, "Any questions?"

Abbie's hand shot up. "Where are the applications?"

He smiled. "In my classroom, Abbie. Stop by and pick one up."

She already knew what she wanted to draw. She couldn't wait to get started.

"I suppose you think you'll win that stupid scholarship?" Jessica said as she pushed past Abbie.

"I have a better chance than you do," Abbie said, looking out of the corner of her eye to catch a glimpse of Jeremy. But he was already gone.

"That's because I don't want it," Jessica said.

"Good thing. You can't even draw a circle," Heather said.

Jessica flipped her hair over her shoulder and smiled at Heather. "*You'll* never get it. Good luck, Drabigail. You have as much of a chance at getting that scholarship as you do getting Jeremy to the dance."

"Oh, yeah?" Heather said. "Just watch her."

"Yeah," Abbie said. She was tired of Jessica's superior attitude. She wasn't drab. She wasn't beautiful either, but she could draw. And she never walked away from a challenge. "Just watch."

But later at home as she worked on her sketches, Abbie wondered if she'd temporarily gone insane. Jeremy hardly knew her. Everybody in the school liked him, and Sadie Hawkins was less than three weeks away.

CHAPTER TWO

A LIGHT FROST SWIRLED Aspen Grove into a kaleidoscope of color. This was the time of year Maxine loved best — clear, crisp mornings followed by sunny afternoons marking the beginning of a month-long Indian summer. As she worked in her garden, gathering the last of the zucchini, tomatoes and bell peppers, Maxine found herself thinking about Larry Fisher again. Approaching her sixty-fourth birthday, Maxine was growing careless. Just last week she did something she'd never thought she would do. As she discussed children, grandchildren, and thoughtless husbands over coffee with Helen and Shirley, Maxine mentioned Larry and how much she once loved him.

"You should write a letter and tell him," Helen said between bites of lemon cream pie.

"Don't be ridiculous," Maxine said. "And I suppose I should send it to heaven, right?"

"Unless he's in hell," Shirley added trying to be funny.

But Shirley hadn't lightened Maxine's mood. On her knees pulling weeds from carrots, Maxine couldn't help but wonder. What would happen if she were to write him a letter? She didn't have to show it to anybody. She didn't have to seal it in a bottle or toss it into the Aspen River and send it out to sea. Weren't those doctors on TV always saying you needed to write things down to get them out of your system? Maybe if she wrote him a letter, it wouldn't hurt so much every time she thought about Larry and what she'd lost.

Maxine sat back on her heels and brushed her limp hair out of her eyes. After all these years, she should have been over him. But her heart hurt when she remembered the way he had kissed her and said, "Later, lover."

Maxine shifted her weight and studied the plants. The garden was neat, the carrots weeded, the leaves raked and bagged waiting behind the shed to serve as mulch when the temperature dropped. She used the back of her flannel sleeve to wipe the sweat from her face. "Crap," she said when she tried to stand, grimacing at the pain in her hip. "Maxine Foster, you're getting old and fat." In that moment, she was glad Larry wasn't there to see how her hair had thinned and grayed, or how her trim waist was now a series of rolls around her belly.

That night Maxine was crankier than usual. Herb had picked at his dinner, a dinner that took some time preparing given the fact that Maxine was out of hamburger and had to walk to the store. She knew cabbage rolls were not his favorite, but she wanted to use up the garden produce. She thought if she smothered the rolls in ketchup, he would eat them. She should have known better. After a few minutes of pushing the hamburger, rice and cabbage around on his plate, Herb picked up his beer and plopped in front of the TV.

"Solve the fucking puzzle," he yelled at a contestant on "Wheel of Fortune."

Standing over the sink full of dishes, Maxine muttered, "Shut your foul mouth." She wondered what she'd ever seen in him, why she'd ever married.

The answer was simple. The answer was Grace.

*   *   *

Grace smoothed the skirt to her new suit and slipped her purse into the bottom drawer of her desk. Already in her second week as receptionist, the top of her desk looked like she'd worked there for months. Pictures of Rob sat off in one corner. A bright fall arrangement with flowers and ivy decorated the other corner along with a note from her husband. *I Love You. Have a great day.* She had just poured herself a cup of coffee in the break room when the telephone rang. She hurried to answer.

"Good Morning, Aspen Grove Realty. How may I help you?" Grace said as she picked up on the second ring, remembering to smile. Her employee handbook claimed a customer could hear her smile, so even before she answered the phone she was supposed to put a big smile on her face.

"I'm calling about a house on Cedar Lane." The voice on the phone was masculine and deep.

Grace smiled even brighter. Cedar Lane, he had good taste. "Which one?"

"The three story. At 2122 Cedar Lane. I'd like to see it today."

Her smile faded, and her mouth felt like sandpaper. He had to be mistaken.

She fumbled with the phone and stuttered. "Let me see. If you will let me put you on hold . . ." She didn't wait for his answer. How on earth had she missed the fact that her dream house was back on the market?

She looked through the new listings, noting nothing on Cedar Lane. As the light on her phone blinked, Grace checked each of the realtors' offices until she found the papers on Trudy's desk, signed the night before. Everyone was attending a one-day sales conference out of town, leaving Grace alone to manage the office.

Hoping she'd been gone so long he'd hung up, she forced a smile. "Thanks for holding."

"No problem."

She frowned when she heard his voice. "I'm sorry," she said. "All our agents are busy today. I can schedule an appointment for you with Trudy Watson on Wednesday." That should give Grace enough time to lock in a sale. It was more than they could afford, but she was sure she could find a way to convince Rob. After all, she had a job now. That should count for something.

The voice grew impatient. "I'd like to see it today."

"Well," Grace said firmly, "I'm sorry. That can't be arranged."

"Listen," the man said. "Kent assured me I could see that house today."

"He isn't here." Grace glanced at the clock. Her stomach rumbled. Lunch was still three hours away. She started to say she was sorry again, when a thought occurred to her. She'd show the house herself. She'd make sure this man didn't make an offer. "We close the office for lunch. I can meet you there at noon if that will work."

She heard the hesitation in his voice. "Fine."

"Okay, then, Mr. . . . ."

"Lancaster. Michael Lancaster. See you there at noon."

Hanging up, Grace beamed. She'd have to cancel her manicure, but it was worth it. For a moment, Grace wondered if meeting a male client alone might be dangerous. But then she relaxed. This was Aspen Grove, silly girl. She was meeting him at noon. Whatever could happen to her in broad daylight?

"Not one single thing," Grace said later as she locked the door and flipped the sign to "Closed, Be back soon." Unlike her mother who was always pessimistic and cross, Grace couldn't have been happier. She had shown initiative. Why, if she could stall Mr. Lancaster, she could buy her dream house before anyone else knew it was for sale.

*   *   *

"Abigail?"

Abbie looked up from doodling in her notebook to meet her history teacher's gaze. Someone in the back of the room shuffled their feet, and a couple of girls snickered. If she bothered to glance behind her, Abbie knew she would see a smirk on Jessica's pimple-free face.

"Plan on joining us any time soon?" her teacher said.

"Yes." Abbie turned to a clean page in her notebook. U. S. History was so boring. Reading the Articles of Confederation put her to sleep. It wasn't like she wanted to be President of the United States or had a passion to become a political target.

Mr. Shaner turned back to the whiteboard, and it was all Abbie could do to stay awake. She glanced outside, wishing she were sketching sparrows or a haunted castle for her portfolio. She fidgeted and closed her book, ready to dart when the bell rang.

"Miss Buchanan?" her teacher said.

Abbie stopped in the middle of the doorway. "A moment of your time, please."

Abbie walked back into the room. She looked at the clock.

"This won't take long." Mr. Shaner pointed to a seat. "Please, sit."

Crap. She borrowed her grandmother's favorite euphemism. She was going to be late for art class.

"Is there a problem with the homework?" he asked. "You haven't turned in the last two assignments."

"Oh." She'd been so busy with the sketches, she forgot. She pretended to dig through her backpack. "I must've left them at home."

He didn't look like he was buying her lie. "You have until Friday to get them in."

"I will." Students for his next class were already entering the room. And now she wouldn't have time to go to her locker. In a hurry, Abbie dodged students, weaving left, then right, stopping short when she ran straight into Jeremy Blackburn.

"Hey, Buchanan," he said as they collided. "Watch where you're going." Her books spilled out of her hands as the buzzer sounded. It didn't matter that he didn't stop to help her, or that he didn't look back over his shoulder. Abbie's heart caught as she watched him walk down the hall. Scrambling to gather her things, she knew she was late, but she didn't care. He had touched her. He had even said her name.

*   *   *

Grace hummed as she turned the corner onto the wide, tree-lined street. She loved this section of town almost as much as she loved that house. Not that she cared to garden like her mother, but Grace did like the way the large lots were landscaped: tall Japanese yews, bright fire bushes, and freshly mown lawns. The houses were so regal she was convinced perfect, happy families thrived behind each and every front door.

Grace slowed the car as she neared 2122. Sure enough, there was the sign. When had that happened? She pulled beside the white Honda in the driveway. A quick glance told her the car was empty. So was the front yard.

"Here goes nothing." Grace checked her hair in the rearview mirror and freshened her lipstick. "One man, one house. Not a room full of people eating chicken pâté. How hard can it be?"

She grabbed the file on the seat beside her and stepped out of the car. Catching her elbow on the door, she dumped the file's contents onto the driveway. "Oh, dear." Grace couldn't bring herself to say "crap" or "shit" like her mother. And she hated the fact that Abbie was starting to swear, too. "Oh, dear," she repeated as she gathered the papers, stood and straightened her skirt.

"Hello?" She scanned the empty yard and porch. She loved that tree. When she owned this house, she would put a chair there so she could read her magazines and wave at her neighbors.

There was no answer, so she walked to the side of the house and slipped her arm up over the fence to open the gate, which latched from the inside.

Oh, my. He was tall, and perhaps the most attractive man she'd seen since college. She wasn't sure what she had expected, but by no means was it this man with hair so black it looked blue in the sun.

"Hello." He stepped away from the patio window. "Thought I'd look around while I waited."

He smelled like palm trees and trade winds. Grace tried to hide the tremor in her voice. She was forty-three-years old, not some fresh college kid. She willed her hand to stop shaking as she extended it. "Grace Buchanan. Aspen Grove Realty."

"Michael Lancaster." He took her hand. His touch was strong, warm, overwhelming. Embarrassed, she flushed when he reclaimed his hand and motioned to the house. "Shall we?"

"Oh, of course." She fumbled. This was going to be hard, pointing out flaws that weren't there.

He shepherded her around the side of the house and through the gate. She stubbed her toe on a concrete paver, and he grabbed her arm to steady her. "Gotcha," he said.

"Thanks," Grace said. This was wrong, this crazy, heady animal way she was feeling. She was so rattled, she had trouble opening the lockbox to retrieve the key.

Inside, the house smelled of fresh paint and new carpets. The entryway floor was polished marble. Three windows stretched high, at least ten feet to the ceiling, filling the house with sunlight. He was already in the kitchen before she could close the door. Her high heels clattered against the marble entryway.

"May I?" He pointed to the staircase.

"By all means." Grace stilled the desire to follow him, heading instead to the sunken living room. Just as she remembered it. The giant bay window looked out onto the deck. She walked around the room, visualizing her large floral paintings on the walls. Even though her sofa and chairs were less than three years old, she'd need new furniture to fill the big room. In the kitchen, Grace considered the new range and double ovens. Perfect for entertaining and holiday dinners.

"How much are you asking?" He called from the dining room. She was so lost in her fantasy, she hadn't heard him descend the stairs.

She opened her folder to the listing and said with the slightest hesitation, "$350,000. It has central air, five bedrooms, three baths and a sauna off the master bath." She'd always wanted a sauna.

"It's very nice," he said.

"Yes," she said. "But some of these features are impractical. Like those cupboards. The only way you can reach them is from a chair or a ladder." He looked to where she pointed and shrugged.

"And look at this," she tried again. "Carpet in a kitchen? Who puts carpet in a kitchen?" When he seemed unimpressed, she added. "And there is no walk out basement."

He nodded and looked at his watch. "I didn't realize it was so late. I have to go now or miss my plane."

She took another quick look at the living room before she locked the door. Lost in her daydream, Grace looked surprised when he said, "I like it, but it's a bit steep for a high school principal."

"And," she recovered quickly. "It's several miles from the high school."

They lingered on the front steps before he shook her hand. "Thanks for showing me the house. I'm sorry I was so insistent. I'm on a tight schedule."

"I understand." He was nice. She liked him. But he still wasn't getting her house. "Have a safe trip."

"Thanks." He smiled and Grace had to check herself. It would be so easy to get caught in his smile.

She watched him drive away, almost sorry he was leaving. She waited until he turned the corner before she unlocked the door.

Back inside, Grace kicked off her shoes and walked around the kitchen, upstairs and back down again. She feathered her bangs in front of the floor-length mirror in the master bedroom. She stood at the living room window and peered out across the lawn toward the neighbor's backyard, hidden behind the high fence. She hadn't exaggerated. The house was worth $350,000. Too bad that was more than a high school principal could pay.

She recalled the way her hand had trembled when he'd touched her, and she tried to picture him at the high school. He looked nothing like her old principal, Mr. Turner, who wore a toupee to cover his bald head. She and her friends had laughed when the wig flapped in the wind like an old pelt. She wasn't laughing now; she was smiling.

"Nicely done, Ms. Buchanan. Nicely done." She slid the chair under the kitchen table. As part of the staging of the house, it was set with plates, silverware and decorations. She straightened a maroon placemat and repositioned a fork. Somehow they would manage the listing price,

$250,000, even if it meant depleting their savings and most of Abbie's college fund. Besides, Rob golfed every Saturday with Steven Hamilton, the president of Aspen Grove National Bank. Confident she'd be cooking Thanksgiving dinner in that great big kitchen, she hugged herself, giddy with excitement.

Grace took a long look at the house before she backed out of the driveway. She'd stop at the store, make Rob's favorite dinner, and later, put on her most alluring negligee. She'd suggest Abbie spend the night with Heather because she and Rob were going to be busy.

CHAPTER THREE

THE NOVEMBER DAY reflected Maxine's mood: cold and gray. She was grateful for the firewood Rob had delivered, and she had a fire burning in the fireplace to stave off the chill. Before her arthritis took over Maxine's life, they all used to go to the grove to gather firewood. Every year after the winter storms, there was an abundance of downed timber. Unwilling to get dirty or ruin her nails, Grace stayed home. But Abbie always enjoyed helping her father and Herb saw up the logs. Abbie even had her own saw, miniature in size, and used it to remove the branches for Maxine to stack. They made it an annual family outing. Every fall, Maxine baked peanut butter cookies and made ham and cheese sandwiches. She'd do what she could while Herb and Rob ran the chainsaws. But her legs started giving her fits, and after a while she and Herb stopped going. She missed those days. It was hell getting old.

Waiting for Helen and Shirley to arrive, Maxine sipped her coffee and smoked a cigarette. She knew she should quit, but old habits were hard to break. She pushed aside the curtain and stared at the sky. Dark, puffy clouds, a sure sign of snow. Maybe the snow would be blue when it fell, like the snowflakes Elvis sang about in her living room. She set her cup on the kitchen table, downed two extra-strength aspirin, and massaged her fingers and wrists.

If she had trouble believing she would soon be sixty-four, here was the proof. Arthritic hands that ached even when she wasn't holding a crochet hook or scrubbing a toilet.

Why she had volunteered to help Shirley make snowflakes was beyond her, given her sour mood. But she would work on that. Besides, she was happy for the company on such a gray day. Already, they were knocking at the door.

"Look, it's snowing." Shirley shook the flakes from her bleached blond hair like a wet dog. Her face glowed, and it wouldn't have surprised Maxine at all if Shirley suggested they go outside and make snow angels in the front yard. Shirley's would be tall and skinny compared to Maxine's short and misshapen angel.

"Brought that pattern," Helen said as she peeled off her coat and rushed toward the bathroom, her short legs making her waddle like a penguin.

"Much better," Helen said when she returned. "Snow makes Shirley act like she's three. All it does is make me pee." Unlike Shirley, who wouldn't be seen dead with a single gray hair, Helen's head was covered with gray, thick natural curls that always needed trimming.

"This is going to be fun." Shirley settled into the sofa. "I want at least two dozen to hang on my tree. What do we do first?"

Since Helen already knew how to crochet, Maxine focused on teaching Shirley how to hold the hook and thread. Her pattern book lay on the coffee table along with Helen's snowflake patterns, and Maxine picked the simplest design for Shirley. "Hold your hook like this," she instructed. "Chain five and join."

"I can't see the holes." Shirley peered at the tiny stitches, then set her hook aside to find her glasses. With determination, she hummed with Elvis and tried to follow Maxine's instructions. By the time Shirley had completed three rows, Helen had finished two snowflakes.

The record player clicked off and Maxine rose to change the music.

"That's enough Elvis for a while," Helen said. "All he does is make you sad."

"Does not." Maxine turned the record over but didn't flip the lever. Helen was right. The day was gray enough without a lot of depressing love songs.

Helen pointed her crochet hook at Maxine. "What you need, Maxine Foster, is to get out of this house."

"I get out plenty."

"You call going to the grocery store and cleaning houses getting out? You don't even go to church any more."

"What I do is none of your business." Maxine was sorry the minute she said it. Helen and Shirley were her closest friends, the ones she turned to when her life got messy. They knew more about Herb and his drinking than she would ever tell Grace.

"Who put your butt in a pucker?" Helen said. "Is Herb being an ass again?"

"No. Yes. Oh, I don't know." Maxine set her thread aside, bored with the whole snowflake project. She went to the kitchen and returned with the coffeepot and a plate of chocolate chip cookies. "More coffee?"

"Can't." Shirley looked at her watch and shook her head. "Need to get home before the grandkids."

It was later than Maxine realized. She'd have to think about supper soon.

"Friday," Helen said as she slipped into her coat. "Friday, we're taking you to lunch."

"By Friday, we'll be snowed in," Maxine said.

"Nah. This is just a skiff." Helen pulled a red scarf around her neck and tied a neat bow. "It'll be gone by morning."

"Oh, I hope not." Shirley buttoned her coat and put on her gloves. "I hope it snows until Christmas. I can't wait to help the grandkids make a snowman."

"You'll need more snow than that." Helen pointed her finger at Maxine. "Friday. Pick you up at 11:30."

"No, you won't. I'll be watching my soaps."

"That's what you think," Helen said. "Friday, they serve the best carrot cake at the Senior Center, and I know how much you love carrot cake."

"I'm staying right here where it's nice and warm."

"It's warm at the Center," Shirley said. "They have a fireplace. We can take our crocheting. After lunch, we can sit in front of the fire and make snowflakes."

Maxine frowned. The last thing she wanted to do was watch Shirley make more crooked snowflakes or eat with a bunch of old people who had nowhere else to go but the grave.

"You'll like it," Helen said. "Even Ray Miles eats there on Fridays."

"Good for him." Being the retired mayor of Aspen Grove did not make Ray special or someone Maxine wanted to share her lunch with. The only person who might be able to persuade Maxine to eat at the Center on Friday was Elvis Presley, and he was already dead.

Even though she protested, Maxine thought about Friday all week long. She couldn't decide. One minute, she thought it would be nice to go to the Center and eat somebody else's cooking. The next minute, she'd push the thought away. Yes, Helen was right. She should get out more.

And she loved carrot cake. But old people made Maxine nervous. Besides, she had nothing to wear.

Still.

Thursday morning, when she should have been watching her soaps, Maxine dumped all of her clothes in the closet onto the bed and spent several hours trying them on. Most of the tops were too tight, and the few pairs of pants she had that weren't stained were at least two sizes too small. "This alone," Maxine muttered as she pulled off a pair of blue polyester pants that stuck to her legs, "is proof you shouldn't go."

Instead of putting her old clothes in a box for Goodwill, she stuffed them into the closet and slammed the door. That took care of that. She wasn't going.

Later that day with the sun still hiding behind the clouds, Maxine snuggled in a blanket with her crossword puzzle and coffee and thought how Currier and Ives it would be to sit in front of a fire and make snowflakes. The idea had a romantic element, enough to send her back into her bedroom to revisit her clothes.

Searching in the bottom of her closet, Maxine found the sweater she had crocheted for Grace several Christmases ago. "It's lovely, Mom," Grace had said. "But it's too big for me." Those words still stung. Grace had no idea the number of hours it took to make that sweater. Or how long it took Maxine to find that special shade of red. A good daughter would have kept it and thought of her mother every time she wore it. But Grace had returned it like a cheap cardigan from Taiwan. Sometimes her daughter could be such an ungrateful child.

"It's supposed to be big." Maxine pulled the sweater over her head. As she smoothed the red and white sweater over her hips, she realized Grace was right. The sweater was miles too big for Grace, because it fit Maxine. Not perfectly, but loose enough she wouldn't be ashamed to be seen in it, even if her breasts looked like two huge red poinsettias, well, sagging poinsettias.

Settling on the sweater, Maxine searched through her pants again but found most of them stained and threadbare. None of them looked good with the pullover, even though the sweater hid most of her stomach.

Determined to find something suitable, Maxine went to Herb's closet. It smelled musty, of beer and motor oil. Most of his shirts were more than twenty years old. Some he had even worn in high school. Maxine made herself a promise. After the holidays, she would clean house, starting with his closet.

Once heavy, Herb had been losing weight. Most of his clothes were now too big, and it didn't surprise Maxine to find the Levis Grace gave him for Christmas, still in a box. Maxine held them up. Would they fit?

One pair was too tight. The waist was too low, and she couldn't close them, not even when she lay on the bed and tugged at the zipper. But the second pair, though snug, fit well enough to get her through lunch at the Center. She wasn't going to a Christmas gala. She didn't need anything fancy. It was just lunch, after all.

Satisfied her clothes were acceptable, Maxine studied her hair in the bathroom mirror. Once thick and dark, it had thinned over the years. Now, it was a drab charcoal color highlighted with streaks of gray. To say she looked like a skunk would be a compliment.

She wrinkled her nose at her reflection. She could curl her hair—which she'd stopped doing years ago, pull it into a ponytail—which looked ridiculous on a woman her age, or she could wear a hat.

"Maxine," she said to her reflection, "you should have listened when Grace suggested a haircut." She might look younger if her hair didn't hang in striped strings around her face. She twisted her hair into a bun, which made her face look fatter.

Discouraged, Maxine left the bathroom and dropped onto the sofa. She worked a crossword puzzle for a few minutes and then looked toward the bathroom. She didn't have to change her hair. Or her clothes. She could just stay home. But she knew. Protest all she wanted, she'd already decided to go.

Friday morning, Maxine was still fussing in the bedroom when she heard the doorbell.

Before she could answer, Helen pushed the door open and hollered, "Maxine, get your shoes on. It's time to go." Wearing a bright purple dress and red glass beads, Helen looked ridiculous. All she needed was a red hat, and she could be queen of her own crazy hat society. Maybe that's what Maxine loved about Helen. She didn't care what people thought.

"Hurry up," Helen said, "we're going to be late."

"Where's Shirley?" Maxine tucked her hair under a white beret she had crocheted and slipped into her coat.

"In the car."

Not sure how long they would be gone, Maxine sprinkled food into the fish tank and said to her Bala sharks, "Elvis, be good to Priscilla today. No fighting." Then she locked the door and followed Helen. Her stomach burned, and she wished she had taken an antacid, but it was too late for that.

Helen held the car door open. "Your carriage awaits, m'lady. Get in. Let's go."

"Hey, Maxine." Shirley waived as Maxine settled into the back seat. "Ready for some carrot cake?"

"I'd rather try that new restaurant over on Fourth. I hear they have excellent lemon cream pie." Maxine tugged her hat tighter over her head.

"Nice try," Helen said as she backed out of the driveway. "Today, Maxine Zelda Foster, we're going to the Senior Center, and that's that. Besides, you just might have a good time."

I doubt it, Maxine thought as Helen maneuvered into the last parking space at the Center. Helen had neglected to tell her that the first Friday of every month was birthday Friday, complete with cake and ice cream, sure to tempt everyone retired away from their naps and TVs. As Maxine watched the doors open and close, she wondered if there'd be anything left to eat. Or even a place to sit.

She didn't need to worry. The Center was prepared for the large turnout. Clutching her purse close as if everyone wanted to steal it, Maxine followed Helen and Shirley into the building. She didn't look right or left but stared at the floor and then at her watch, wondering how long before she could return to the comfort of her home. But her stomach betrayed her, rumbling at the aromas drifting from the kitchen—ham and scalloped potatoes, Maxine guessed. It smelled wonderful. She could already taste it.

"Hey, Belinda." Helen waved at a woman standing beside a long table, flapping a scarf to catch their attention. "This is my friend Maxine. Maxine, this is Belinda. She works at King's part-time and lets me know when their yarn and crochet thread goes on sale."

They put their coats over chairs to save seats and joined the others already in line for lunch. Belinda stood next to Helen, babbling about the Thanksgiving and Christmas decorations already in stores. Then she turned to Maxine. "I love that sweater. Did you make it?"

Maxine nodded.

"It's pretty. I wish I could do that. I suppose you made that cute hat, too?"

Maxine's hand went to her head, flattered Belinda liked her handiwork. "Yes."

She followed Helen and Belinda through the line. She waited as one of the women behind the counter filled her tray with scalloped potatoes.

"Why, Maxine Foster, I haven't seen you here before. Here, you'd better take another roll. They go fast."

"Thanks." Maxine glanced at the server, embarrassed because she couldn't remember her name.

They settled at a round table decorated with colorful placemats and a paper streamer running down the center of table. The confetti sprinkled on the table made everything festive.

"See, Maxine." Shirley had already finished her ham. She brandished her fork at the people in the room. "Isn't this more fun than staying home? And the food is so yummy." She waved at Mr. Miles who sat with friends a few tables away. "Hi, Ray," she said. He waved, and Shirley tittered.

While Shirley flirted with Ray Miles, the man sitting across the table from Maxine tried to engage her in conversation. Wearing a tan vest over a crisp, white shirt, he looked like a retired schoolteacher. Or a banker. He had kind, sad eyes. She especially liked his thick head of hair, white, but every strand neatly in place.

"Hello." He smiled, but Maxine looked at her potatoes and ham. She flashed her left hand. What did he think that ring on her finger represented?

"Is this your first time here?"

She avoided his question, and after a while, he turned his attention to Helen. "My, that's a pretty blouse."

Geesh, Maxine thought, he couldn't even be original.

"Thanks," Helen said. "Where's Loretta today?"

"Tired from the chemo."

"Sorry to hear that," Helen said. "Give her my best, and tell her if she needs anything . . ."

"I will," he said. "Thanks. I'm taking her some lunch, but I doubt she'll be able to eat."

Maxine gave a weak smile. He wasn't a letch, just a lonely man with a sick wife. Having nothing to say, she chewed her ham in silence.

When her plate was empty, Maxine was ready to go. She rose to put her tray away when a group of servers brought out plates of carrot cake and ice cream. She looked at Helen, who grinned. "Still want to go to that diner on Fourth?"

"No." Maxine sat back down and slid her fork into the cake, enjoying the rich spicy moistness while everyone sang "Happy Birthday." There were no candles to blow out, but those celebrating November birthdays were asked to stand while everyone applauded. Maxine was glad it wasn't March. She'd hate to stand and endure all the fuss. She focused on the cake. "This is so good," she said. "I'd love to have the recipe." She looked around the table, hoping for more.

"I'm sure that can be arranged," Helen said. When they finished eating, Helen stood. "All we have to do is ask."

The kitchen was a hubbub of commotion. Two women stood over a sink washing dishes, while two more packaged the leftover chopped lettuce and tomatoes. Dixie, the cook, checked the stove to make sure the oven and burners were off.

Helen put her arm around Dixie's shoulders. "Maxine here said you make the best carrot cake in the world, and she's an expert on carrot cakes."

Dixie beamed. "Glad you like it. The secret is the crushed pineapple. Keeps it nice and moist."

"It's delicious," Maxine said. "Would you mind sharing your recipe?"

"Not at all." Dixie wiped her hands on her apron. She opened a large binder of loose recipes, and it didn't take her long to find the section on cakes. She took the recipe into the office and returned with a photocopy.

"Here you go," Dixie said. "Enjoy. And I expect to see you next week. Monday we're serving beef and bacon stroganoff."

"Thanks." Maxine hugged the cook. She never hugged a stranger before, but this felt right. Everything about this lunch felt right and worth repeating.

"See you Monday," Dixie waved.

"Okay," Maxine said.

But on the way home, she told Helen and Shirley she couldn't go back. "It's cheap enough," she said, "but I can't afford it."

As the car idled and Maxine climbed out of the back seat, Helen said, "I'm disappointed in you, Maxine Foster. Don't you think you're worth three dollars a day?"

Maxine shook her head.

"Well, that's a pity."

"But thanks," Maxine said. "I had fun."

"Bye," Shirley said. "See you soon."

Later, as Maxine slipped out of her red sweater and into her sweats, her mood shifted. It had been fun to talk to Belinda about crocheting. It had been nice to eat someone else's cooking. And the carrot cake was better than any she'd ever baked. She poured a cup of coffee and turned on the TV, still thinking about Helen's comment. Was three dollars a day too much to ask for the cleaning, cooking and laundry she did in this house? She was sure Herb spent more than that on beer.

Maxine lit a cigarette and sank into the sofa, clicking the remote until she found Dr. Phil. Then she picked up her knitting. The more she thought about the injustice, the faster her needles clicked through the stitches.

*   *   *

Abbie rarely ate lunch in the school cafeteria. Usually she and Heather walked to Frosty Burger and gobbled fries and Cokes, but today Heather was sick and Abbie didn't want to walk to the diner alone. Having skipped breakfast, she was hungry, and her stomach growled at the whiff of cafeteria tacos. So, instead of skipping lunch, Abbie filled her tray with lettuce, tomatoes, meat, and cheese. Then she found an empty table in an inconspicuous corner and sat down. When she finished her tacos, she pushed her tray aside and pulled out the application for the summer art scholarship her art teacher Mr. Young had given her earlier that morning. The extra copy she promised to get for Heather fell to the floor. Bent over to retrieve the application, Abbie looked up when she heard Jessica snicker, "Watch this."

Abbie had no idea why Jessica and her cheesy friends were eating lunch in the cafeteria where it was totally uncool. But there they were, laughing and walking toward Jeremy.

"Hi, Jeremy. Can we join you?"

Jeremy looked at his best friend Charles Kennedy and said, "It's a free country."

"That would be a 'yes.'" Jessica put her tray on the table and slid next to Jeremy. He looked at Charles, shrugged, and kept on talking as if she wasn't there.

Abbie narrowed her eyes. Since when was Jessica interested in Jeremy? With his dark bangs masking half his face, Jeremy was nothing like Jessica's old boyfriend Lane. Jeremy didn't drive a new car. He didn't have a lot of money. He wore black turtlenecks instead of polo shirts from Abercrombie. Abbie glanced around the cafeteria. Sure enough, Lane sat across from Cindy Lawrence, leaning so close to her face he could kiss her.

Jessica moved closer to Jeremy and whispered. Jeremy's face turned red, even his ears.

What was she doing? She didn't want him. She should just leave him alone. Abbie picked up her tray and made it a point to walk by their table.

"Hey, Charles," she said. "Hey, Jeremy." Her voice was strong, but her knees were shaking.

"Hey, Abbie." Jeremy's eyes met hers for what seemed like forever before he turned his attention back to his food. Tacos with lots of cheese, just like hers. Jessica moved closer, her face only inches from his. Abbie wanted to look away, but her eyes were fixed on his face, his eyes so blue she could easily lose her way. He was so hot, not to mention the best artist in school. Heart pounding, Abbie tried to move, but her legs were two wooden stilts.

Jeremy said something to Charles, and Jessica laughed.

Phony. You're just trying to make Lane zealous. Abbie glanced at the other table. Didn't work. Lane was still talking to Cindy. He didn't even look their way.

Abbie's feet felt like they were glued to the floor. Standing so close to Jeremy made her dizzy.

"What are you gawking at, Drabigail?" Jessica leaned in closer to Jeremy.

Abbie's fingers clenched her tray. "Not you, that's for sure."

Charles and Jeremy snickered.

"Then get lost," Jessica said.

"My pleasure." When she finally got her feet to move, Abbie put her tray away, and even though it took every nerve in her body, she walked out of the cafeteria without once looking back.

She was on her way to class when she passed a poster advertising the Sadie Hawkins dance.

What if Jessica was asking Jeremy to the dance right this minute?

Panic rose inside her like her grandmother's bread yeast. She'd have to come up with a plan. Soon. But that wouldn't be easy, not when she had so much trouble moving her feet.

*   *   *

Sitting across the table from Trudy, Grace studied the menu. Her usual luncheons involved meeting friends or planning events and stretched long into the afternoons. But today she was having a business lunch with her co-worker.

That wasn't exactly true. They may have worked in the same office, but in reality, Grace worked more *for* Trudy than *with* her. A primary realtor at Aspen Grove Realty, Trudy had offered, on this rare occasion, to take time for lunch. What it really meant was Trudy had no house to show, and she was bored. "Let's go to lunch," she'd said to Grace. "I'm hungry." Flattered, Grace had accepted.

"You know," Trudy said as she surveyed Hart's dining room for familiar faces, "the one thing we have to offer is quality customer service. We don't have an expensive van to help customers move. We can't justify mass mailings that get tossed in the trash. But, if we act in a professional manner and make our customers feel like we care about them, they'll remember and refer us to their friends."

Trudy took Grace's menu out of her hand and gave it to the waiter. "We'll have two California salads and two raspberry teas. No lemon." Then she addressed Grace.

"Take for instance, yesterday. You displayed initiative, Grace, showing that house when I couldn't. But don't do it again. It's unprofessional. Kent could lose his license letting a secretary show houses."

Grace looked at her water glass. What she thought was going to be a pleasant lunch was turning into a reprimand.

"That said, I talked with Mr. Lancaster last night. He's interested. Apparently, you quoted him the wrong price."

Grace swallowed, afraid to look at Trudy.

"He needs to settle in soon so he can get on with his job at Aspen High. I think we have a sale."

Grace choked on her water. At this very moment, Rob was supposed to be meeting with their banker Steve Hamilton to arrange a loan.

"...Isn't that so?"

Confused, Grace looked at Trudy. Caught up in her own thoughts about the house, she hadn't been listening.

No longer hungry, Grace picked at the avocado in her salad. If Trudy had asked, she would have learned that Grace was allergic to tomatoes. And raspberries made her sick. But they were dining at Hart's and smiling at accountants, doctors and attorneys. That should have made her happy instead of miserable. She returned from lunch with a stomachache.

Later that evening, Grace was still thinking about lunch at Hart's when the phone rang. "Hi, hon," her husband said. "Forgot to tell you. I won't be home for dinner."

"But we're having salmon."

"I'm sorry. I have to work. "

"Rob? Did you ---" He'd already ended the call.

Grace hurled the salad she was fixing across the room. "Work. Work. Work. If I changed my name to Work, maybe I'd get to see you once in a while!"

Wanting to ignore the salad on the floor, but hating a messy house, Grace threw the lettuce and cucumbers in the garbage. When the floor was clean, she opened a bottle of wine and poured a large glass.

Pacing the kitchen, she stopped and said, "Hi, sweetheart. How was your day?" She took a sip. "Hart's you say. Bet that was nice. By the way, I talked with Steve. We're getting that loan."

Grace downed the glass of wine. Then poured another. She had just emptied her second glass when Abbie entered the kitchen. "Let me guess. Dad's working late again."

Grace feigned a smile, imitating her husband's voice. "Some of us have to work." He wasn't a general manager for a car dealership when she married him; he was a boy who loved to read. She took the half-empty bottle of wine into the living room, folded into the sofa and wondered. If Rob had pursued his dream to teach, would he be home more? Probably not. He'd just hole up in his office with his books.

"Can I go to Heather's? I promised I'd help with her homework. She was sick today."

"What?" Having forgotten her glass in the kitchen, Grace drank from the bottle.

"Heather's. Can I go?"

"What about dinner?"

"I'll grab something at her house."

"Fine." Grace took another drink from the bottle. Husbands. Kids. Thank God they didn't have a dog.

*   *   *

Sitting on the floor with her back against Heather's bed, Abbie flipped to the notes Heather wanted to copy. "Are you sick, or were you faking so you wouldn't have to take that test?"

"I *was* sick," Heather said. "But not any more. Look. Do you like this?" She held a picture of a brightly colored dress, cinched above the waist.

"Where are you going to get a hundred dollars?" Abbie said when she looked at the picture.

"From my dad. He's feeling guilty about leaving us."

When Heather's father walked out on his family, taking up with his secretary "The Whore," according to Heather's mother, all Heather could do was cry. But that was a month ago, and now Heather found ways to make her father's abandonment pay. Already she had a new iPod, and she was working on a car for her birthday.

"Tyler's going to love it. Look, you should get this one."

Abbie glanced at the dress. Blue, almost the color of Jeremy's eyes.

"That's all he wears, that blue sweatshirt," Heather said.

"Is not." Mostly, he wore black turtlenecks. They were part of the reason everyone noticed him. Every day, rain or shine, he had on a turtleneck shirt. Abbie liked them; they made him different and mysterious.

"Did you ask him?" Heather said, still ogling the picture of the dress.

"No."

"What are you waiting for?"

"Christmas."

"Don't be a smartass."

Abbie pantomimed. "Want me to get dumb?"

This made Heather laugh. "You should ask him before someone else does."

Abbie frowned. *Like Jessica.* She reached into her backpack. "Here."

"Sure you don't mind?" Heather glanced at the art scholarship application. "I know how much you want this."

Abbie shrugged. "Why would I mind?" She loved Heather, but Heather had one chance in a million of winning a scholarship. If she had any competition, it was from Jeremy Blackburn. Mr. Young said two would get the scholarship — she and Jeremy, if Abbie had her way.

Standing in front of the mirror, Heather piled her hair on top of her head.

"You should make him fall in love with you like Tyler and me. Then we could do everything together."

Abbie gave a nervous giggle. She and Jeremy? In love?

"I want everything to be perfect." Heather unclipped her hair, letting it fall to her shoulders. She bared her midriff and pinched her skin. "I need to lose a couple of pounds before the dance."

If Heather needed to lose a few pounds, Abbie needed glasses. Heather was so thin, Abbie could count her ribs. The last thing Heather needed to do was lose weight.

And the last thing Abbie needed was to fall in love. But with a boy like Jeremy, it would be so easy...and so worth it.

CHAPTER FOUR

"**COMING!**" Setting aside her needlework, Maxine wondered who'd be crazy enough to venture out on such a stormy day. She groaned and pushed herself off the sofa, stopping at the stereo to turn off Elvis and his Hawaiian Wedding Song.

"Helen? Good Lord. What are you doing out in this snowstorm?"

"Waiting for you to open the damn door." Helen's red hat and purple coat were covered with snow. Her face was almost as red as her hat. Snowflakes stuck to her eyebrows and glasses. In each hand, she held a large bulging sack.

Maxine eyed the bags suspiciously, but moved out of the way. "Come in. Come in."

Helen dropped the bags, and then peeled off her coat and gloves. "Coffee hot?" She rubbed her hands together and headed to the bathroom.

"Just getting ready to make a fresh pot."

While they waited for the coffee to brew, Maxine asked, "What's in the bags?"

"A present for you. Open them."

Maxine untied one of the bags and looked inside. It was full of clothes. Confused, she turned to Helen. "What's this?"

"Kendra and I went to the yard sale at the Presbyterian Church yesterday, and when I saw these, I thought of you. So here you are. Merry Christmas."

Maxine felt a twinge of jealousy. She wished Grace was more like Helen's daughter, eager to spend hours shopping at bazaars with her mother instead of sitting in a chair having her nails and hair done.

Without saying thanks, Maxine unfolded the clothes. Blouses, slacks, and even a couple of dresses. Most of the clothes still had tags. Maxine didn't know if she should feel grateful or insulted. She wasn't used to getting presents and wasn't quite sure how to act. She wasn't a charity case or needed some stranger's hand-me-downs.

Still.

The lime-green pants were pretty.

"Thought you might like those," Helen said. "Try them on."

Maxine was afraid to look at the size, sure they would be too small. She started to refold them, then hesitated. They were so pretty.

In her bedroom, Maxine slipped into the colorful slacks. In spite of the smaller size marked on the tag, they fit. She studied her butt in the mirror and smiled. It had been a long time since she'd had something brand new, something so nice.

Next she tried on the matching top, an off-white peasant blouse with a green vine embroidered around each wrist. It looked too froufrou for Maxine's tastes, but when she slipped it over her head and saw how nice it matched the pants, she changed her mind. Besides, it hid her fat rows. She took one more look in the mirror and came out of the bedroom. "How do I look?"

"Like Grace Kelly. Saw them hanging on that rack and knew they were you."

"Thanks," Maxine said. "What do I owe you?"

"Not a thing." When Maxine hesitated, Helen added, "It's no big deal. They had a two for one sale."

Even if Helen was telling the truth, that didn't make the clothes easy to accept. Maxine didn't like owing anyone, especially her friends. Even if it was an early Christmas present.

"Go on," Helen said. "Look in the other sack. You'll like the sweaters."

Maxine loved the sweaters, the red blouse and the black slacks. To her surprise, everything fit. Some of the pants were a bit tight, but with a little tug, she managed to close those with zippers.

When Maxine finished modeling for Helen, she slipped into the green pants and offered more coffee along with a tray of the oatmeal cookies she had baked earlier that morning.

"Mmmmmm." Helen took a bite, pointed her cup at Maxine, and said, "Now you have no excuses."

"For what?"

"To stay home. Now you can go to lunch with us at the Center on Wednesday."

Maxine shook her head. "I don't think so."

Helen finished her cookie, then set her cup down hard. Good thing it was empty. "Maxine Foster. You're in this damned house all day long waiting for that no good husband of yours to come home and pass out. It's time you started living your life instead of resenting it. All you do is sit here and wait for something to happen. Hell, you're still young enough to make it happen."

Maxine stiffened. "I do more than sit. Today, I'm making snowflakes."

Helen glanced at the crochet work lying on the table. "You think I don't see how unhappy you are? I don't know why you don't leave him. You could do so much better."

Maxine took a pensive drink and curbed her temper. "If I leave, he gets it all. I didn't stay this long just to hand him everything so he can drink it away."

Helen went to the kitchen and returned with the coffeepot. She refilled their cups and took another cookie. "You don't have to live like this."

"What do you suggest I do, shoot him?"

Helen laughed and choked on her coffee. "No. Then I'd have to visit you in prison. Maybe you should lock him in the closet until he dries out."

"That would kill him for sure." Maxine turned serious. "He isn't eating. He gets all his nutrition from a beer can. His liver has to look like Swiss steak. One of these days he'll keel over, and I'll be free."

"If you say so." Helen put her cup in the kitchen sink and picked up her coat. "In the meantime, look what this is doing to you. Maxine, if you aren't careful, you're going to die before he does. And then all this waiting for him to die will have been a waste of time."

It wasn't funny, but the way Helen said it, her hat bopping back and forth like a dead pheasant, made Maxine laugh. She laughed so hard, she spilled coffee all over her new pants.

Later, as she stood by the sink in her underwear letting the cold water wash away the stain, she realized what Helen said could very well come true. It was time for a change.

She began with the pair of stained gray sweats. Instead of putting them on, she tossed them in the garbage. Wasn't much, but it was a beginning.

*   *   *

Grace and Rob were dining at her favorite restaurant, Rudy's. She had just finished her salad when Michael Lancaster entered the restaurant and followed a waiter to an empty table adjacent to theirs. When he saw her, he smiled, and her fork clattered to the floor.

"Someone you know?" Rob said.

Grace coughed and took a sip of water. "He just bought the house on Cedar Lane." If silence had been a loaf of bread, Grace could have sliced it with her icy recrimination.

"I'm sorry, Grace. I know you wanted that house."

Grace blotted her lips and folded her napkin. "A lot you care."

"That isn't fair. You and Abbie are always my first concerns."

"Right after your precious job."

Rob put his knife down. "Don't do this. I wanted to enjoy a quiet evening without a lot of drama."

Grace stood. "I have to use the restroom."

She ran cold water over her wrists to stop the angry tears. Nodding at a slight woman washing her hands, Grace touched up her lipstick and returned to the dining room. She needed a drink, a bottle of wine. But instead of a vintage chardonnay waiting at the table, she discovered Michael.

"Honey," Rob indicated with his hand. "This is Michael Lancaster. He was dining alone so I asked him to join us."

Michael stood. "I hope you don't mind. Your husband insisted."

"Of course not." The evening was already ruined, what did it matter?

"I want to thank you."

"For what?" Grace looked from Michael to Rob, trying to ignore the question in her husband's eyes.

"I had a tight schedule last week," Michael explained. "Your wife was kind enough to show me a house. And I made an offer they accepted."

Rob broke the awkward silence by raising his glass. "Well, then. Congratulations."

Grace stiffly lifted her glass. "Congratulations." She took a deep long drink. The wine burned. She took another.

"Michael tells me he's the new principal at Aspen High," Rob said as he refilled their glasses. "From Kansas City."

"Kansas City." She'd never been to Kansas City. Never had the desire to see the flat Midwest or the prairie.

"I heard they were replacing Greg Anderson. That heart attack did him in," Rob said.

"Sad," Michael said. "But he seems to be in good spirits. I met with him this afternoon and he's planning a lot of camping trips come summer."

They had just finished eating when Rob's cell buzzed. "I'm sorry," he said. "I have to take this."

If Michael hadn't been sitting at their table, Grace would have protested. But Michael nodded. "I know all about intruding phone calls. Had a few of those myself today."

"So," Grace struggled with the uncomfortable silence. "You got the house?"

"I did, thanks to you." He raised his wineglass. "To new beginnings."

He had a nice smile and even though she tried, she found it hard not to like him. "To new beginnings." She clinked her glass against his, relaxing under his smile.

His manner was easy-going, not overpowering like Rob's. He laughed as he talked about losing the keys to the rental car. "I'm making a fine first impression here in Aspen Grove," he said.

He was certainly making an impression on her. She smiled and listened attentively as he talked about his job and settling in. She caught herself wondering what it would be like to be his wife, off on a new adventure. Lost in her daydream, Grace missed what he said about Greek waffles.

"Oh." Grace took a drink to cover her embarrassment. "Ah, do you get a lot of snow in Kansas?"

"Our fair share."

He was easy to talk to, and she wanted to ask a hundred questions. Why was he moving? Why Aspen Grove? Was he married? She didn't see a ring. "When will you move in?"

"As soon as possible."

"How do you like the neighborhood?" If Rob had acted sooner, she'd be the one unpacking boxes.

"Love the trees. Especially the lindens."

"Me, too." Their eyes met and held. She was the first to look away.

They finished the wine and sat in awkward silence. When he looked at his watch, Grace said, "Please. You don't have to stay on my account. Rob will be back any minute."

"I don't mind," he said. "Besides, I enjoy your company."

Was he flirting? She didn't think so. Yet, in a strange way it felt like flirting. She didn't need a mirror to know she was blushing. Her stomach fluttered; her fingers tingled. "You might be sorry. He could be gone most of the evening."

"I don't mind." Michael flagged the waiter. "Chardonnay?" he asked Grace.

"I prefer Merlot."

"Bring us a bottle of your best Merlot," he told the waiter. When they were alone he pulled his chair closer. "So, tell me Grace Buchanan, have you always lived in Aspen Grove?"

There was a strong physical attraction. She wondered if he felt it, too.

Every time she asked him a question, he turned the conversation back to her. What kind of music did she like? Did her eyes always sparkle? Did she like to walk in the rain?

It had been a long time since anyone was interested in Grace and she eagerly answered his questions. Face flushed from the wine, she was talking too much, but he never looked away or appeared bored. In fact, he encouraged her. She was describing her relationship with her father when Rob appeared.

"Sorry." He turned to Grace. "Ready?"

"No." She was having a good time. He could just wait.

Rob remained standing, making it clear that he wanted to leave. She was ready to tell him to sit down when he said, "Grace. We need to go."

An uncomfortable silence followed until Grace rose. She extended her hand. "Nice talking with you, Michael. Welcome to Aspen Grove." She genuinely meant it. She could have spent the rest of the evening in his company.

They drove home in silence. Grace had no idea what Rob was thinking, and frankly, didn't care. She was too busy thinking about Michael. His warm hand. Strong. Hard to let go. She could still smell his cologne. She thought about that and the flutter in her stomach all the way home.

*   *   *

"Abbie?" Her mother knocked before opening the door. "I thought you were spending the night with Heather."

Scrunched in the middle of her bed squeezing a pillow, Abbie rounded into a tighter ball. "Go away."

Any other mother would reach out and hug her daughter. Any other mother would sit on the edge of the bed and offer her shoulder, but not Abbie's. *Her* mother stood in the doorway as if she were afraid to enter the room.

"What's wrong?"

"Nothing."

"Did something happen at school?"

"No."

"Did you have a fight with Heather?"

"NO." Abbie threw the pillow to the floor so hard, it bounced. Then she pulled her knees up under her chin and hugged them close.

Her mother watched with that stupid pained expression.

"What?"

"Are you going to tell me what's going on?" her mother said. "Or should I call your father?"

"IF YOU HAVE TO KNOW, Heather's mom and dad are SO SELFISH."

"Why, because they need some time apart?"

"It's called a separation, Mom. And they're making Heather choose who to live with."

"It can't be that bad."

"Shows what you know. Every weekend, Heather's supposed to go to her dad's. Fifty miles away. I'll never get to see her."

"Well, if that's true, then I'm sorry. I'm sure the Winters aren't happy about this either. Sometimes people fall out of love. Sometimes it's better if they live apart."

"You think it's better if Heather moves away with her dad?" Abbie unfolded her legs and stood. "I don't know why I tell you anything. You never understand." Sketchbook and red pens in hand, she pushed past her mother. "If you EVER divorce Daddy, I will hate you for forever!"

Abbie stomped down the stairs and opened the door to her father's study. "Can I come in?"

"Sure, Pumpkin," her father said. "What's up?"

"Nothing. I just need a quiet place to draw."

"Have a chair. I'd like some company."

"Thanks."

While her father worked on his book—he was writing a mystery novel—Abbie curled into the overstuffed chair. The first picture she drew was an image of her mother, which Abbie scribbled over until the paper looked like it was covered in blood. Then she wadded the drawing and tossed it at the garbage can. Bingo. Score six points for Team Abbie.

She drew another sketch, and another. By the time Abbie finished her third drawing—this time a picture of a grove of aspen trees covered with starlings in winter—her hand was calmer, her fight with her mother almost forgotten.

Occasionally she would look up from her sketches to watch her father. Every time, he looked at her and smiled. He knew her so well, loved her unconditionally. Unlike Heather, if she had to choose, she knew exactly whom she'd pick.

*   *   *

Fine, Grace thought. Run to your father. He can fix anything. She flinched at the click of the study door. Four more years. Maybe even less before Abbie was out of the house. Then she could stop censoring everything she said.

Sometimes, when Grace fought with Abbie, she'd think of her own mother and feel guilty. In the kitchen, Grace poured another glass of wine and looked at the clock. Nine o'clock. Maybe her mother was still awake. The phone rang five times before her mother answered.

"Hello?" Her mother sounded tired, sleepy.

This was a mistake. Grace sank into the sofa. "Hi, Mom. Just checking to see how your week went. Sorry it's so late."

"What time is it anyway?" Grace could hear her mother fumble for her glasses.

"A little after nine. I didn't mean to wake you. I'll call tomorrow so we can catch up."

"I'm talking to you now," her mother said. "What do you want?"

"Mom, please don't fight with me. Not tonight."

"I'm not fighting with you. I asked what you wanted."

Grace reached for her wine. Why was it always so hard to talk to her mother? She shouldn't have called. Now it was too late to hang up without a fuss.

"What's wrong?" her mother said.

"I just had a fight with Abbie. I don't understand that girl."

"What's wrong with Abbie?" Her mother was instantly awake and alert.

"Oh, you know. Teenage hysterics. Heather's parents are separating, and Abbie's carrying on as if planet Earth just exploded. You'd think Rob and I were getting a divorce, the way she's acting." Grace switched the phone to her left hand and took a sip of wine. "Not that I haven't thought about it."

"What's wrong with you, Grace?" her mother said. "Are you in the bottle again?"

"What makes you think anything's wrong? Maybe I just wanted to talk to my mother."

"Since when? Sometimes, Grace, I wonder about you. Rob's a good man. You don't know how lucky you are."

"You're right, Mom. I never had it so good. Sorry I woke you." Grace clicked off the phone.

After refilling her glass, this time cutting the Merlot with club soda to save calories, she settled on the sofa and stared at the walls in the living room. Her house always felt so cold. She heard Abbie and Rob laughing in his office and turned on the TV. Louder. Sipping wine, she walked around the living room, straightening the pillows and pictures. This was her home, everything she'd ever wanted. She'd worked hard to make it perfect. Yet, in spite of all her hard work, it felt like the inside of a freezer.

She settled on the sofa, pulling the blanket close and thought about the house on Cedar Lane. Even sparsely furnished, it was warm and inviting. She imagined lounging on a couch, enjoying talking for hours with Michael.

She was tempted to track down his cell phone number, to use any excuse to hear his voice again. If she had his number, she might even call him and thank him for the pleasant evening and the extra bottle of wine at Rudy's.

The door to Rob's office opened and closed, and Abbie pattered up the stairs without so much as "goodnight."

Grace folded the blanket and stared at her maroon walls. Kansas City. Greek waffles. She wanted to slip into her shoes. Drive to the house on Cedar Lane. Instead, she turned out the light and went to bed before she did something stupid.

CHAPTER FIVE

TODAY. BEFORE SHE LOST HER NERVE.

Abbie stood near art class waiting for Jeremy. Talking with Charles Kennedy, he would have walked right by her, but Abbie stepped forward. "Can we talk?" Charles raised an eyebrow and proceeded into the classroom, leaving Abbie and Jeremy alone by the door.

Now that she had his attention, she didn't know what to say. *I was wondering … would you like … are you busy …* "I, um, I was wondering." Her heart beat so fast her tongue wouldn't move. "Next week is . . ." Her voice squeaked like a mouse's. What was wrong with her? She wasn't afraid of boys. Many of her friends were boys. But today, standing next to *this* boy, she forgot how to talk. Maybe Jessica was right. Maybe she *was* pathetic.

The warning bell rang, and Jeremy nodded to the door. "We're going to be late."

Abbie darted into the room and took her seat. Total humiliation. *Thank you, Mr. Young, for not assigning seats according to last names.* If she had to sit beside Jeremy all period after that disaster, she would die.

Class over, Abbie gave a relieved sigh when she saw Jeremy walking away with Charles. He wasn't Degas, Matisse or Escher. He was just a boy. But asking him to the dance was harder than she thought it would be.

That night Abbie decided it might be easier to ask Jeremy over the phone. That way she wouldn't lose her mind every time he looked at her. He had a cell, but she didn't know his number.

Since his father was an electrician, his number was easy to find. Abbie waited until after dinner before she called.

"Hello?"

She startled at the gruff voice. "Um. Hello. Could I. Could I speak to Jeremy?"

"No." The man huffed and slammed down the phone before Abbie could say anything further.

"Asshole." Abbie yelled at the phone. What a crappy father.

The next day at school when Heather asked about Jeremy, Abbie said, "This dance thing is stupid. I don't want to go anyway." Lie.

"Want me to ask him for you?"

"NO."

"There has to be a way." Heather wrinkled her forehead. "I know." Her face brightened. She ran to the bulletin board and unpinned the poster for the dance. "Give me a pen."

Heather folded the poster in half and wrote in big red letters: TO JEREMY BLACKBURN. FROM ABBIE BUCHANAN. WILL YOU GO TO SADIE HAWKINS WITH ME?? When Heather slipped the poster between the chevron slits in Jeremy's locker, Abbie giggled, and then actually squealed as she and Heather ran away from the locker.

"He'll say yes," Heather said. Abbie hoped so. Maybe he'd even think she was clever for the way she offered the invitation.

All weekend long, when Abbie should have been working on her sketches, she caught herself daydreaming. Had he found it? Did he smile and think she was cool, or did he show it to Charles and laugh? Wad it up and kick it around the halls like a football? Ignore it and pretend he never saw it?

Monday morning Abbie woke with a stomachache. She thought about skipping school. As soon as she saw Heather, she would tell her that she wasn't going to that stupid dance, even if Jeremy said yes. Just thinking about it made her miserable, twisted and jumpy.

Art class was torture. Jeremy nodded to her on his way in but said nothing. Not yes, not no. Not even hello. She tried to focus on her sketches, but every line she drew looked wrong, like something a three-year old would draw. Unlike her—an unfocussed mess—every time she glanced his way, Jeremy was bent over his drawing, working diligently until the bell rang. Never had fifty minutes lasted so long.

He was waiting for her at the door. "Hey, Buchanan."

"Blackburn." Her heart hammered; her hands were ice.

"Lose something?" He flashed her the poster.

"No." She grabbed the paper, shoved it into her sketchbook and rushed away.

Later, alone in her room when she was supposed to be studying, she looked at the poster. She could no longer recognize the message Heather had written. Instead, intricate drawings surrounded Heather's letters, each one depicting the dance. A tub of apples. A stack of hay. A barnyard of animals. Mayor of Dog Patch and Marryin' Sam scarecrows. Abbie and Jeremy dressed like Li'l Abner and Daisy Mae, dancing on top of an old truck. Below the drawing he had written, *Sorry. Can't go. Grounded. J Blackburn.* Beside his signature, so tiny she almost missed it, was an elongated loop, a sign she recognized as infinity.

Crushed, Abbie pushed the poster aside. She shouldn't have wanted this so much. She should have known better. When Jessica found out, she'd tell the whole school Abbie got what she deserved because she was such a loser.

Abbie's cell phone buzzed, and she glanced at Heather's text.

HE SAID NO, Abbie replied and switched off her phone.

Later, when she crawled into bed, Abbie studied the poster. It wasn't that he didn't like her. He was grounded. He wouldn't be going with anyone, not even Jessica. Besides, he had written, *thanks for asking.*

In spite of her disappointment, Abbie was fascinated with the picture. She wished she could draw like that. No doubt about it, if he applied for the scholarship, she'd have no way of winning first place. He was a master. Look at the way he'd already captured her heart.

Well, maybe he was grounded. That didn't mean they couldn't hang out. That didn't mean they couldn't be friends. Instead of going to the dance, maybe they could meet at the library, and he could show her how to draw those scarecrows.

She could have fallen asleep with sorrow on her pillow. But her head was filled with images of horses, cows and apples. Anyone could go to a dance. But no one could draw like Jeremy.

*   *   *

"Whoever said the first time is the hardest doesn't know what they're talking about," Maxine muttered. Instead of drinking coffee, knitting or watching soaps, Maxine spent the morning curling her hair and pressing her lime-green outfit. Her arguments with Helen and Shirley about the Senior Center were a waste of energy now that she couldn't say she had nothing to wear.

She wasn't young anymore, but she wasn't sure she wanted to spend her days with old people either. What did they do all day at the Center anyway? "Sit around and talk about all their aches and pains, that's what," Maxine said as she slipped into the polyester pants. She had better things to do than spend all day with a bunch of drooling senior citizens.

Maxine looked at the clock. Helen said eleven-thirty sharp. She still had half an hour. She went to the kitchen for a glass of water. Sprinkled food in the fish tank. Went to the bathroom. Tried to crochet, but every few minutes she'd run to the mirror to check her reflection, to make sure her hair was as perfect as she could make it. She fussed with her makeup and reapplied waxy lipstick that was at least ten years old, so red, it made her look clownish. She wiped it off. Put it on again. Checked her clothes. Her hair. Her face over and over until it was finally time to go. Coat buttoned and a new crocheted hat on her head, Maxine met Shirley at the door.

"You look great," Shirley said.

"Like anyone's going to notice." Maxine patted her pocket to make sure her house cleaning money was still there.

When they arrived at the Center, everyone greeted Maxine with honest camaraderie. "Where have you been? We've missed you." She answered their questions with shrugs and hugs, enjoying the attention. It had been a long time since someone seemed happy to see her.

"I thought I poisoned you with my cooking," Dixie said when Maxine went through the lunch line. "Did you make that carrot cake yet?"

"Not yet. But I'm gonna."

Linda, the director of the Center, stepped in line behind Maxine. "Today, we're not going to let you slip away so fast. You're staying for bingo."

Bingo? Maxine hadn't played bingo since she was a kid.

After filling her plate, Maxine followed Helen and Shirley to their usual table. Shirley waved to Ray Miles, and Maxine noticed that the man who had commented on her blouse during her last visit sat alone. This time she didn't ignore him, but said, "How are you?"

He beamed. "Fine. Thanks for asking."

There were three empty seats at their table, and Helen waved him over. He smiled and took a seat across from Maxine.

The Swedish meatballs and homemade noodles Dixie fixed for lunch were so good Maxine returned for seconds. She was tempted to go back for thirds. It was nice to eat something someone else had cooked.

"It's been a long time since I've had homemade noodles," Maxine said. "I forgot how good they are."

"Loretta used to make noodles," the man said. "Made them every holiday to go with the turkey or ham."

"I'll bet they were tasty." It would be nice to cook for someone like him who appreciated good food.

"They were. I miss her cooking. Especially at holidays."

Instead of hiding behind her sweater and mumbling in monosyllables, Maxine tried to be more sociable. This man's wife had cancer. He could be sitting home feeling sorry for himself. But here he was, making an effort to be pleasant. Unlike her husband, he wasn't passed out in front of the TV.

She wondered what Herb would do when he retired. The Center was the last place he'd be, commenting on someone's homemade noodles, that's for sure. She stabbed a meatball and chewed it to bits.

With lunch over and the tables cleared, Linda brought out the bingo cards. Even though she thought she was too old for the game, Maxine could play for fifty cents a card, and they had great prizes. There was a box of Russell Stover Chocolates, an artificial bouquet of red poinsettias that would look good on her coffee table, a bottle of lotion with aloe for chapped hands, a tin of shortbread cookies, and Christmas ornaments. Maxine had her eye on a particular ornament. Elvis stood inside a snow globe and sang "Blue Christmas" when a plastic button was pushed.

Still early November, Maxine was in no mood for Christmas. She wasn't ready for it at all, but at that particular moment she wanted that ornament more than she wanted Herb to disappear. She dug out her money and asked for two bingo cards. She wouldn't leave the table until she was broke or the ornament belonged to her.

"You know," a gray-haired woman on Maxine's left said. "Bingo is good for your brain. It prevents Alzheimer's because you have to count."

Shirley ignored the chatty woman while Maxine just stared at her as she babbled away even though no one listened. This was one of the reasons Maxine avoided the Center. They were a bunch of old fools waiting to die or go crazy.

"Bingo!"

Maxine had been so preoccupied with her neighbor that she had missed the last three numbers. Ray Miles waved his hand to claim his prize. Thank God he chose the chocolates. Maxine glared at the woman beside her, determined not to be distracted again. She even refused to look up when the woman said, "Don't forget to mark the center. It's free, you know."

Nothing's free, Maxine almost said but stopped before the woman could engage her in another conversation.

"B-14," Linda called.

"Did she say B-13?" the woman to Maxine's left said. Maxine tried to ignore her.

"I-25."

"Yea!" Shirley clapped her hands. "Come on Linda, give me just one more."

"N-40. N-39. G-50."

"Bingo!" A man waved his hand to claim his prize, settling on the lotion for his wife.

"I think this game's rigged." Helen set up two more cards. "Why are all the men winning today?"

"Because the women can't keep their mouths shut." Maxine scowled at the woman beside her before moving to the other side of Shirley where she could concentrate. She had enough money for three more games, and she didn't want to lose.

Linda called the numbers for the next game. Maxine lost by two numbers. The following game was worse. She had only marked three spots when someone yelled, "Bingo!"

She looked hard at the Elvis ornament and concentrated. Once, on TV, one of her soap opera leading ladies said if you wanted something, all you had to do was envision it, and it would come to you. Maxine stared at the ornament and saw a Christmas tree standing in her living room. She concentrated harder until she saw the ornament hanging from a branch. She focused until she could hear Elvis Presley singing.

"Bingo!"

"Crap." Maxine pushed her cards away as Helen waved her hand to have her card verified.

Once approved, Helen took her time selecting a prize. She looked at the poinsettias, the tin of cookies, settling on the Elvis Presley ornament.

No, Maxine wanted to say. That's mine! But she didn't. If she couldn't win the ornament, it may as well be Helen. At least that way she could see it when she stopped in for coffee.

Out of money, Maxine said. "I'm done."

"Same here," Shirley said. "I need to get home before the grandkids get there."

They were buttoning their coats when Linda stopped them in the hallway. "Maxine, I wanted to ask you about your hat. It's so pretty."

"Thanks," Maxine said. She was proud of her hat, one she'd made without a pattern.

"Would you teach me how to make one for my sister? Is there time before Christmas?"

"Me, too," Dixie said, coming from the kitchen with a fresh pot of coffee.

"I'd like to learn." The gray-haired woman who kept talking during bingo added. "Be good for my Alzheimer's."

"Roberta," Linda said. "You don't have Alzheimer's."

"I know," Roberta said. "And I want to keep it that way."

"Tell you what." Linda took Maxine's arm and pulled her away from the others. "If you'd be willing to lead a class once or twice a week, I think we could pay you. It wouldn't be much, maybe ten dollars a week. I know our members would enjoy it. They're always looking for something new to do."

"I don't know." Maxine had never seen herself as a teacher. Once she'd wanted to be a nurse. But that was long ago, before she'd married Herb.

"We wouldn't have to start with a hard project, maybe something simple. Like those snowflakes you made the last time you were here. We would love those."

"Can I think about it?"

"Of course. Take all the time you need. But I hope you say yes." Linda hugged Maxine. "Come back soon."

It was after three before Helen pulled into Maxine's driveway. As she waved goodbye, Maxine had to admit it had been a long time since she had had so much fun. Her sides ached from laughing.

She put her coat away and pondered. Herb would never have to know she took the job at the Center. She could teach right after lunch and be home long before he left work.

Maxine looked at the clock. Two more hours before Herb would be home. She flipped the lever on the stack of Elvis records and turned up the volume. Then she looked through her crochet books. She didn't need a pattern for the snowflakes or the hat because those were already in her head. But she wanted to have more than two projects ready when she called Linda and told her yes.

*   *   *

Grace stared out the window at the gray November sky and tapped her pen against her desk. No matter how hard she tried, she couldn't stop thinking about Michael and how much she'd enjoyed his company. If only Rob would be as attentive. Taking this job to rouse Rob's attention had worked against her. Instead of being angry with his wife for not conferring with him, Rob had been happy, glad she'd found something to occupy her time.

It wasn't that she didn't like working at Aspen Grove Realty. Sometimes she did, like the days they had potluck or celebrated birthdays. But days like this when the weather was too cold to be outside showing houses, most of the brokers were gone, leaving Grace alone to answer the phones, which was just flat boring.

She needed an adventure. A trip out of town with someone she desired and who desired her. She flipped through the calendar, looking ahead for a long weekend. Thanksgiving was a week away. Maybe she could convince Rob to spend the holiday someplace romantic.

She let the fantasy play in her head. They'd check into a ski lodge, happy, aroused, and breathless. After a long soapy shower, they'd tumble onto the clean sheets, hungry for each other—the way they did before Abbie was born. Their skis would never leave the room while they discovered new ways to please each other. They'd make love on the floor in front of a fire.

They'd make love in the snow, in the hot tub. They'd sleep late, make love again for hours, and feed each other chocolate-covered strawberries from bowls on their pillows.

Grace grew warm just thinking about it. She dialed her travel agent. Then she poked her head into Kent's office. "It's quiet this afternoon. Do you think I could leave early?"

Busy at his computer, Kent looked up. "Sure. Take the rest of the day off."

"Thanks."

In less than ten minutes, Grace was in Victoria's Secret, trying on lingerie.

When Rob arrived home that night, the salad was tossed. Brown rice was cooking in the steamer. Grace had scrubbed the outdoor grill and had steaks marinating.

"Ahhhh," Rob said. "Something smells good."

"I hope it's me and not just the food," Grace teased.

"Of course, it's you." Rob tipped her chin and kissed her. She wrapped her arms around his neck and held him tight, wanting more moments like this.

"Where's Abbie?" Rob motioned to the table set for two.

"Spending the night at Heather's."

"Again? Maybe we should start paying the Winters rent." He loosened his tie. "Abbie's growing up too fast. I never get to see her."

You would if you were home more. Grace bit back the urge to complain. He was home. In a good mood. She didn't want to ruin the evening.

"Would you do the honors?" She handed him a bottle of wine and held glasses while he poured.

"To us." She clinked his glass and took a sip.

"To us." He toasted and kissed her before going to the bedroom to change.

She was tempted to follow, to slip into her new negligee, but decided to wait. They could eat first. There was plenty of time after dinner.

They had just finished eating and were enjoying another glass of wine when Grace handed him an envelope.

"What's this?"

"A surprise." She grinned.

"I like surprises." He opened the envelope, and his smile turned into a question. "Grace?"

She snuggled into his lap. Arms around his neck, she kissed him. "A trip, honey. A romantic getaway."

"I can see that." He pulled out of her embrace. "For two. Next week."

Grace waltzed around the room. "I know. Cathy worked magic to get us that deal. We're all set. I've already started packing."

Rob pushed away from the table, upsetting his empty wine glass. He took three steps toward the sink and turned. "You know we can't go."

Grace stopped dancing. "What do you mean, 'we can't go'. I made all the arrangements."

Rob leaned against the counter and folded his arms across his chest. "You'll have to unmake them. I can't get away. We're having a big sale."

"You can get out of it." She refilled their glasses and smiled. He refused the wine and stepped away.

"I don't know what the big fuss is anyway." Grace smiled and tried to ease the tension in the room. "You can get away if you want to."

He stiffened when she tried to kiss him. "Don't."

"Fine." Grace grabbed his wine and drank it. She snuffed the candles and put the glasses in the dishwasher. Then she cleared the table, banging plates and dropping silverware on the floor.

"You should have asked me first," Rob said. "I can't go."

"I heard you," Grace said. "I'll call Cathy tomorrow and cancel."

"Why don't you take Abbie? It would be nice for the two of you to get away. Have some quality mother-daughter time."

Like she wanted to spend a romantic weekend with her daughter. Grace filled the dishwasher with soap, slammed the door and snapped the ON button. For several minutes the only sound in the kitchen was that of running water.

"I'm going to bed," Grace said when the kitchen was clean.

"Maybe she can schedule it for another time," Rob offered.

Maybe she should find someone else to go. Like Michael Lancaster.

"My head hurts. I need to lie down." It sounded like a weak excuse, when in fact the wine had gone to her head. A migraine pounded in her temple.

Alone in their bedroom, Grace slipped into a nightshirt without glancing at the new silk negligee draped on the chair. With a damp cloth over her eyes, she lay on the bed in the dark, unable to move. It took every inch of resolve to stay still, when what she really wanted to do was break a window and scream.

CHAPTER SIX

THE BEAUTICIAN WITH PINK HAIR teased higher than a space needle stared at Grace's reflection in the mirror. "Are you sure?"

"I'm sure," Grace said.

"But—but---"

"But what?" Grace looked around the shop for another stylist. She didn't have time for this one; she was too skittish.

"Your hair is . . ."

The stylist looked as though one cross word would send her into a fit of tears. "It's my hair," Grace said. "If I want to dye it blond, why can't I?"

"You're right, lady, you're right." The stylist fumbled as she fastened Grace's shampoo cape. "Okay. Let's get started. But—but—do you know how many women walk through that door and beg me to give them color like yours?"

"Please." Grace was harsher than she needed to be, but the fact was it took all night to decide. Yes, her auburn hair was pretty. Grace took special care to keep it shiny and silky. But she wanted something new that would turn a man's head.

Grace gave the stylist a picture she tore from a magazine. "After it's colored, I want it cut. Like this."

The stylist laid the picture on the counter. "Maybe we should cut it first."

Grace looked at the clock. "Do it." She hated having to schedule appointments around her lunch hour. No more long lunches with Brenda and Carmen. No more late morning massages or pedicures. Even though Grace liked working at Aspen Grove Realty, there were times working had its disadvantages.

The stylist picked up her scissors. "Here we go."

Grace closed her eyes. She could have taken the picture to her own beautician, who'd been styling Grace's hair for years. But Angie loved Grace's hair just the way it was, and Grace wasn't sure Angie would cut it so short, let alone dye it blond.

Snip. Snip. Snip.

Grace tensed with each clip of the scissors.

"Done." The stylist handed Grace a mirror and spun the chair so Grace could see the back of her head. "What do you think?"

The short pixie style made Grace's face look younger. She relaxed her shoulders. She liked it, very much.

"Ready for that color?"

"Actually." Grace looked at her watch. "We can color it another day. I have to get back to work."

The beautician smiled. "Told you. Your hair is pretty just the way it is." Using a brush and blow dryer, she finished. "Check it out."

"Thanks." Grace tipped the stylist, took one last look at her reflection and smiled.

At the office, Trudy turned Grace in circles. "Look at you. If I saw you on the street, I wouldn't recognize you. It's very chic. Very you."

"Nice." Kent whistled. "If I wasn't married, I'd ask you for a date." Grace beamed, pleased with the attention.

She was standing at the copy machine when Michael Lancaster walked through the door.

"Excuse me," he said. "I'm looking for . . ." His mouth formed a round O when he saw her. "Grace?"

She nodded, feeling suddenly awkward and shy.

"I'm here to sign the papers on the house. We're closing today." He whistled. "Look at you."

Just then, Cheryl Adams, the escrow officer, stepped out of her office. "Hi, Michael. This way."

Michael followed Cheryl to her office, but when he passed Grace, he said, "Nice haircut. Makes your eyes sparkle."

Grace blushed, her heart racing. She smiled and wondered if her husband would be as complimentary.

But when she got home, no one noticed her hair. Abbie was busy with her sketches, and Rob was still working.

After changing clothes, Grace poured herself a glass of wine, and turned on the TV. Nothing held her attention, not even the commercials advertising nail polish. Bored, she flipped through several magazines on the end table, finally focusing on the latest real estate guide. She enjoyed looking at new houses and fantasizing on how nice it would be to move in, to start over, fresh.

Grace turned the pages to the house on Cedar Lane and sighed. She liked Michael. If she couldn't have the house, she was glad it was his. And she was going to tell him.

She clicked off the television and pulled an unopened bottle of wine from the wine rack. After touching up her makeup, she yelled up the stairs to Abbie. "I need to run to the store. Be back soon." Then she drove to Cedar Lane. The front-porch light beamed into the night, welcoming her in.

Smiling, Grace rang the doorbell. In a perfect world, this would be her house. But her world was far from perfect. A bottle of wine and pleasant conversation was sure to make it better.

She rang the bell again and stood straighter when she heard approaching footsteps. Expecting Michael, she smiled wider.

"Hello?"

Grace stared at the thin woman answering the door. About Grace's age, if Grace had to guess, the woman was pretty without makeup. Her hair was pulled back in a ponytail. "I, um." The words of welcome went out of her head. Her smile faded.

"I'm sorry," Grace said. "I was looking for the Peterson's. I must have the wrong house." She turned abruptly and left the woman standing in the doorway, a silhouette in the kitchen light.

Grace drove home without noticing the stoplights or the trees. She pulled into her driveway without seeing anything but the woman standing at Michael's door. Flushed and shaking, she knew she had no right to be jealous, but she was. She threw her keys on the table. "What were you thinking, Grace. What on earth were you thinking?"

She opened the wine and drank a glass, then another. By the time her husband came home and turned out the lights, Grace was passed out on the sofa. She wasn't thinking at all.

*   *   *

While Heather and Tyler enjoyed the dance, Abbie sat on her bedroom floor and studied Jeremy's drawing. So he couldn't go. No dejection there. Rather, more like intrigue—why was he grounded? Had he lied to his parents—had he wrecked his car or stayed out too late? And how did he make that amazing drawing? The whole picture looked like one continuous line. Full of questions, Abbie tried to find where he lifted the pen, but even with her nose all but touching the paper, she couldn't. Determined to discover his secret, she opened her sketchbook.

The pumpkin patch was easy, but the Dogpatch scarecrows proved more challenging. When she tried to duplicate Jeremy's picture of them dancing on top of the old truck, Abbie's hand faltered. Would he pull her close—would she lay her head on his shoulder? Would he kiss her? Her hands turned sweaty, her heart beat so fast she was light-headed.

She set her drawing aside and went to the mirror. As Heather had earlier, Abbie lifted her thick hair and twisted it in a knot. She plaited it into braids, combing them out with her fingers. Imitating Jessica, she tossed her hair over her shoulder. Did Jeremy like long hair? Did he prefer blondes to brunettes? Should she dye it, streak it blue to match the color of his eyes? Maybe even get a tattoo?

An unsettled feeling invaded her stomach, making her edgy. In the kitchen, Abbie filled a glass with water, took a sip, and poured it down the drain. She opened cupboards. Bran flakes. Wheat Thins. Raw almonds. Choosing the leftover lasagna, she zapped it in the microwave, not sure she was even hungry.

"Abbie?" Her mother called from the living room where she sat on her white sofa and read *Vogue* and interior design magazines. If they'd been a real family, Abbie could take her lasagna into the living room, plop down beside her mother, and ask about the first time she fell in love. But even if Abbie's mother allowed her to eat in the living room with its white carpet—strictly forbidden—the last thing she would discuss with her daughter was falling in love.

She took the lasagna to her room and thumbed through the latest issue of *Seventeen*. She studied the clothes and hairstyles. She read an article about moods and makeup and made a list of things to do the next time she saw Jeremy: always smile but don't be pushy; don't act like an airhead; try to be his friend and bolster his ego. She even considered layering her hair and changing whatever it took to make him like her.

She felt desperate like the women in Dogpatch. "Just call me Daisy Mae," she sniffed at her sorry reflection.

Thinking about Jeremy was messing with her head. She always wondered what Heather saw in boys. Now she knew.

Abbie picked up her cell. She wanted to call him, but chickened out. Instead, she called Heather. "How's the dance?" Abbie asked when Heather picked up.

"It's so cool," Heather said. "You should have come, even without Jeremy. We're on our way to the apple tank. We're going to dunk for apples."

"Sounds fun," Abbie said half-heartedly. It would have been so much fun bobbing for apples with Jeremy.

"So," Abbie said. "Who's all there?"

"Jessica's hanging on some guy I don't know, and no, he isn't here," Heather said.

"Who?"

"You know who. I gotta go. Talk to you later." Heather clicked off her cell and Abbie smiled.

Jessica might be at the dance, doing who knew what, but she wasn't doing it with Jeremy.

Monday afternoon, Abbie watched Jeremy laugh and crack jokes with Charles in the school parking lot. She ached with envy and tried to remember what the magazine said. Smile, then look away. Smile and say, "Hi." Smile, then walk away, but turn and wave. All the advice seemed contrived so she just stood there until he noticed her.

"Hey, Buchanan." He waved. "How's it going?"

She shrugged. "All right. I, um..." Brilliant. Here was her chance. She needed a breath mint. Heather. Her head examined. Courage.

"I, um, was wondering, um, if we could talk about your drawing. Maybe you could show me how you do that." There. Bold, but not too bold.

She grew paranoid as he studied her face. Did she have a new pimple? Were her eyebrows too bushy? Standing so close to him she could hardly breathe.

"Sure," he said. "I'll give ya a call. Maybe this weekend if I don't have to work."

Abbie dug a pen from her backpack. Her hand shook as she wrote her number in the palm of his hand. It was warm, wet. She'd never done that before, but she'd seen other girls do it at school, at the mall. Looked easy enough, but then, why was her heart beating as if it wanted to leap from her chest?

Trying to sound casual, she said, "'K. See ya." She smiled and walked away. But after taking a few steps she had to know. She peeked over her shoulder. He *was* watching her. He even smiled back. Face flushed, head covered with snow, Abbie was so excited, it could have been summer vacation.

But Saturday was still five days away, which made for a very long week.

Saturday morning, Abbie was up, showered, and ready. It took a while to decide what to wear. The gray sky promised snow, so she settled on a soft blue sweater and jeans. She plucked her eyebrows and carefully applied makeup — not too much — just enough to enhance her natural features like the magazine said. She was lucky she didn't have freckles to cover like Heather. Or thin flyaway hair. She wondered if her eyes were too close together, scrutinized her nose, glad it was small and not protrude-y. Then she grabbed her sketchbook and waited.

When he hadn't called by noon, Abbie's hair started fraying from all the knots she'd twisted it into.

"I'm making a chef salad for lunch," her mother said when Abbie went to the kitchen for a soda. "Would you like one?"

"Not hungry."

"You have to eat."

Only her mother would eat a salad in the middle of winter. "Can I have tomato soup instead?"

"Sure." While the soup heated, her mother fixed two salads heaped with crisp greens, hardboiled eggs, and turkey.

"There you go." She put the soup and salad on the table in front of Abbie. "This is nice. We should do this more often."

"What?" Abbie looked at her mother as if she were crazy. "Eat salad?"

"Spend time together on the weekends. You're always so busy."

"Well, yeah. Some of us have a life." Abbie took her soup to her room where she could wait for Jeremy to call without having to talk with her mother.

One o'clock. Two o'clock. Three o'clock. Not a single call. Not a single text. No day had ever felt so long, worse than a trip to the dentist. She waited. Waited. And waited. Every few minutes Heather would text. HAS HE CALLED YET?

NO, Abbie would answer and glare at her phone as if that hopeful energy was enough to make him call.

Should she call him? Should she text? Maybe he was still grounded. Or lost her number. She didn't want to appear needy like her mother, so she didn't call. After a miserable day checking her phone for messages that never arrived, Abbie turned it off and shoved it away.

It was after nine when Abbie put on pajamas and brushed her teeth, but she was afraid to go to bed. Just in case, she turned her phone back on. She texted Heather and listened to music. She sketched. She stared at the walls and willed her cell to ring. But all of her wishing wouldn't make a boy call or text if he didn't want to.

*   *   *

It was late when Maxine finished her work in the kitchen. When she finally had time to relax and watch television, Herb was passed out on the sofa.

"What's that awful smell?" Maxine sniffed the air, trying to locate the source of the foul odor. "Smells like something died." Or Herb forgot to flush the toilet.

She rushed to her aquarium. But the constant whir of the filter reassured her it was working. Priscilla and Elvis swam lazily, unaware of Maxine's concern.

Maxine circled the room sniffing before she stopped at the sofa. Crap. Her good-for-nothing husband was stinking up the room.

"Herb." She shook him. "Dammit Herb. Wake up. You're ruining my couch."

Herb snorted and struggled to open his eyes. "Stoph it." He pushed her hand away and rolled onto his side.

"Get up." She slammed him with a pillow. Again. Again.

"Stoph it!" He tried to stand, fell against the coffee table and toppled to the floor. Now the stench was so strong Maxine had to hold her nose.

"What the---" Maxine stared at the wet spot on her sofa. She turned toward her husband, sprawled on the floor and snoring, unaware that he was no longer on the sofa, or that his pants were stained and smelly.

Maxine kicked him. He didn't move. "Herb. Get up, you drunken bum." She kicked him again. He snored louder.

Maxine was so angry she would have taken a hammer to his head if she had had one. Instead, she pulled his winter coat off the kitchen chair and wrapped it around him like a diaper so he wouldn't ruin her carpet. Then she tugged and pulled and pulled and tugged until he was on the bathroom floor. She slammed the door, then went straight to the kitchen and mixed a solution of carpet cleaner and scrubbed the soiled sofa best she could. When she finished cleaning the sofa and the carpet, she dumped all the alcohol she could find in the house down the drain.

Sitting at the kitchen table with the phone book, Maxine searched the Yellow Pages until she found a listing for Alcoholics Anonymous. With a black marker, she wrote the phone number in big letters on a piece of paper and put it on the counter where she used to place his lunch. Then she locked the doors and turned out the lights. But she was too angry to sleep.

For hours, Maxine sat in the dark, staring at the bathroom door, wondering how she could have married such a loser. By the time she went to bed, just before daybreak, she had decided. Things were going to change even if it meant packing everything he owned into his truck and sending him back to his mother.

CHAPTER SEVEN

INSTEAD OF RISING TO FIX Herb's lunch, Maxine stayed in bed until she heard his truck leave the driveway. When she was sure he wasn't coming back, she slipped out of bed and into the kitchen for her morning coffee. Herb's empty lunch pail sat on the counter, and her note with the number to Alcoholics Anonymous was crumpled beside it. Didn't surprise her. Herb stopped paying attention to her years ago.

But today she had better things to do than worry about Herb. Today the Senior Center was holding a Christmas Bazaar, and Maxine had agreed to bring in some of her handmade items to sell. With Christmas three weeks away, she had no time to make anything new, but she had boxes of knitted hats, crocheted potholders, and doilies that would make wonderful presents. Not to mention the sack of crocheted snowflakes leftover from the classes she'd been teaching twice a week at the Center for almost a month. At that particular moment, Maxine was content, even happy. She had her job cleaning houses, the classes at the Center, and good friends. She yawned and looked at the clock. Best get her big butt moving. Helen would be there any minute.

While the coffee brewed, Maxine went to the bathroom to shower. But the foul smell beside the toilet was so strong, she had to hold her hand over her nose. Damn that crappy man. Herb's dirty clothes were heaped in a pile near the hamper. His shit was all over the floor.

Furious, she gathered his soiled clothes and marched them out to the trash even though it was thirty-two degrees outside and snowing. Dressed in robe and slippers, Maxine was so angry, she didn't care if her neighbors saw her bare legs or ratty hair. This was one set of clothes she was never putting in *her* washing machine ever again. She was so angry, she didn't even check the pockets for loose change.

Maxine used her anger to scrub the bathroom floor. This was her house, too. She might be married to a slob. That didn't mean she had to live in a barn.

When the floor was clean, Maxine stepped into the shower. She let the hot water pulse against her neck, releasing some of the tension. As she shampooed her hair, she wished she could go back in time and marry Larry, or that Herb would drive off the road and into the river. Maybe this was her fault. Instead of harping about his drinking, she should encourage him to drink more. With his diseased liver, it was just a matter of time. Maybe she should give him a case of beer for Christmas.

As she dressed, Maxine pushed Herb from her thoughts. He'd already ruined most of her life. He wasn't going to ruin one more day. Donning her Christmas sweater with the red poinsettias, Maxine was dressed and ready when Helen and Shirley pulled into the driveway. She had even found a pretty, plastic poinsettia for her hair.

Three months ago, if anyone had told Maxine she would be standing behind a card table selling hats and potholders at a Christmas Bazaar, she would have laughed. But by ten a.m. that's exactly what she was doing. While Christmas carols played in the background and the smell of cinnamon rolls and brownies wafted through the building, Maxine encouraged customers to try on hats and rummage through her box of potholders. Singing along with the carols, she was having a grand time and enjoyed every minute visiting with the people who stopped to chat. Two months ago Maxine could have counted her friends on two fingers. But today everyone was cheery, and almost everyone who stopped at their table bought something. Potholders and doilies from Maxine, brownies or fruitcake from Helen, or used books and cast-off jewelry from Shirley. They were busy during the noon hour when secretaries on lunch breaks and tellers from banks stopped in for last minute gifts.

"Thank you," she said between bites of fudge, to a woman who purchased a dozen snowflakes to hang on her tree. Maxine had to eat standing up, which wasn't hard to do. Instead of eating something healthy like the Center's lunch special—chicken noodle soup or a tuna sandwich— Maxine munched on caramel popcorn, chocolate-covered pretzels, and homemade fudge. None of it healthy, but every bite delicious.

Things slowed down after three. By then, Maxine was tired—a happy tired. While she and Shirley took down the table, Helen tallied their earnings. After deducting the five dollars they owed the Center for their space, they had made a nice profit.

"Not bad." Helen handed Maxine an envelope containing her share of the earnings. Ready to leave, they were halfway out the door when Linda stopped them.

"Maxine, wait." Linda ducked into her office and returned with a check. "I should have given this to you yesterday, but I forgot."

"What's this for?" Maxine stared at a check for twenty-five dollars.

"Last week's classes. We added an extra five because we like you so much. And," she said with a wink, "it's almost Christmas."

"You're kidding." *Twenty-five dollars for having fun and laughing?* "Thank you." Maxine grinned. Who'd have thought she'd get paid for doing something she loved?

She waited until she was alone inside her house before she opened her envelope. Five. Ten. Twenty. Thirty. She counted out the money and sank into her sofa. Between what she sold at the bazaar and Linda's check, she had more than three hundred dollars. More than enough money to buy something special for Abbie and Grace for Christmas.

She added the check to the cash and kissed the envelope. "Fa la la la la, la la la la," she sang as she danced around the room. For once, they would have a nice Christmas.

*   *   *

Even though Grace found it inconvenient to reschedule her haircuts and manicures, everything considered, she was glad she had a job to go to. Now that it was December, she'd have something else to decorate besides her own house, which was decorated the day after Thanksgiving. When she asked Kent if they were going to put a tree in the office, he said yes, they always did, and would she like to be in charge? "Yes," she said, already planning the decorations. Gold and ice blue were the year's popular seasonal colors, and instead of an angel or a star, she'd make a huge gold and blue bow to put on top of the tree and cascade to the floor like a river.

Humming "Silver Bells," Grace was standing on a chair trying to attach the bow to the tree when the front door opened, filling the lobby with a cold breeze and the smell of snow and ice. "Be right with you," she said, adjusting the bow. When she looked down, there, holding a huge double white poinsettia and grinning, was Michael. She almost fell off the chair.

"Careful!" He dropped the plant on the counter and rushed toward her.

"I'm fine." The minute he touched her, Grace forgot all about the pretty woman who had opened his door. So what if he was married? She was, too. Didn't mean they couldn't be friends.

"Gotcha," he said with a smile.

If he hadn't been there to catch her, she would have been sprawled on the floor. He was always coming to her rescue, just like he did that night when Rob was too busy to finish his dinner. "I'm such a klutz." She loved his smile, the way he smelled like vacations in Paris and island breezes.

"You," he said, "are many things. But a klutz isn't one of them." He made sure her feet were solid on the floor before he let go.

"Thanks." Grace smoothed her skirt, making sure everything was neat and in order.

He pointed to the plant. "For you. And your office. To say thanks for helping me get the house."

"You didn't need to do that."

"Yes, I did." He looked at his watch. "You wouldn't be free for lunch, would you? I'd like to celebrate."

When he smiled like that, she couldn't resist. Besides, she was starving. "Let me get my coat."

Instead of taking her to Hart's where Rob liked to dine, Michael suggested the nearby Italian diner tucked between the floral and jewelry stores, her favorite place, Rudy's. He held her hand, so she wouldn't slip on the ice as they navigated the short two blocks in the snow. She wasn't cold; she didn't feel the flakes at all. It was like walking in a romantic wonderland until her foot hit an icy patch. She grabbed his arm before she fell.

"Looks like we're making a habit of this." Michael caught her, and they both laughed. Outside, the diner was decorated with blinking red and green lights. Inside, it smelled like cinnamon and mulled wine. The air was festive, full of Christmas.

Unlike Rob, who always made observations about the menu, often suggesting foods Grace hated, Michael asked, "What looks good to you?"

She met his gaze without speaking.

Moments later, studying the menu, she tried to calm her shaking hands. Her heart was beating so fast she was sure he could hear it. Lasagna. Ravioli. Tortellini. Michael. She tried to keep her thoughts on food, which was hard to do with him sitting across the table.

"We'll have the cheese fondue appetizer," he told the waitress. "Grace?"

"Grilled chicken salad." Grace closed the menu.

"You want more than a salad."

Yes, she did. Grace lowered her eyes. "No, a salad's fine. And a glass of tea, please."

"The house ravioli," Michael said. "And a bottle of Merlot. Two glasses."

They sat in awkward silence until the wine was served. Grace's mouth was dry. She could already taste the woodsy flavor. She wondered what it would be like to kiss him. She watched his hand on the bottle, the long steady fingers cupping the wine glass. He clicked her glass and took a drink. She raised her own glass and all but inhaled the wine, hoping it would calm her.

Refilling her glass, he said, "You didn't stop by my house the other day, did you?"

"I, um." Grace froze.

"The woman from the cleaning service said a pretty lady stopped by but seemed confused. I was hoping it was you."

The cleaning lady? Grace relaxed. "When are you moving in?"

"The van arrives in the morning. I'll have a busy weekend."

Grace circled the rim of her wineglass with her finger, making it sing. He'd be in by Christmas.

"You're suddenly quiet."

"Wishful thinking," she said. "I love that house."

"Good. You can help me decorate it."

"Me?"

"Of course. You worked magic on that tree in your office. Ah," Michael smiled as the waitress put the fondue in the middle of the table. "Dive in."

Grace avoided cheese. Like mayonnaise, milk and other fattening foods.

"Don't be shy." Michael pushed his plate across the table and settled beside her. Dipping a piece of bread into the warm cheese, he held it to her lips. "Open."

She savored the salty explosion. She licked cheese from her bottom lip and dunked a cube of bread and offered it to him.

"Delicious." He swallowed in a slow sensuous bite. "Another?"
She nodded, unable to deny the heat rising inside.

They lingered over the fondue. By the time the waitress delivered the ravioli, they were no longer hungry. Fuzzy with wine, Grace would have sat beside him all afternoon, but she finally remembered her job. "What time is it?" she said with a start.

He looked at his watch. "One-thirty."

She stood. "I'm late. I have to go."

They walked back to the office, touching, but not speaking. She stopped at the door. "Thanks for lunch."

"You're welcome. Have a nice weekend. I'll be busy moving in."

She stalled, unwilling to let him go.

"If you get bored, I have some boxes that need unpacking," he said, as if reading her thoughts.

She shot him a quick glance to see if he was teasing. She couldn't tell. "Thanks for lunch," she repeated.

"My pleasure." They might have stood there all day if it hadn't been for the phone. "I have to get that." Grace moved toward her desk, waving goodbye. "Aspen Grove Realty." She couldn't focus on her job or the person on the phone. All she could think about was Michael. His new house, his hands, his lips and his smile.

*   *   *

Jeremy was standing by his locker talking with Charles and a few of his friends. Determined to ignore him, Abbie clutched her books closer. When she passed him, she diverted her eyes. He wasn't worth the energy. Jessica could have him.

But all that changed after art class. She was all but out the door when he stopped her. "Hey, you mad at me?" He looked totally sincere.

"No."

"Then what's wrong?"

"You said you would call."

"I know," he said. "But I had to help my dad. All weekend."

"Is there a law saying you can't pick up a phone for three seconds?" Her voice was shaking.

"You're right," he said. They were almost at her English class. "Next time, I'll do better." He smiled, and she forgave him, just like that. Just like Saturday had never happened.

"Catch ya later," he said, then walked on down the hall, taking her heart and good intentions with him.

Three weeks before Christmas and Abbie still hadn't persuaded Jeremy to show her how to draw that picture. Any other girl would have given up. But she wasn't any other girl. In many ways, she was like her father—a hard worker, a good student—but she was also like her mother, determined to win in spite of rejection.

To make matters worse, Heather would be spending winter break with her father. That meant Abbie would have to spend most of Christmas vacation alone. But in the meantime, she and Heather had this week, this weekend.

On their way home from school, Tyler said, "Jessica's having a party at her house Friday night. Wanna go?" They were in the front seat of Tyler's car, Heather cuddled next to Tyler. Abbie sat beside her, next to the door.

"No," Abbie said.

"Jeremy's going," Tyler teased.

"Is not." Abbie said. "Is he?"

"Of course, he is," Tyler said. "Everyone cool is going."

"Are you?" Abbie said.

Tyler squeezed Heather's hand. "If I don't have to work."

"Since when did you start hanging out with Jessica and her stupid friends?" Abbie said.

"Who's hanging out?" Tyler said. "It's a party."

Later, after Tyler dropped them off at Heather's, Abbie said, "Are you going to go?" They were eating day-old pizza, drinking sodas, and lounging on Heather's bed,

"Go where?" Heather reached for another slice of pizza.

"Jessica's party."

"Depends."

"On what?" Abbie said.

Heather wrinkled her nose. "Well, if Tyler's going, he's not going alone." She wiped the grease from her hands and closed the lid of the empty pizza box.

"Can I go with you? Abbie said.

"If we go. Lucky I don't have to go to my dad's this weekend. And watching my mom cry makes me crazy."

"Settled." Abbie tried to high-five, but Heather shrugged her hand away, sinking into her pillow texting Tyler. Abbie thought about the day she'd be as relaxed texting Jeremy. The thought made her giddy.

Abbie spent the rest of the week thinking about the party. She hated Jessica, but on the slightest chance Jeremy would be there . . .

She was wearing a new pair of jeans. Her hair was curled softly around her face and her heart felt like the motor in a racecar. Jessica's house was lit up like a carnival in honor of Christmas. Cars were parked on either side of the street. But not Jeremy's. His Camaro wasn't there. They approached the front door, and Abbie hesitated. If he wasn't there, why suffer through what would promise to be a miserable evening? But Tyler had already pushed the door open, and he was waiting for her to enter.

Inside, the fake tree near the window with synthetic white and gold poinsettias made everything feel as phony as Jessica's laugh. The music was so loud the windowpanes rattled, and even though she had never smoked pot, Abbie could smell it coming from the kitchen. Clearly, Jessica's parents were gone, and probably weren't coming back any time soon.

They put their coats on the pile in the living room. "Hey, Tyler. Heather." A history nerd from school cornered Heather almost the minute they arrived. Keeping an eye out for Jeremy, Abbie left them to discuss the Spanish Inquisition. She got enough censorship at home; she didn't need another lesson in persecution. She circled the house, listening for Jeremy's laugh. Once she thought she heard him in the den, but when she looked in the room, all she found were some guys playing cards and munching corn chips.

Upstairs, five boys were eating Cheetos and playing *Dungeons and Dragons*.

"You are walking down a dark hallway," Charles Kennedy said.

"Is there a door at the end of the hallway?" the boy beside him asked.

"A heavy door," Charles said.

"Is it locked?"

Abbie had never played D & D. It had the reputation of being the devil's game, and she wasn't enamored with killing people. But if Charles was here, Jeremy was bound to be, too.

"Look what the dog dragged in," Jessica stood behind her. "If it isn't Drabigail."

He'd better be here. He'd better be worth it. Abbie didn't back away.

The D & D game stalled. Everyone was watching. Someone snickered, "Cat fight. Cat fight."

Rick Chapin, a senior, stepped between the girls and put his arm around Jessica's shoulders. "Play nice."

"Yeah," Scott Lander said. "Come on, Abbie. Let's get something to drink." He took Abbie's arm and all but pulled her toward the kitchen, where the room was filled with snorts and testosterone. "Somebody get this girl a drink."

The keg sat outside on the patio, surrounded by snow. Rick filled a cup and handed it to her. "Bottoms up, pretty lady."

"No, thanks," Abbie said. Jeremy wasn't in the kitchen, or outside by the keg either.

"Go on," Scott said. Someone behind her called, "Chicken."

It wasn't like she'd never tasted beer before. She had, a couple times when her parents hosted summer barbeques. But that was tasting. This was guzzling. "No," she put up her hand as Rick tipped the cup to her lips. Everyone was watching. It was just one cup. She didn't want to make a scene.

"No," she said, pushing her way out of the kitchen. She knew Jessica was watching. Watching and laughing.

She'd been through the whole house and found everything but Jeremy. She was on her way back down the stairs when she saw him. Jessica had her arms wrapped around his neck. They were sharing a beer at the bottom of the stairs.

She couldn't move. She felt numb.

Jeremy hadn't seen Abbie at the top of the stairs, but Jessica had. She smiled that sick sweet smile and flipped her hair like a prom queen before she led Jeremy to the kitchen.

"Slut," Abbie muttered as she navigated the stairs. In the living room, she dug through the pile of coats until she found hers. The white lights on the fake Christmas tree blinked off and on. She was suffocating. Needed air. Was going to be sick.

"Hey, Buchanan." Jeremy stepped closer. "I didn't expect to see you here."

"'Spose not."

He was standing too close. She wanted to . . . If she were smart she would . . .

He stepped closer. She moved back and fell over the ottoman. "Come on," he said, helping her stand. "Let's blow this scene."

"I have to find Heather." She pulled away from him.

"Last time I saw her, she was upstairs with Tyler."

"But . . ."

"Trust me," he said. "She isn't going to miss you."

He helped her into her coat while the Christmas tree lights twinkled behind them. Off. On. Off. On. They silhouetted Jeremy in an enchanting holiday glow. He held out his hand and she took it. Backlit by the lights, he was her Christmas wish come true. Her head pounded. Her heart surrendered, and she knew she'd never look at a Christmas tree the same way ever again.

She expected him to take her straight home. Instead, he drove across town and stopped at Burt's Diner. They ordered Cokes and fries and talked about school, art and cars. He had this old Camaro he was fixing up. His dad wanted him to be an electrician, but he wanted to be an artist. He wanted to go to Europe after high school and study the great artists. Dipping a fry into ketchup, he said, "And what about you, Abigail Buchanan. What do you want to do after high school?"

"Go to San Francisco."

He nodded. "Like that old song says, you'd be pretty with flowers in your hair."

Corny, but she laughed anyway.

"How's your portfolio coming along?" He waved at the waitress to refill their sodas.

Abbie shrugged. "I'm almost done."

"Yeah," he said. "Can I see it?"

Maybe. "Sure. If I can see yours."

"No problem."

Before he took her home he drove out of town, stopping on a hill that overlooked Aspen Grove. He let the car idle while they watched the town's lights flicker. He reached for her hand.

"I like your car," she said.

"Thanks. I hope to have enough money by summer to get it painted."

By summer. If everything worked out, they'd be studying at the art institute in San Francisco.

He leaned over and kissed her.

They might even be lovers.

CHAPTER EIGHT

"**COME BACK TO BED.**" Rob pulled Grace under the covers. "Mmmm. I love the way you smell after sex." He buried his face in her hair and kissed her neck. "Even if your new do makes you look like you're ten years old."

Grace ran her hand through her hair. Michael liked it short. Said it made her eyes sparkle. "Don't." Grace untangled her legs from Rob's. "I'm going to be late."

"For what? It's Saturday. I thought we'd spend the day together. Do a little Christmas shopping for Abbie."

"That's what you get for thinking." Grace smiled as she pushed his hand away, slid off the bed, and stepped into the shower. There was a time, years ago, when, after making love, she wouldn't bathe for days, willing Rob's musky scent to permeate her skin, marking her as his. But that was years ago, before waiting for him to notice her, hold her, or make love to her had turned everything sour. She tried to remember the last time he had told her he loved her and couldn't.

Grace turned off the water. What was she doing? Just when she got what she wanted, she pushed it away like yesterday's green beans. Her head was confused. One minute she wanted Michael; the next, she wanted Rob.

Wrapping her hair in a towel, Grace dove back into bed, surprised to find it empty. "Rob?" She looked around the room. "Rob?"

Slipping into her bathrobe, Grace padded down the stairs and found her husband at the kitchen table, drinking orange juice and buttering a piece of toast for Abbie, who was laughing at something he'd said.

"You're up early." Grace glanced at her daughter. Even with dark circles under her eyes and her hair looking like a rat's nest, Abbie was pretty. In that moment, Grace hated her.

"Abbie and I are going shopping." Rob winked at his daughter. "Too bad you're so busy you can't come along. We're even talking about lunch at Rudy's."

Any desire Grace may have had for Rob at that moment disappeared. The last time she was at Rudy's, she and Michael had snuggled in a booth. She shrugged away the piece of toast Rob offered. Good wife, bad wife, should she stay or should she go? Wanting some time alone so she could think about Michael, Grace settled on a shower and a new sweater. Pale pink, the cashmere made her feel pretty and feminine. She styled her hair, grateful she no longer had to spend an hour curling it. "There." She blotted her lipstick. "You don't look half bad." As a matter of fact, she looked quite good. Better than her daughter with her unruly hair, even if she said so herself.

Grace hummed as she planned her day. First the massage, then a manicure. In the living room, she stood back to inspect her tree. Like the one at work, this one was perfect. So unlike the smaller tree she put up in Rob's office, adorned with the rudimentary ornaments Abbie made in elementary school and with her grandmother—old candy canes supposed to look like reindeers; cardboard gingerbread houses held together with school glue; faded satin balls displaying each of their names. She adjusted the garland and admired the gold bow that cascaded to the floor.

Rob stepped into the room, buttoning his coat. "Sure you won't join us?" Before she could answer, he called up the stairs. "Abbie, you ready?"

"Coming." Abbie dashed down the stairs and into the coat her father held open for her, a sure reminder that if Grace *had* wanted to go along, she would just be in the way.

"Have fun." She waved them out the door.

"Ho, Ho, Ho. Merry Christmas." She picked up the extra boxes of crystal ornaments still sitting under the tree. She thought of Michael and tried to manufacture a reason to see him. The ornaments. As usual, she had too many for her tree. She'd give them to him as a house-warming present. After her massage, and after she dropped off the yarn she'd found on sale for her mother.

In spite of the wind and blustering snow, Grace smiled when her mother opened the door. "Hi, Mom."

"Why, Grace?" Her mother peered out the door. "Are you lost?"

"Funny, Mother." Grace closed the door and brushed the wet snow from her coat. "Brrrr. Can't a daughter visit her mother without making an appointment?"

Maxine said. "It's been a long time since you just dropped by."

"I have a job now, you know." Grace pulled off her gloves and stuck them into her coat pocket.

"Don't I."

Grace handed her mother the bag of yarn. "I didn't come over to fight. I thought you'd like this."

Maxine took the sack to the sofa. "Sit down. How about a cup of coffee?"

"No thanks. Where's Daddy?"

"Where he always is on weekends." Maxine nodded to the bedroom. "Can't you hear him?"

Her father's uneven snoring echoed down the hallway. Grace knew why he slept all weekend. She even understood his need to drink.

"What do you want me to do with this?" Maxine pulled out several variegated skeins of yarn. "Make something for Abbie? You realize Christmas is just two weeks away."

"No, I don't want you to make something for Abbie." Grace tried, but she couldn't keep the edge from her voice. "I thought you'd like it. If you don't, take it to your Senior Center. Maybe someone there can use it." She glanced around the room, at the hideous Christmas tree with its red and green lights, so old they were antiques. It stood in the same corner every year, draped with the same paper garland, pipe-cleaner reindeers, crocheted angels, and plastic canvas rocking horses. She wasn't surprised to hear Elvis Presley crooning, "I'll be home for Christmas."

"I don't know why you always have to turn your nose up at everything I do," Maxine said. "I swear, Grace, there's no satisfying you. No wonder Rob's never home. Would you please sit down?"

"Can't stay." Grace walked over to the fish tank and peered in at the silver Bala sharks. "I see you still have Elvis and Priscilla." She tapped at the two-inch hapless hostages until they swam over to the glass.

"Just a smidge." Maxine handed Grace the fish food. "I already fed them once this morning."

Grace lifted the lid to the aquarium and sprinkled flakes on the water. "Here fishy, fishy."

"What did you do to your hair?"

Grace dropped the lid. "Cut it. Don't you like it?"

"I do, unless you're having a mid-life crisis." Maxine lit a cigarette and went to the kitchen to refill her coffee.

"Why would you say that? You're the one who said I needed to change."

"I'm surprised you heard me," Maxine said.

"I hear everything you say."

"If that's true, where's the Christmas list I asked for last week?"

Mother and daughter stared at each other, each guarded and defensive. In less than ten minutes, Grace was thirteen again. She stood in the middle of the room considering the gurgle of the fish tank, the Elvis Presley music playing on the stereo, the ticking of the clock over the fireplace, and her father's snoring in the other room. She was so glad this was no longer her home.

"Anything you give us is fine." Grace pulled on her gloves. "I have to go. Tell Daddy 'Hi'." She was out the door and down the steps before her mother could thank her for the yarn.

Grace dashed through the snow and slammed her car door. So much for trying to do something nice. She backed out of her mother's driveway without looking toward the window, without seeing her mother standing on the porch, waving goodbye.

Across town, Grace pulled into the driveway at the house on Cedar Lane. Tire tracks leading to the front door indicated the moving van had come and gone. She turned off the engine and stared at the house.

She smoothed her hair and gathered the boxes of ornaments. She would deliver them and leave. Unless he still wanted her help. Her hands shook like she was still in high school, waiting for her one true love.

He must have been watching from the window. Before she could ring the bell, Michael opened the door. "Ah, she comes bearing gifts."

"I hope you like them." Grace handed him the boxes.

"Come in. Come in." He put the ornaments on an entryway table that hadn't been there before and asked to take her coat. As she shrugged out of it, his hands lingered on her shoulders. She liked the way they felt—warm, confident. "Coffee?" He hung her coat in the closet.

"Sure." Grace stepped past the foyer and boxes waiting to be unpacked. If these had been her moving boxes, there would have been twice as many, and each would be labeled. Kitchen. Bathroom. Bedroom. Pantry. But this was Michael, and his way seemed more fun. Opening each unmarked box would be a surprise, maybe even an adventure.

Sipping coffee, she said, "How can I help?"

"In here." He led her to the sunken living room with a vaulted ceiling.

"Oh, my goodness." Grace stared at the giant fir, so tall it touched the ceiling. She had no idea how he'd gotten the tree through the door, let alone into a stand.

"Do you like it?"

"I love it." Perfectly shaped and pine-scented, the tree all but filled the room. It must have taken him all night to attach the thousands of blinking lights. Scattered across the floor were boxes of decorations. Gold. Silver. Blue. She was glad she brought the ornaments. They would work nicely here.

She looked from the tree to the unopened boxes. She wanted to do both. "Can I help you unpack?"

"Nope." He handed her an ornament. "You're commissioned to decorate the tree." She couldn't see the radio, but Christmas carols transformed the room into a romantic refuge. All she needed was hot buttered rum and gingerbread to make it perfect.

"Well," he said. "If you need anything, I'll be in the kitchen, unpacking those boxes."

"Yes, sir." She saluted him with a smile, not at all sorry she wasn't ogling over presents with Rob and Abbie at the mall. This would be a lot more fun. "It's beginning to look a lot like Christmas," Grace sang along with the radio as she hung ornaments on the fragrant branches.

"Everywhere you go." Michael sang behind her, and she jumped. He had opened an unmarked box and discovered tinsel, garland, and peacock feathers. "Look what I found."

Funny how things appeared when she needed them without once having to ask. There was the ladder, right beside the tree. More coffee before her cup was empty. A welcomed change to soft rock music when she grew tired of the carols. Even as he worked in the kitchen putting dishes and utensils away, his thoughts seemed to be on her. Was she too warm? Was she too cold? Did she want him to hold the ladder?

Grace glanced over her shoulder to watch Michael rummage through the boxes. He was comical as he held up a mixer, a toaster and scratched his head as if he didn't remember packing them. Arresting, he made her smile. Besides, he was easy to look at. Her heart felt lighter than it had in years.

"Break time." He handed her a steaming cup; this time, not coffee.

"Hot buttered rum," he said to her questioning gaze. "Old family recipe."

Grace sipped. "Delicious." Their eyes met; her face grew warm. Because there were no chairs, they sat on the floor in front of the tree. "To Christmas." Grace clinked her cup against his.

"To Christmas," Michael said. "The help's not bad either." She blushed.

When their cups were empty, Michael said, "Guess it's back to work." He stood and offered his hand. Tipsy from the rum, Grace swayed into him. There was an awkward moment of silence before he kissed her. She didn't pull away. In fact, she put her arms around his neck and kissed him, too.

They kissed with eyes open, and she liked looking into his eyes, knowing he was thinking of her instead of work or a child.

"Do you want to stop?" he said.

"No." She played with the buttons on his shirt. His chest was warm and strong. Hungry and starved for attention, there was no name for what Grace felt. Love or lust, it didn't matter. She wanted the closeness of his body, the heat and his desire. She quivered as he touched her and closed her eyes, riding the waves of emotion like a carnival ride, higher, faster, again, don't stop. Again. Again.

Afterwards, spent and sweaty, they lay in each other's arms. He tipped her head and looked into her eyes. "Sorry?"

Grace snuggled against his shoulder. "No."

By the time she fastened her bra and slipped into her clothes the sun was setting, making everything in the room rosy and enchanted. She didn't want to leave, and she drove away from his house reluctantly, hoping her husband and daughter had stopped somewhere to eat. After such a lovely day, the last thing she wanted to do was to go home and cook. In fact, she didn't want to go home at all.

*   *   *

All morning long, Maxine worried about Christmas. Less than two weeks away, she still hadn't settled on gifts for Grace and Abbie. The sweaters she'd knitted and planned to give them were gone, sold at the Christmas bazaar.

She opened her purse and took out the envelope she hid from Herb. While he slept, she counted the money—three hundred dollars—enough to buy Grace a bottle of perfume with plenty left to get something nice for Abbie. But what? What did you buy a teenager who already had everything? She had asked Grace for a Christmas list, but didn't get one. "Anything you give us is fine." Maybe she should give them nothing. See how fine that was. Maxine sighed. No matter what she did, it was never good enough for Grace.

She poured a cup of coffee, settled in the sofa, and looked through the pile of mail-order gift catalogs. The Swiss Colony offered a nice assortment of holiday gift baskets, petit fours and chocolate covered nuts. A basket might make a nice present. It could take the place of the baking Maxine hadn't had time to do.

Maxine pushed the catalog aside. Grace would never eat candy or cake, let alone keep the tempting desserts in the house. Maxine looked through the flyers she'd saved from Sunday's paper. She spotted a nice dress shirt for Rob. It even had a tie. She looked at sweaters, purses, gloves and scarves. Some would look nice on Abbie, but others were downright ugly. Maxine flipped through the electronics ads, but the new gadgets confused her. She knew nothing about electronic notebooks or iPads. Nor could she afford them.

Maybe a CD.

She had no idea what kind of music Abbie listened to lately.

A new backpack.

No.

An easel.

Abbie already had two.

Who knew spending money could be so much work?

Frustrated, Maxine called Shirley. "Do you still want to go shopping?"

"Absolutely," Shirley said. "Give me an hour, and I'll be ready."

Maxine looked down at her own clothes. A baggy pair of jeans and a sweatshirt that was clean but splotched with old paint and bleach. Her hair lay flat against her head. She could cover her hair with a hat. But she'd have to change her clothes.

Herb snored as she entered the bedroom. Mindful not to wake him, Maxine tiptoed to the closet, eased the door open, and took down a clean sweater. As she pulled the sweater over her head, she glanced at the bed. *Good, he was still asleep.* When she opened the dresser drawer to take out a clean pair of socks, the lamp tipped, and she scrambled to catch it before it fell to the floor. She closed the drawer as Herb rolled onto his side.

"'S time to eat?"

Shit.

"No," Maxine said. "Go back to sleep."

He made a congested gurgle in his throat like he was swallowing a cat. "Call me when dinners s'ready." He rolled over and started snoring again. If she were lucky, he'd go back to sleep and stay that way for the rest of his life.

But she wasn't so lucky. She had just opened the door for Shirley when Herb lumbered out of the bedroom, his rumpled undershorts hanging off his hips.

"Where's my dinner?" He slurred his words.

"Go." Maxine shoved Shirley out the door.

"Oh, Maxine," Shirley said between laughing and trying to catch her breath. "I had no idea." She was laughing so hard, she couldn't get her key in the ignition. "You told us he drank a lot, but . . ." Shirley whooped. "Oh, my God, Maxine. You should take his picture." Tears ran down her face, streaking her mascara.

"It isn't funny," Maxine said. She might laugh too if she wasn't married to the sorry slob. "Go before he comes outside and shares all his glory with the neighbors."

This brought another howl from Shirley, who was laughing so hard she couldn't back out of the driveway. When her laughter subsided and she was more composed, she said, "It's a good thing Helen didn't see that. She'd drive you to divorce court today. What I wouldn't give for a picture."

What Maxine wouldn't give if he would just go away.

The streets and sidewalks were busy with people scurrying to find perfect gifts. "Let's go to Macy's," Shirley said as she parked the car. "I need a new purse."

It had been a while since Maxine had been shopping in the mall. The number of bustling people overwhelmed her, but the Christmas carols streaming over the loud speaker put her in the Christmas spirit. She even stopped to watch a jovial Santa pose for pictures with hopeful children.

"If I sit on his lap, do you think he'll grant my wish?" Maxine said.

"You never know," Shirley laughed. "Give it a try."

Maxine imagined herself on Santa's lap, telling him she wanted Herb to die. She wondered if he could pull that one out of his gift bag.

On their way to look at purses, they passed a display of sunglasses. *Who bought sunglasses in winter?* Maxine wondered. But Shirley had stopped and was trying on several different frames. "What do you think?" She turned to model a blue pair trimmed in rhinestones. Maxine thought they looked like something Marilyn Monroe might have worn in one of her movies, but Shirley bought them anyway, saying they looked nice against her skin.

"Here we go." Shirley led Maxine to the purses. "Oh, look. Isn't this cute?" While Shirley checked out the purses—opening zippers and posing before a mirror—she asked Maxine, "Does Grace like perfume? Christian Dior's on sale."

"I'm sure she does," Maxine said. "But I have no idea what she wears."

Settling on a blue shoulder bag that matched her new sunglasses, Shirley pointed to the cosmetic counter. "Bet this nice girl can help us." She selected a tester and sprayed her wrist. "What are your top sellers?"

The clerk slid a tray of perfumes toward them. "Chanel No. 5 is always a favorite." She sprayed it on Shirley's opposite wrist.

"What do you think?" Shirley held her wrist for Maxine to smell. Maxine wrinkled her nose. "Too strong and flowery."

Shirley turned to the clerk. "What else do you have?"

"We sell a lot of Cinnabar for Christmas."

Shirley offered Maxine's wrist. It smelled like cinnamon, only spicier. "Ummm, I like that." Shirley said. The perfume made Maxine sneeze.

"Or," the clerk said, "Opium is still popular." Maxine sniffed her wrist and tried to imagine the oriental fragrance on Grace.

"Do you think Abbie would like it?" Shirley said.

"Abbie's too young for perfume," Maxine said. "Isn't she?"

"I wore my mother's Tabu in junior high," Shirley said.

"Pathetic," the clerk said, and rolled her eyes. "Then you might be interested in these." This time she didn't spray their wrists, but set out a selection of pretty bottles. Shirley helped herself, trying one fragrance after another. By the time Maxine had sniffed six or seven more, the perfumes all smelled the same, and she had a pounding headache.

"Think I'll wait," she said.

"I'll take this one." Shirley pointed to a bottle of Cinnabar. "What the heck?" She handed the clerk a bottle of Opium. "I'll take this one, too. After all, it's Christmas."

Maxine stared. The perfume purchases totaled more than one hundred and thirty dollars. Unlike Maxine, spending money wasn't hard for Shirley.

Next, they went to JC Penney's. While Shirley tried on sweaters and corduroy pants, Maxine walked the aisles, trying to find something for Grace or Abbie. But everything was too bright, too tight, or too sloppy. She found a top with beads worked in a circle around the neck and wondered what it would look like on Grace.

"Oh, that's cute!" Carrying an arm full of clothes, Shirley fingered the beads. "Are you getting that for Abbie?"

"No."

"Good." Shirley snatched the top.

Before leaving the store, they stopped at the jewelry counter where Shirley tried on rings, watches, and bracelets. "What do you think?" She modeled a necklace with large gold links. "Would Grace like this?" Maxine shook her head. "How about this?" Shirley held a jeweled parrot pin bigger than a silver dollar.

"I don't think so."

While Shirley paid for her clothes, the beaded top, and the pin, Maxine said, "I have no idea what to get them."

"There's a cute teen boutique. Bet we can find something there for Abbie."

By now, Maxine was done with shopping, but she followed Shirley into the store anyway, even though it was filled with giggling teenagers, and the music blaring in the shop made Maxine's head hurt more. She looked at a short jacket Shirley thought would look good on Abbie. But when Maxine read the price, she shook her head. "Let's go." Her feet hurt, her head hurt. She wanted a cup of coffee and a cigarette.

As if reading her mind, Shirley said, "Let's get something to drink. My treat."

In the mall coffee shop, they shared a maple doughnut the size of a dinner plate. Shirley doctored her coffee with sugar and cream, but Maxine preferred hers black. It felt good to sit.

While Shirley watched people, or rather, the men, trying to guess who was still single, Maxine studied the teenagers. So many of the girls wore faded jeans that looked like they'd been washed in acid, or eye makeup so black, it made them look like vampire hookers. Many had tattoos and piercings. Thank God Grace didn't let Abbie dress like that.

Maxine took another bite of the doughnut. She was a bad mother. She should be kinder to Grace.

She was watching a girl about Abbie's age drape herself all over a boy when she noticed a sign in the window of an adjoining store. *Senior Special. Book now for a once in a lifetime trip to Graceland.*

Maxine was on her feet and in the travel agency before Shirley could ask where she was going. "How much?" she asked the travel agent.

"It's a Christmas special," the agent said. "Four hundred and fifty dollars."

Maxine pulled out her envelope. She had three hundred dollars. But she knew where she could get the rest.

*   *   *

"What about this? Or this?" Abbie and her father were standing in front of the jewelry counter at JC Penney's. Her father pointed to a tennis bracelet with small silver hearts jeweled with diamonds. The bracelet was marked fifty percent off, and one look was enough for Abbie to know it would never be good enough for her mother. Not compared to the other bracelets that were more delicate with larger diamonds.

She didn't want to hurt his feelings, so she lied. "Nice. I think Mom will like it."

"All right, then." Her father motioned to the bracelet. "We'll take that one. Can we get it gift-wrapped?"

The cashier pointed to a table near the door where Girl Scouts wrapped presents. On their way, they passed a shelf of porcelain figurines. Her father picked up a Santa. "Do you think your mother would like this for her collection?"

"Nope," Abbie said. "She already has one."

"She does?" her father said. "I didn't know that. What do you say we head over to Rudy's and get something to eat after we get this present wrapped?"

"Hang on." Abbie stopped to answer her cell. GOING 2 MALL, Heather texted. COME W ME.

ALREADY THERE, Abbie replied. SHOPPING W DAD. ALMOST DONE. COME MEET US? Ten minutes later, Heather appeared.

"Hi, Mr. Buchanan. Nice to see you."

"Nice to see you, too. We were just talking about lunch. Care to join us?"

"No thanks. Abbie said she'd help me find a gift for my mom."

Abbie turned to her father. "That okay?"

"Guess I know when I've been replaced," her father teased.

"Aw, Dad. No one can replace you."

"Butter me up." He tapped his cheek with his finger.

Abbie gave him a kiss. "Thanks. Mom's going to love her present." He was always so happy. She loved the way he whistled as he walked away.

"Okay," Abbie said to Heather. "Let's do it so I can get something to eat. I'm starving."

They were looking at scarves when Heather said, "Where'd you go last night?"

Abbie picked up a plaid scarf. "What about this one? It looks like Christmas."

"Don't change the subject. We looked for you, and you were gone."

"Well," Abbie hesitated. "You were busy."

Heather didn't blush, not like Abbie would have. "How'd you get home?"

"Jeremy."

"Really?" Heather tied a green scarf around her neck. "'Bout time. What do you think?"

Abbie shrugged. "Nice."

"What else did you do?"

"Nothing," Abbie said. "Why are you so mad?"

"Who's mad?" Heather said as she paid for the scarf. "Why would I be mad?" Before Abbie could answer, she added, "Thanks for telling me you were leaving. Next time I won't waste my time looking for you."

Minutes later, they were sitting at a table eating fries and drinking sodas. "He's really nice, Heather. I'm sorry I didn't tell you we were leaving. It just sort of happened."

Heather smirked. "The next time it just sort of happens, I'm gone."

"It won't," Abbie said. "I promise."

"Better not." Then she winked. "By the way, I'm glad you two finally connected." They giggled.

"Did he kiss you?"

"Yes," Abbie squealed.

"She kissed the boy, she kissed the boy," Heather sang until her phone beeped. "Shit. Have to meet my dad. And his new girlfriend." She made a face and Abbie laughed. "Want to come along?"

"No thanks."

"Please. It should be a riot." Heather dumped her empty cup in the garbage. "Need a ride?"

"Nope. I'll walk. Have fun with your dad and his new squeeze."

Heather rolled her eyes, and Abbie laughed.

She was less than a mile from home, and there was an eagle's nest by the river she wanted to draw for her portfolio. She had to get it done by the first week of January if she wanted to win that scholarship. Even in the snow, it didn't take her long to get home.

"Mom?" she called. The house was empty. Abbie collected her car keys, camera and sketchpad, and drove to the river. Settling at a picnic table near the nest, Abbie open her sketchpad. The low-angled winter light cast strange colored shadows on the snow she hoped to capture. It took a while to get started, and at first all she could do was doodle as she recalled last night's events. Fries. Cokes. Jeremy's hands. His kiss. She ripped the sheet of paper from her sketchpad and began again.

She started with the top of a tree and tucked the nest below the crown near the trunk where the branches were thick and strong. She worked until her pile of sticks, grasses and moss took shape, adding a few feathers and scavenged twine. As often happened once Abbie put pen to paper, she lost track of time. When she looked up from her drawing, the sun was lower in the sky, the air cooler. She stretched and put her drawing away. Where most would have expected black or charcoal, she liked red ink. She'd finish it later at home.

Walking back to her car, Abbie took a path that followed the partially frozen river gurgling under the ice. The snow crunched under her feet, and a sparrow bobbed out of her way. She kept walking but stopped abruptly when she saw him. He was standing on a log fallen precariously over the river. His sketchpad lay on the bank in the snow.

"Jeremy?"

She startled him, and he almost fell into the water. "Be careful." She rushed closer and offered her hand.

He waved her away. "Move."

She did, and he jumped. Slipping on the ice, he landed at her feet. An awkward grin filled his face. Abbie picked up the sketchpad, soppy with snow and ice. "It's good." She glanced at the drawing slowly turning into a blurry mess.

"I can do better."

She gave him back his drawing. "Well, I wish I could. What were you doing out there on that log anyway, trying to kill yourself?"

He laughed. "Trying to get a better look at the water."

"Well, you almost did," she said, and they both laughed.

They sat down at the picnic table. Because his sketchpad was wet, he used hers. "It's easy," he said, taking out his pen. "It just takes concentration."

Abbie sat beside him and watched the short, almost nonexistent dots become images. She took a piece of paper and started to draw, imitating him the best she could.

"No," he corrected over her shoulder. "Hold your pen like this." Amazing what a slight tilt to the hand could do. Soon, they had both drawn the same image, an empty teeter-totter half covered with snow, only his was blue and hers was red. With a few minor corrections, they were a perfectly matched pair. She even copied his insignia, the lopsided infinity he drew in the corner of the picture.

The sun was setting, leaving behind an icy stillness. It would be dark soon. When Abbie moved to stand, she brushed against his shoulder. One moment they were gazing into each other's eyes; the next, he was brushing her hair from her face. Her once cold fingers tingled. Her breath caught in her throat as she closed her eyes and felt his lips, gentle and soft, touch her like butterfly wings. Behind her closed eyes, she was lost in an explosion of color. She felt his arms around her and leaned in closer, her heart hammering as she kissed him back. Shy, she pulled her head away, looked into his eyes, and kissed him again, wanting the moment to last forever.

Awkwardly, he ended the kiss and fished his car keys from his pocket. He held her hand as they walked toward the parking lot. She couldn't feel her toes. Her nose was running. But there was no place she'd rather be.

Her phone beeped. "It's my dad," she said. "Wondering when I'm coming home.

"Yeah, my old man is probably having fits." Jeremy tucked her into her car and kissed her again. Her head was fuzzy, her face flushed. With fingers resting lightly on her lips where he kissed her, Abbie watched him walk to his car. She waited until his taillights flashed before she backed away, thinking this is what it feels like to love someone who believes in infinities, in things that have no beginnings and no ends.

CHAPTER NINE

GUILT WASN'T A FEELING Maxine was familiar with. If she felt anything, it was anger. Because her husband was a sorry alcoholic. Because her daughter was selfish and unfeeling. Because she hadn't gone to college or studied nursing, thinking being a wife and a mother would be enough. She should have followed her mother's suggestion and worked in the library. But her mother was always giving bad advice.

What did she do to merit this guilt in the first place—put leftovers in a lunch that would just get tossed out? Watch soap operas when she should have been washing windows? No, guilt was something Maxine rarely felt. But once she bought that ticket to Graceland, all she felt was guilt.

First, there was the money she owed Shirley. Maxine didn't like to borrow from friends, and the owing bothered her the minute she got home from the mall. Herb was still asleep, even though there was evidence that he'd been up while she was away. A half-eaten sandwich lay on the table beside an open bag of potato chips and three empty beer cans. *Worthless*, Maxine thought as she cleaned up his mess.

After tucking her ticket in the bottom of a drawer, Maxine rummaged through the house looking for loose change. She opened the envelope she kept in the kitchen drawer for groceries, but it held less than ten dollars. She checked the pockets in all the clothes in the hamper. She searched her purse again, hoping to find a hidden dollar or two, but she knew even without looking that she had spent every penny she had and then some. Even though Shirley said not to worry about the money, that's what Maxine did as she paced the living room, trying to will the extra cash to appear. She studied the room, searching for something to sell. But even if she were to discover anything of value, no one would buy her hand-me-downs at a yard sale two weeks before Christmas. She could call the doctors' wives to see if they needed extra holiday cleaning, but that felt too much like begging.

She had no other choice. She had to return the ticket and get a refund. But how was she going to get to the mall? She couldn't call Shirley—that would be too embarrassing. She recounted the change from the kitchen and Herb's pockets—$5.65 would barely pay for a taxi.

Outside the streetlights flickered, illuminating the falling snow. Herb was still asleep. Maybe . . .

She found the keys to the truck on the dresser. It had been years since she drove the vehicle, hating the fact that it was a stick shift and not automatic. She could take the back roads across town, return the ticket, and be home before he even knew she was gone.

She had to turn the key three times before the truck shuddered to an idle. The "check engine" light was on, but Maxine ignored it as she inched out of the driveway, shifted into first gear and chugged to the end of the block. Carefully turning the corner, she slipped into second gear, but didn't like how fast she was moving on the slick roads. So she shifted to first and chugged along until a car behind her started beeping.

"Hold on to your pants!" Nervous and shaking, Maxine pulled to the curb where the engine died.

"Drive it or park it, lady!" A teenage boy shouted from his open window as he sped by.

"Up yours," Maxine yelled. She waited for her hands to calm before she turned the key in the engine. Nothing. She tried again. The engine light wouldn't stop blinking.

Crap.

Maxine clicked the key to Off. If it hadn't been so cold, or if she hadn't been so far from home broken down in a worthless truck, she might have enjoyed the snow falling in huge soft snowflakes. While it was very pretty, it was also very cold. She must have sat there ten minutes before she tried the truck again.

Dead. Nothing. She could leave the truck and walk home. Or she could walk to the mall and refund her ticket. *How,* she thought, as she braced for the cold wind, *could something as simple as spending money become so complicated?* If this was what having money was all about, maybe she didn't want any.

The sidewalks were slick under the snow. The wind whipped her face, but she hugged her coat close and began walking. Cold. Wet. Slippery. But the snow was also beautiful, and Maxine enjoyed the winter weather, always had, even as a kid. The flakes sticking on her nose reminded her of when she used to catch snowflakes, and she stuck out her tongue. When Grace was little, Maxine had tried to get her to play outside in the snow, but Grace would always run back inside, complaining of the wet and cold. The snow tasted like her childhood. Maxine had fun until the wind kicked up, making her shiver. She discovered the faster she moved, the warmer she was.

Trying to keep her head down and out of the wind, Maxine stepped off the curb onto a patch of ice and landed flat on her stomach. Her purse flew into the middle of the road and would have been run over if a man driving a black sedan hadn't spotted her and stopped.

"Are you all right?" His emergency lights flashed as he rushed to her side.

"I'm fine." Maxine tried to stand but had to grab his arm for support.

"Do you need a doctor?" The man brushed the snow from her coat and face.

"No. I'm just a clumsy old woman." Her attempt at laughter was less than enthusiastic. She was cold. Everything hurt.

A woman, Maxine assumed the man's wife, appeared beside them. "You dropped your purse."

"Thanks," Maxine said, her right arm starting to numb.

"Can we give you a ride?" the man asked.

"No." Maxine pointed to the mall. "I'm almost there."

He helped her cross the road before he drove away. Too embarrassed to watch the line of traffic that had gathered behind them, Maxine pulled her coat close and hobbled to the mall entrance. Her side was sore where she had hit the curb, but soon she'd have her refund, and everything would be better.

Inside the mall, Maxine limped through center court toward the travel agency. But when she got there the office was dark. The door was locked and the sign on the door said CLOSED.

"Crap." Maxine hobbled to a chair in the food court and plopped down. Her elbow hurt so much she wondered if she had broken it. Her nose ran like the Aspen river, and every muscle in her body ached. She sat for a long time, hoping to spot someone she knew. Grace. Maybe Abbie. Helen or Shirley. Even though the mall was busy, full of shoppers, she didn't know a single one.

The longer Maxine sat, the stiffer her bottom grew. She knew she should start moving, but when she stood, her knees creaked and the pain brought her back to her chair. A phone, she thought, wishing she'd let Grace buy her one for her birthday. One by one the lights in the stores signaled the mall's closure. She had to move.

Every step hurt. Maxine was tempted to hide in the bathroom, to stay there until morning or until she could summon help, but she had more pride than her husband. She wasn't sleeping in a bathroom.

She was standing outside the mall, watching the snow fall and trying to ease off the curb when a police car pulled along side. "Ma'am, can I help you?"

"Yes." Feeling less anxious, Maxine explained about the truck and her fall.

"I can take you home, or call a tow truck. Which would you prefer?" the policeman said.

She would have preferred that this day had never happened, but that was not a satisfactory answer. "Tow truck," she shivered.

The policeman dropped her off at Herb's truck and waited with her until the tow arrived. "Looks like we're going to have a white Christmas," he said.

He looked so young. She wondered if he had a family. She should have known him, his family, too, but he didn't look familiar.

"Thanks," she said, when the tow truck arrived. She waved to him. "Have a good Christmas."

"You, too," he said, and drove away.

Maxine waited on the sidewalk while the driver hooked a metal yoke under the rear of the truck. While she was gone, someone had slid into the truck, denting the right fender. If Herb noticed it, she would say he must have done that on his way home. That was a problem she would deal with later. Right now, she had a bigger problem: how to pay for the tow. She didn't carry a credit card. She'd have to write a check, which would overdraw their account.

"Where do you want it?" the driver asked when they reached her house.

"Can you can get it off the street, maybe into the driveway?"

"Not a problem."

Maxine watched him back the truck into the driveway. Except for the dented front fender and a pile of snow accumulated under the truck, Herb would never know it had been moved.

"Thank you." Maxine handed him a check. Now, besides worrying about how to repay Shirley, she'd have to get money into the checking account before Monday morning.

But she couldn't do anything about that tonight. Tonight all she wanted was a hot bath and something to take away the pain.

Hobbling to the kitchen, Maxine opened the refrigerator and looked for something to drink. Water. Milk. Beer. She reached for the beer. After the night she'd had, she was entitled. She settled on the milk and used it to wash down two aspirin. She went to the bathroom, filled the tub, and lowered her body into the steamy water. Someday, life wouldn't be such a struggle. Someday, she'd catch a break.

Or, maybe not. Maybe this was as good as it was going to get.

*   *   *

Regret was nothing new to Grace. At forty-three, she knew a lot about regret. She regretted being forced into having a child when she wasn't ready. She regretted marrying a man more interested in books and cars than her. She regretted throwing away her life before she'd had a chance to experience more of its pleasures. And now, as she brushed her teeth and thought about Michael, she regretted having to lie to her husband.

Climbing into bed, Grace said, "Rob? Honey, you still awake?"

"Hmmmm?" He stirred.

She snuggled against his chest and pulled his arms around her. "Sorry it's so late. I got bored and went to a movie. I was hungry and stopped for a sandwich." He didn't ask where, or what movie, but she had names on her tongue, ready to lie again if he asked.

"Good."

She snuggled closer and kissed his chest. He kissed the tip of her nose, something Grace had enjoyed when they were dating. But when he did it now, she felt like he was dismissing her.

"'Night." He rolled over. Soon, he was snoring. She laid still, humiliation flushing her face. She could die, and he wouldn't even notice.

Grace turned her back to her husband and tried to sleep. But her thoughts kept drifting to Michael—the way he unbuttoned her blouse. The way he kissed her. The way he made her feel important, sensuous, wanted.

The next morning, Grace woke with resolve. She would try harder. She took a shower, then went downstairs and started the coffee. Pulling eggs and oranges from the refrigerator, she fixed Rob's favorite breakfast— eggs benedict, hash browns, and fresh squeezed orange juice. He was in the shower when she set the tray on the dresser.

"Breakfast is served." She locked their bedroom door and slipped out of her clothes and back into bed. When he came out of the shower, she was under the covers.

"Oh, Grace," he said. "I thought I told you. I have to work."

"On a Sunday? You can at least have breakfast." She patted his side of the bed. "Please, Rob. Sit down and eat."

"Just a bite." He drank the juice and ate part of his eggs standing up. "Thanks, honey." He moved toward the door. "Love you. Go back to sleep."

Like that was going to happen. Grace waited until she heard the front door click. Pushing the curtain away from the window, she watched him drive away. He didn't look up or wave goodbye.

"You're going to be sorry." She wanted to throw the uneaten food at the door and scream, but, instead, she took the tray downstairs and dumped the food in the trash. She was sitting in the living room, reflecting on her Christmas tree and disappointing marriage, when the telephone rang. She let it ring thinking it was Rob. She'd show him.

"Mom." Abbie yelled down the stairs.

"What?"

"It's for you. Some guy I don't know."

Grace picked up the phone.

"Good morning."

Her voice faltered. "Michael?"

"I hope it's all right to call you at home. I wanted to make sure you were okay."

"I'm fine." Her heart beat faster.

"Good." Then he said, "There's a tree over here calling your name." She looked at the lights flashing on her own tree.

"Grace?"

"I'm sorry, Michael." This was hard. "Listen, I can't do this."

"Do what? Talk on the phone?" He sounded confused.

"No. This. Whatever it is we're doing." She had to stay firm. She couldn't give in, no matter how much she wanted to.

"What are we doing?"

"I can't," she said. "I'm married."

He lowered his voice. "You weren't married last night?" He didn't wait for an answer. "I'm sorry. That was rude. What happened? You were happy when you left."

She looked at her tree, at the pictures hanging on the wall. "Nothing. Everything. Oh, I don't know. I have to go."

"I'm sorry. I didn't mean to upset you," Michael said. "I just wanted to make sure you were all right. Would you like to go someplace? Would you like to talk?"

"No," Grace said. She replaced the receiver and went about erasing him. In the kitchen, she slammed cupboard doors as she unloaded the dishwasher. She pulled out the vacuum and cleaned the living room rugs until every fiber stood up straight. She Lysoled the bathrooms and scrubbed the toilets until they shone like glass.

"Hold down the noise," Abbie called from the stairs. "Some of us are trying to sleep."

Grace yelled back. "Keep working on your beauty sleep. You need it."

She put the vacuum away and took a long hard look at her living room, her Christmas tree, her empty house. Then she grabbed her coat and drove straight to Michael's.

"This is a surprise," he said as he opened the door.

"Today," she smiled awkwardly, "I'm full of surprises."

"What's going on?" He stepped aside to let her enter.

"I'm sorry. I was confused."

"You aren't anymore?" He hesitated.

"No." She took his hand and led him straight to the bedroom. She kissed him until her lips were bruised, and the last thing she felt was regret.

Later, as she lay naked beside him, she said, "I've never had my tubes tied." It was an embarrassing way to say it, but the last thing she needed was another baby, and there was no easy way to ask if he'd had a vasectomy like Rob. So she just blurted it out. They couldn't have another afternoon of unprotected sex. He was lying on his side, up on one elbow, tracing her nipple with his finger. Even after two orgasms, she still ached when he touched her.

"I can wear a condom."

She reached up and kissed him because he offered and she didn't have to ask.

*   *   *

"He kissed me again," Abbie yelled into the phone.

"You slut!" Heather laughed. "When?"

"Down by the river. We were working on our sketches. Heather, he's so good."

"I know he can draw. What I want to know is can he kiss?" Heather teased.

"Yes."

"That's awesome" Heather said. "I need all the details."

When Abbie clicked off her cell, she danced around the room, hugging her pillow. She didn't plan to fall in love. She planned to win that scholarship and go to college. She was sixteen, *just a baby*, her father kept reminding her, but once she kissed Jeremy she didn't feel like a baby. She didn't feel sixteen, either. She felt euphoric. Like dancing in the rain. Like singing in the shower. Like ignoring what others less in love would have noticed.

Like the turtlenecks he always wore, no matter what. Or the fact that he always had a new bruise on his face after a weekend. She didn't want to think about these things. Whatever it was, they would figure it out together.

Unable to sit still, Abbie took her sketchpad into the living room, sat on the floor beside the Christmas tree and tried to draw. But all her pen would create were pages of infinities, hearts filled with *Jeremy* and *Abbie*, or variations of their names.

Abbie set her drawings aside and rubbed her arms. This room never felt warm, even when there was a fire in the fireplace. She hated those awful colors, the rose and mauves her mother favored. They reminded Abbie of a funeral parlor. The only thing that made the room bearable was the tree with its blinking lights and presents. Sitting on the floor with legs crossed, Abbie reached under the tree and picked up a package. She loved Christmas.

"I wondered where you'd gone to." Her mother entered the room. Abbie put the present back. "Just in here. Trying to draw."

"When is your portfolio due?"

Abbie stared at her mother. Did her mother actually say that? Did she actually care? "First week of January, when school starts."

"Well, then, better get busy." Her mother rearranged the presents under the tree, holding up one with her name. "I love presents. Nothing makes me happier." She rattled the box, held it to her nose and smiled at Abbie. "Any guesses?"

"Nope," Abbie said. "Maybe it's a mink coat."

Her mother laughed and put the present back under the tree. But she had given Abbie an idea.

The mall was busy, and Abbie enjoyed the festive commotion. With Christmas two weeks away, the excitement in the air tasted like peppermint and chocolate. Everyone was singing with the Christmas carols streaming from the hidden speakers, and children stood in line to see Santa. If Heather were there, they'd be laughing and trying on clothes and cosmetics. With Heather's help, she'd have already settled on something cool for Jeremy—a hoodie, an iPhone cover, or maybe a watch. But Heather was spending the weekend with her father, and if Abbie was going to find something nice, she'd have to do it alone.

At the cosmetic counter, Abbie sampled colognes and found one she liked, but what if Jeremy thought she was suggesting he didn't smell good? She looked at nail clippers and comb sets, a blue and white striped scarf. After an hour of second-guessing, Abbie selected the perfect gift: a sketchpad to replace the one he'd dropped in the snow.

At home, Abbie wrapped the present and put it under the tree. Singing Christmas carols, she danced circles around the room. He would be surprised. He might even kiss her again. She would even let him.

She texted Heather again and settled in front of the tree with her sketchbook. She drew clouds that looked like rose petals, aspen branches that reached past the moon. Dragonflies and fairies. Jeremy's face and the lock of hair that wouldn't stay out of his eyes. She drew a big heart around his face and kissed his picture.

So Heather was fifty miles away with her father. So what? Who needed Heather when she was busy falling in love?

Apparently Abbie did, because she agreed when Heather suggested they double date. "I want to see this boy up close and personal," Heather said. "See if he meets my approval."

When Abbie asked Jeremy, he said, "No. I don't like to double."

"Come on," Abbie said. "It'll be fun. We'll go out to eat and then see a movie." She was standing by his locker, holding his hand. "Please?"

"I'd rather not."

"Ah, go on," Charles said, walking up beside them. "It isn't going to kill you to be sociable."

"Only once," Abbie begged. "I'll never ask again."

"Once. But never again."

They took Tyler's car because there wasn't enough room in Jeremy's. That was the first mistake. The Honda Accord was nothing like Jeremy's Camaro.

"Nice car," Jeremy said when they picked him up. "What year?" He settled into the back seat with Abbie.

"2010," Tyler said.

"Didn't they have a lot of problems with that year?" Jeremy said.

"Not that I know of." Tyler turned to Heather. "Where do we want to eat?"

"Red Robin?" Heather said.

Tyler glanced into his rearview mirror. "That okay with you?"

"Fine with me," Abbie said.

"That place is for kids and old farts. It'll be busy and loud," Jeremy said.

"Well," Heather said. "Everything's going to be busy on a Friday night. Let's give it a try."

Just as Jeremy had suggested, Red Robin was busy, but then, when wasn't it? While they waited for a table, Heather held Tyler's hand and said, "Glad you two finally hooked up."

Abbie smiled and expected Jeremy to say something. But he didn't.

"So," Tyler said. "You're fixing up that old Camaro."

"Yeah," Jeremy said.

"What color are you going to paint it?"

When Jeremy didn't respond, Tyler added. "You work for your dad, right. An electrician?"

"Yeah."

"Bet it pays good," Tyler said.

"Hardly."

Heather and Abbie tried to fill the painful silence talking about school until they were seated.

Everyone was studying the menus except Jeremy. "Well," Tyler said. "Jeremy must already know what he wants. What ya having, Bro?"

"A milkshake. The food here sucks."

Abbie and Heather exchanged surprised looks.

"They have good onion rings," Abbie volunteered.

"I hate onions," Jeremy said.

"Yeah," Tyler laughed. "Not so great if you're kissing a girl."

Heather laughed and snuggled closer. "I'm having a salad so I can have popcorn later."

"I'll have the same," Abbie said, closing her menu.

"Not me," Tyler said. "A big burger and onion rings."

The restaurant was noisy, making it hard to hear. "What's that you say?" Tyler said.

"Nothing." Jeremy rolled his eyes at the commotion coming from the next table. There must have been ten or eleven children celebrating a birthday. Between the yelling and the screaming, they could barely hear their cell phones ring.

"Ah, finally," Tyler said when the waitress brought the food.

"So, Jeremy," Heather said as she slipped her fork into her salad. "Are you still working on your portfolio?"

"Yes," Abbie said. "Tell them about that cool picture you're doing. The one with the starlings and the water."

"It's nothing," Jeremy said.

"Pen or ink?" Heather said.

"Neither." He pulled the straw out of his milkshake and tipped the cup to his mouth.

"Then what are you using?" Heather said. "Water color, oils?"

"My imagination."

Heather looked at Abbie. "I need to use the bathroom."

"Me, too," Abbie said. "Be right back."

"What's his problem?" Heather said when they were alone.

"He's just tired," Abbie said. "He's been working lots of hours with his dad."

"Well, he doesn't have to be so rude." Heather washed her hands and checked her reflection in the mirror. "If he doesn't stop it, I'm going to clobber him with Tyler's onion rings."

Abbie laughed. "Then you'd be wasting perfectly good food."

"Not according to Jeremy." They laughed, trying to ease the evening's tension.

Back at the table, Abbie tried again. "Jeremy's thinking about starting an art club. Tell them Jeremy."

"You have to be able to draw to get in."

"That shouldn't be too hard," Heather said.

"You'd be surprised," Jeremy said.

"When do you meet?" Tyler said.

Jeremy shrugged.

Abbie snuggled closer to Jeremy. "I'm so looking forward to Christmas. It'll be nice to have a break from school."

"Yeah," Heather said, "except I have to spend most of my time with my dad." She laid her head on Tyler's shoulder. "But Tyler promised he'd drive over to see me.

"Maybe you and Jeremy can come along and we can hang out," Heather added.

Jeremy had finished his shake and was drumming his fingers on the table. "Why would we want to do that?"

An uncomfortable silence followed.

Heather put down her fork. "I'm done."

Tyler pushed away his plate, leaving his burger half eaten. "Me, too."

Abbie looked at her cell. "Maybe we should go then. The movie starts in twenty minutes."

"My head hurts," Heather said. "Think I'll skip it."

"Yeah," said Tyler. "Maybe we can do this again, some other time."

The ride home was painful. No one spoke. Abbie held Jeremy's hand and wondered what went wrong. She was glad when Tyler turned up the radio.

They dropped Jeremy off first. He kissed Abbie goodbye. "See you at school."

"Okay," Abbie said. "Bye."

"What was that all about," Heather said the minute they drove away. "That guy is a jerk."

"No, he isn't," Abbie defended.

Tyler pulled into Abbie's driveway. "Good luck with Mr. Attitude."

Abbie waved as they drove away. The date had been a total disaster. But then it was her own fault. He'd said he didn't want to double date.

The night wasn't a total waste. She'd learned a valuable lesson. She'd never force Jeremy to do something he didn't want to do ever again.

CHAPTER TEN

SUNDAY MORNING, Maxine woke arthritic and achy. Hobbling to the kitchen, she turned on the coffeepot and looked out the window. Herb's truck had a huge dent, she owed Shirley money, and if she didn't find a way to get some cash into their checking account, the check she gave the tow truck driver would bounce. She moved away from the window, hoping the fluffy snowflakes would cover Herb's dented fender before he woke.

Maxine found the name of the travel agency in the phone book. She dialed the number and got a recording. "We're sorry. Our office is closed. Call back during business hours or leave a message." She waited until they were open and called again.

"I was in there yesterday and bought a ticket to Graceland, the senior's special. I fell and broke my foot, and now I can't go. Can I cancel and get a refund?" Maxine rubbed her foot, not broken, but clearly swollen.

The woman on the other end of the phone was firm. "If you read the fine print, you know all sales are final. No, we cannot refund your ticket." The phone clicked off in Maxine's ear.

"If you read the fine print." Maxine looked at the ticket. Sure enough, there it was, stamped on the back in red letters. ALL SALES FINAL. NO REFUNDS OR EXCHANGES.

She tucked the ticket in her purse. Shirley could wait, but the bank couldn't. There was no extra money in the house, and Herb wouldn't get paid for another week. There was only one thing left to do.

Grace wasn't home, so Maxine talked to Abbie instead. "Hi, Gramma. How's it going?"

"Can't complain."

"That's good. Ready for Christmas?"

"Almost. Just need a few more things," Maxine said. "Can you tell your mom I called?"

"Will do. But don't hold your breath for her to call you back." Abbie took a drink from something. Soda, Maxine guessed. "She's too busy and distracted these days."

"Thanks for the warning," Maxine said. "I'll try again later."

In the meantime, she'd better settle on what to give Abbie, Grace, and Rob for Christmas.

Deciding to use the yarn Grace dropped off earlier, Maxine searched through her patterns. Many of the sweaters she'd already made for Abbie and Grace. She'd even made a few for Rob. One pattern she wanted to make for Abbie required two different colors of yarn. But Grace had bought variegated yarn, lavender and gray. Maxine put the pattern back. Even if she had enough yarn, it would take months to finish. She searched until she found a pattern with three matching vests, a simple cable stitch. She could use the yarn Grace gave her and have enough left to make a beret for Abbie. They weren't the presents she wanted to give, but they would do.

Her fingers flew through the yarn as she knit one, purled one toward the end of each row. The stitches were so familiar her mind wandered, settling on the senior trip to Graceland. For the first time since she'd bought the ticket she let herself imagine the journey. In less than a month, she would be touring Elvis's home. Maybe she'd touch the table where he ate his peanut butter and banana sandwiches. Maybe she'd even see his bedroom.

Knit one. Purl one. Maxine hummed some of her favorite Elvis songs as she stitched. She couldn't get a refund. She didn't know anyone who would buy the ticket from her, even if she could force herself to sell it. Maybe life didn't end at sixty-three. Maybe at sixty-three, her life was just beginning.

*   *   *

Grace plugged in the Christmas tree and stood for a moment, watching the lights. She knew she should think about dinner but was reluctant to cook just yet. She poured a glass of wine and curled up on the sofa. If she were still at Michael's, they'd be feeding each other strawberries in bed.

She studied the living room. The mauves and blues would look nice at Michael's. The floral paintings would accent the wall leading to his master bedroom. Funny how things changed. One minute she was waiting for Rob to remember he was married. The next, she was wondering what it would be like to marry Michael. She might have felt guilty if she hadn't had such a wonderful afternoon.

Returning to the kitchen for another glass of wine, Grace noticed Abbie's note on the table. *Gramma called. Call her back.*

The phone rang twice before her mother answered. "Hi, Mom. Abbie said you called."

"I did. She said you've been distracted."

"I'm not distracted, just busy with Christmas."

"Christmas," her mother said. "That's why I'm calling."

Grace heard the hesitation in her mother's voice. "What? You don't want to come here for Christmas?"

"No. No. That's not it. It's . . . I did something foolish. I bought something for your father. It was more than I expected and if I don't get two hundred dollars in the bank by tomorrow morning, my check is going to bounce. I don't want him to know. It'll ruin the surprise."

Grace waited for her mother to continue. When she didn't, Grace said, "Am I supposed to read your mind?"

"I'll pay you back as soon as your father gets paid."

"Two hundred dollars?" Grace said. "Consider it an early Christmas present."

"I will pay you back," her mother repeated. "And Grace? There's something else."

"What?"

"Could you make a deposit for me tonight so it will be there in the morning?"

Grace fought to keep the irritation from her voice. "Sure."

"I'll get a deposit slip ready," her mother said. "Thank you."

Her mother was waiting for her at the door. "Your father's sleeping," her mother nodded to the bedroom. Like this was something new. "I'll pay you back," her mother whispered.

"Don't worry about it." Grace took the deposit slip from her mother.

"Do you want to come in?" her mother said.

"No, I've got to go." Grace left without telling her mother goodbye.

The evening wasn't a total waste. After depositing the money in her parents' account, Grace went to the bookstore. She browsed while waiting for the clerk to find the rare copy of *The Faerie Queene* she had ordered for Rob for Christmas. She wanted to get Michael something, but she didn't know him well enough to know if he liked books, or if he had any hobbies other than golf. She wanted to give him something nice, something that would make him think of her when she wasn't there.

She looked at a book. *How to Make Him Beg for More.* Then another. *How to Please Your Lover.* Still tingling from her afternoon of lovemaking, Grace settled on *I Love the Way You Love Me.* The cover was eclectic, an abstract painting of a naked couple embracing. She had both books gift-wrapped and headed home.

Rob greeted her at the door. "How was your day? I see you've been shopping."

"No peeking." Grace swung the bag out of reach. She should have left the books in the car. She would slip them under the tree and deal with them later.

"Need help with dinner?" Rob said.

"No." Grace moved toward the stairs. "I'm going to change, then fix a salad. Nothing fancy."

Later, Grace replayed the afternoon as she chopped lettuce and grated carrots. If she was going to continue this relationship with Michael— and she was—she was glad they'd discussed birth control, glad she wouldn't have to use pills because they always made her cramp and bleed. She nibbled on a carrot. Strange, worrying about birth control after all these years. Before, when she discovered she was pregnant with Abbie, she had briefly considered an abortion. She hadn't been ready to be a mother, but Rob had insisted. She'd learned her lesson. This time she'd be more careful. She'd been confused, but now her head was clear. She'd sleep with Michael for as long as he wanted her. And that meant he wore a condom, or she started the pills again. It would be a nuisance, but he was worth it.

*   *   *

Abbie hurried to art class, wanting to be the first one in the room. She opened Jeremy's art drawer and put the sketchbook inside. If nothing else, this should make him happy. She didn't sign her name to the card, writing instead "Merry Christmas to the boy who believes in infinities." Already the last day of class before Christmas break, she didn't know how she'd spend Christmas vacation. But she had visions of him holding her sketchbook and drawing, and that made her happy.

She ran into Heather after second period. "Where were you this morning?"

"I had something to do," Abbie said.

"Have anything to do with Jeremy?" Heather said sarcastically. "Is he your new best friend?"

"No," Abbie mumbled. Heather would always be her best friend.

But Heather was changing. Since her parent's divorce, Heather was distant, slower to laugh. And she spent most of her time with Tyler, leaving Abbie to entertain herself or spend time thinking about Jeremy.

"Well, I'm off to my dad's," Heather said after school.

"Text me," Abbie said.

"I will." Heather gave her a hug. "Have a great Christmas."

"You, too," Abbie said. "I'll miss you."

Abbie tried to pass the long days before Christmas by writing poems and drawing pictures in her sketchbook. She tried to text Heather, but Heather was slow to reply, and hanging at home with her parents was lame. She'd spent a long day doing nothing. There were no movies she wanted to see, and it was no fun going to the mall alone. She was thinking about Jeremy, when, as if by magic, he was knocking at her door.

"Can you go for a ride?" he said.

A thousand things ran through Abbie's head. She should have washed her hair. She wasn't wearing makeup. Her jeans were too baggy. But he smiled anyway and reached for her hand. "Don't forget your coat."

"Be back in a while," Abbie yelled to her parents and rushed out the door before they could ask a hundred questions.

"Where are we going?" She loved riding in his car even though it still needed a lot of work.

"You'll see." He drove through the snowy roads toward the river. He didn't stop until he reached the cluster of trees outside town called The Grove.

The first thing Abbie thought as he pulled the car to a stop and pushed back his seat to give himself more leg room, is that this is where she and Heather used to come hiking in the summer before the rumors of hangings and suicides scared them away.

"Thanks for the sketchpad." He reached into the back seat and retrieved a large envelope. "Merry Christmas."

Abbie's heart pattered as she opened it. A picture. Of them. Sitting by the river drawing, their heads bent over their sketches and touching. It was amazing, something she would cherish forever. She couldn't wait to show it to Heather.

"Hope you like it," he said.

"I love it." She kissed him.

The last time she'd been in The Grove her father scolded her and told her to stay away, that there was nothing there but danger. But tonight there was something else. There was electricity, love, and excitement. When Jeremy kissed her, Abbie couldn't help but believe she was proving everyone wrong. Here in The Grove, under the hanging tree, there was something more than danger and death. There was Jeremy, hope, and desire.

CHAPTER ELEVEN

THE WEEK BEFORE CHRISTMAS Maxine was busy with presents to wrap, a husband to feed, and loans to repay. From Herb's paychecks, Maxine was able to scrape together enough money to repay Grace, but she still owed Shirley fifty dollars.

"Don't worry about it," Shirley said. They were at the Senior Center sitting around one of the tables decorated with green tablecloths and large plastic poinsettias. One of the directors played Christmas music on the old piano while Linda, dressed as Santa Claus, passed out plates of fruitcake and frosted sugar cookies.

"Merry Christmas," she said, moving from table to table to refill coffee and water cups. Maxine, Helen and Shirley took this occasion to have their own Christmas celebration.

After Mrs. Miller's third grade class presented their Christmas program and sang, "You'd better not pout," shaking their fingers at the senior citizens, Maxine reached under the table for the large bag and presented her gifts.

"Thank you." Helen modeled the purple beret. A row of variegated red roses adorned one side of the hat, which looked perfect on Helen.

"I love them!" Shirley ahh-ed over the crocheted bells and stars Maxine made to go along with Shirley's lopsided snowflakes. Maxine also gave them each a knitted scarf, zebra striped for Shirley and purple for Helen. The woolen thread had been expensive, and as they tied them around their necks, Maxine was proud of her work, that she hadn't skimped on the thread.

"What's this?" Maxine said when she opened her gift from Shirley, a digital camera. Helen gave her an accompanying gift, a nice camera bag.

"You can take it to Graceland and get instant pictures," Shirley said. "See?" She aimed the camera at Maxine and Helen and snapped their picture. "If you don't like that one, you can take another." Shirley showed Maxine how to scroll through the pictures and delete the ones she didn't want to keep.

"This is too much," Maxine rewrapped the camera and tried to give it back.

"Stop it," Shirley said. "Or I'll give back my scarf. Which I love."

"Thank you." Maxine flushed. "I'll take good care of it."

Shirley poked her. "You'll takes lots of pictures and have a wonderful time."

People were buttoning coats, ready to leave. Since the Christmas party was over, Maxine stood and reached for her purse.

"Hold on, Nellie," Helen said. "Not so fast." She handed Maxine a small box. "Merry Christmas."

"You already gave me a gift," Maxine said.

"Shut up and open it."

Maxine unwrapped the present and laughed. In fact, they all laughed because she was holding the Elvis Presley ornament she had coveted, the one Helen won at bingo.

"You're the best." Maxine hugged Helen.

"Didn't think I was going to keep that ugly thing in my house, did you?" Helen smiled.

Not to be outdone, Shirley handed Maxine an envelope. Inside was a gift certificate for fifty dollars. Shirley had pasted a sticker of Santa in the middle of the certificate and wrote, One Loan -- Paid in Full.

"I can't accept this." Maxine pushed it back.

"Oh yes you can." Shirley crossed her arms over her chest. "You'll need it when you go to Memphis. I want the best souvenir you can find."

"I don't deserve you." Maxine hugged them both and wished them Merry Christmas.

The next day as she gathered the presents she would take to Grace's to be opened after their Christmas Eve dinner, Maxine reflected. She still had to tell Herb about the ticket to Graceland, and she dreaded the conversation. But wasn't it better to "throw caution to the wind" like Shirley said, and make one of her dreams come true?

All afternoon she had her hands full trying to keep Herb sober. Andy's shop closed at noon, and Herb had been underfoot most of the day. He tried to sing the songs from Elvis's Christmas album to Maxine, which made her angry.

She snapped off the stereo. "Take a shower. You stink."

She didn't want to go out, she didn't want to celebrate Christmas, but if she had to, she was glad they were going to Grace's. He may have liked his beer too much, but around his daughter and granddaughter, he tried to behave.

While Maxine waited for Herb to shower, she sat on the sofa and stared at her tree. Christmas wasn't fun anymore. Not like when Grace and Abbie were little. She missed icing sugar cookies and cleaning up the mess their little fingers left. Grace was always so precise in her decorations, so much so no one dared to eat them. Abbie, on the other hand, leaned toward covering everything with red icing. "Here, Grampa," she would say, always offering Herb her first creation. Now Grace was always on a diet, and Abbie was covering canvases with red ink.

Maxine sighed and lit a cigarette, blowing smoke at the tree.

"Ready." Coming from the bedroom, Herb's hair was combed. His clothes were clean.

"Let's go then." She turned out the lights and followed him to the truck. He never mentioned the dented fender, which didn't surprise Maxine. What surprised her was that he could even start the piece of junk, given the trouble it had given her before.

They were silent on their way to Grace's. The new snow made everything white, perfect for Christmas. But a perfect Christmas was the last thing on her mind. Herb parked the truck in Grace's driveway. They sat a moment watching the snow. Maxine knew Herb wanted a cold beer, while the thing she wanted most was out of her marriage.

* * *

Grace was full of angst and longing the week before Christmas. She had planned a special surprise for Michael, one with wine, presents and lovemaking. She had even bought a new negligee. They would read the book together. They would linger over wine. They would look into each other's eyes and pledge their love. Christmas would be perfect.

But Michael had a surprise of his own. The minute school dismissed for Christmas vacation, he had to fly to Kansas. "I have to go," he had said hurriedly on the phone. "Something's come up. I'll call you later."

She tried to hide her disappointment. "I'll miss you, but we can celebrate Christmas when you get back. I love you."

Grace sat at her desk and stared out the window. No one bought houses the week before Christmas. Last year, she was home fussing with decorations and Christmas menus. This year, she was staring at the snow and fussing with her wedding ring. She should be in Kansas, sipping wine and planning a quiet romantic Christmas and New Year with Michael.

Two months ago, Mrs. Rob Buchanan would have never considered an affair, let alone adultery and divorce. But Grace Buchanan, petite secretary and receptionist for Aspen Grove Realty, caught herself thinking about affairs and divorces at the oddest times, like setting the table. Or picking up a suit at the dry cleaners. Or slipping into bed. Mrs. Rob Buchanan had a cleaning lady to clean the toilets and dust the furniture. But Grace Buchanan, Michael Lancaster's lover, would clean her own toilets and dust her own furniture, keeping their home a sanctuary from anything that might hurt them, like prying eyes or wagging tongues.

The ringing phone jarred Grace from her thoughts. "Hello," she said, forgetting for a moment where she was, or that she was answering her cell instead of the office phone. So lost in her daydreams about Michael, she even forgot to smile. "Excuse me." She smiled into the phone. "Let's try that again. Aspen Grove Realty. How may I direct your call?" A part of her hoped Michael would be on the other end of the phone saying how much he missed her. She was disappointed to discover it was only her husband. She thought she heard laughter in the background.

"A few of us are heading over to Hart's for a little Christmas cheer. Care to join us?" There it was again, the laughter. This time, Grace recognized Jill's voice. It wasn't bad enough that Michael had left without giving her a present; now, Rob wanted her to sit in a room with strangers and watch a secretary ogle her husband.

"I can't," Grace said. "Trudy and I have plans. Oops. There's the other phone. Have fun." She frowned as she clicked off her cell. There was no incoming call, and Trudy had already started her Christmas vacation. Grace wasn't having drinks with anyone after work, not even Michael. Tonight, she'd be drinking alone.

The next morning while arranging the house for her Christmas Eve dinner, Grace pulled Michael's present from under the tree. She had planned to give the book to Michael before he left. Now she'd have to wait until he returned. She was headed to her bedroom to hide the gift when the doorbell rang. Grace set the present on the entryway table and opened the door.

"Grace Buchanan?" A messenger hid behind a large wicker basket.

"Yes?" She stepped to one side, trying to see.

"For you." A teenage boy, not much older than Abbie, put the basket on the floor. "I tried to deliver it to your office, but it was closed. Merry Christmas."

"Merry Christmas," Grace said.

The basket was huge, overfull with olive oil, pasta, a cheese grater and everything she needed to make ravioli. There was also a book, *The Pasta Lover's Guide to Nutritious Eating* and a bottle of Merlot. She smiled and thought of Michael and the ravioli he had fed her at Rudy's.

She took the basket to the kitchen and untied the red bow. Someone had gone to a lot of trouble. She opened the book and a smile flooded her face. There, on a small piece of paper, Michael had written, *Enjoy♥*.

Grace hugged the book to her chest. "I love you, I love you." Here was the proof that he loved her, too. She folded the note and put it in her pocket. The basket she hid in a closet where Rob would never look. Her life was complicated, but almost complete.

While Rob showered and Abbie fussed in her bedroom, Grace hummed Christmas carols and straightened the napkins and silverware. She rearranged the placemats and centerpiece. The table looked nice, straight out of *House Beautiful*. Michael would love it.

"Brrr." She rubbed her arms and looked for a sweater. Even though she had just adjusted the thermostat, the house felt cold, as if suffering from loneliness or neglect. Grace took another look at her dining room to make sure everything was in place, then walked over to the Christmas tree and plugged in the lights. Next year, Grace would be living with Michael in the new house on Cedar Lane. He'd help decorate the tree, and *their* house would never feel cold and empty.

*   *   *

Until she fell in love, Abbie hadn't paid a lot of attention to waiting or loneliness. An impatient child, she always got what she wanted, or received a suitable answer from her father as to why it was prudent to wait. For instance, she couldn't have a credit card until she got a job. Things like that that made sense. But there was nothing about falling in love that made sense. Whenever she was with Jeremy, the sun shown brighter, even on cloudy days. Or, whenever she wrote his name on a piece of paper, her hand grew so hot, it almost burst into flames. Or, when he called her name, she forgot who she was.

Or why, when she couldn't be with him, she turned moody and temperamental, like today. Even though it was Christmas Eve and she should have been looking forward to celebrating and enjoying the dinner her mother spent all day perfecting, Abbie was restless, withdrawn and mopey. Jeremy was gone and would be until the first week in January when school started again. In the meantime, he was spending the holidays in Montana with his mother. Heather wasn't the only one whose parents no longer lived together.

"Call me," Abbie said.

"I'll try," he said. "But my dad smashed my phone."

She would miss him. Every minute he was gone would feel longer than ten thousand years.

When she grew tired of drawing, Abbie sat in front of her mirror and experimented. She rarely used makeup, but now played with black mascara and eyeliner. Drawing thick dark lines under her eyelashes the way Jeremy did when he drew her picture, Abbie outlined her eyes until each line met, giving her the appearance of a cat. Trying for a beautifully mysterious look, Abbie softened the lines and with her finger blended a charcoal eye shadow over her eyelid. She dusted her eyelashes with powder, a trick she learned from her mother and applied two coats of mascara. Using an opalescent shade of white, Abbie highlighted each brow, then stood back and admired her work. Not bad. It had taken more than an hour, but she ended up with something striking, if not attractive.

Next, she turned to her mouth. Using black eyeliner, Abbie outlined her lips the way she watched her mother do numerous times before she started locking Abbie out of the bathroom. Abbie smudged the inside edges with her finger and applied a ruby red lipstick. Over this she put a blush lip-gloss and blended the colors the way she blended colors on a canvas. Then she fluffed her hair with her fingers. "Hey, beautiful," she said to her mirrored image. She wasn't a masterpiece yet, but she'd get better with practice.

Abbie searched for something jolly to wear. She glanced at the pile of clothes accumulating in the bottom of her closet, all from her mom in her mother's favorite pink shade. One of these days, Abbie would get rid of them. She hadn't, nor would she ever, wear one of those awful things. She looked through her drawers until she found a black turtleneck. She'd forgotten she'd bought it to wear to a Halloween party a couple of years ago. She knew her mother would have a fit, but Abbie didn't care. Wearing the shirt made her feel closer to Jeremy. But just to be festive, she tied a red scarf around her neck, took one last look in the mirror and went downstairs.

The minute her mother saw her, she stopped mashing the garlic potatoes. "What did you do to your face?"

"Love you, too, Mom." Abbie picked an olive from the relish tray and popped it into her mouth. "What's for dinner?"

"Nothing until you wipe that crap off your face."

Abbie smiled. She finally made her mother say "crap."

Her mother threw the potato masher into the sink and said, "Right now. You will not sit at my table looking like that."

"Now, Grace." Her father put down the knife he used to carve the prime rib and walked over to his daughter. He tilted her head one way, then the other. He gave her a squeeze. "Did you change your name, too? Morticia or Lilith?"

"Oh, Daddy," Abbie giggled.

"Here." He handed her the relish tray. "Help your mother and put this on the table."

"Rob," her mother said.

He put his arms around his wife. "Relax. She's just experimenting. You think that looks bad, you should see some of the college kids."

"I won't--"

"Grace, it's Christmas. Can we just not fight today? Please."

Her mother reached for the butter and slammed the refrigerator door.

The doorbell rang and Abbie said, "I'll get it." She plunked the relish tray in the middle of the dining room table and opened the door. "Hi, Grampa. Hi, Gramma."

"Ummm," her grandmother said. "Your house smells like holly berries, pine boughs, and..."

"It's okay," Abbie said. "You can say it. Lysol."

They both laughed, and while her grandparents slipped off their coats, her grandmother said, "Good Lord, Abbie, has your mother seen your face?"

"Oh, yeah, Gramma. She's already pitched a fit."

"Teenagers," her grandfather said. "Always trying something new."

Abbie wrapped her arm around her grandfather's waist. "Yes, we are."

He gave her a hug. "When do we eat?"

"Merry Christmas." Her father took their coats. "Hope you're hungry, Herb. Grace's been cooking your favorite dishes all day." He led them to the dining room where Abbie's mother was rearranging the relish tray and filling the crystal goblets with ice water.

"Merry Christmas." Her mother retreated into the kitchen.

"Grace," her grandmother called after her. "I thought we were cutting back this year. What's with this fancy dinner?" Abbie's mother didn't answer as she returned with the green bean casserole.

"Look," her grandfather said to Abbie's grandmother. "Your favorite."

"Look," her grandmother replied as Abbie's father poured the wine and prepared for a toast. "Your favorite."

When everyone was seated around the table, Abbie's father raised his glass. "To my beautiful family. I love you all. Merry Christmas."

"Merry Christmas." Everyone clinked glasses.

Abbie smiled. "Merry Christmas." She could have alcohol on special occasions like this. She took a sip and wondered what all the fuss was about. She doubted she'd ever like wine as much as her mother did. Diet Coke, even water, tasted better.

"I always get confused when I eat at your house, Gracie." Her grandfather put his empty wine glass beside his plate. "What am I supposed to do with all these forks?"

"Eat," her grandmother said, and Abbie giggled.

They continued the meal in half-silences. "So Herb," her father said, "How's work?"

"Can't complain."

"Maxine, they keeping you busy at the Center?"

"They are. We've been running all week. Next week--"

Abbie's mother interrupted. "Daddy needs some mashed potatoes. Please pass these to him."

"They're garlic, Grampa," Abbie said. "Don't you like them?"

"I'll save them for you," he said, passing them on. "So," he teased, "got a steady boyfriend yet?"

"She's too young for boys," her mother said.

"No she isn't. I was dating your ma when I was just about her age."

"We all know how well that turned out," her mother said.

Abbie's father's fixed stare brought her mother to her feet. Abbie'd seen her do this a million times. First, she'd stand over the sink with her hands planted hard and count. One. Two. Three. Then she'd reach into the cupboard and pull out the bottle of aspirin and take four with a full glass of wine, shake her head like a dog trying to get the water out of its ears, take a deep breath and return to the table. It never made Abbie's mother any nicer, but at least she'd shut up.

They were finishing their meal when her mother returned. "Dessert?" she said with a forced smile. "I have your favorite, Daddy. Pecan pie."

"Let's wait," Abbie's father said. "Until we open the presents." He slapped his father-in-law on the back. "What do you say, old man, ready to hit that tree?"

"Sure am," her grandfather said. He finished his wine in one gulp. "Let's do it."

Pretending to be Santa, her grandfather handed out the gifts. "Here, Abbie, this one's for you." He crawled around under the tree, sending the ornaments spinning.

"What do I do with this?" her grandmother said after opening a mandolin slicer.

"You use it to slice carrots, Gramma."

"Or julienne jicama," Abbie's mother added. "It's very handy and very sharp."

"Jicama," Abbie's grandmother said. "Thanks."

Her father held up a knitted vest and said, "Thanks, Maxine. It's nice."

"Damn fine work that woman of mine does, don't you think?" Abbie's grandfather said.

"Yes." Her father pulled the vest over his head and said, "Your turn, Pumpkin."

Abbie hated it when he called her that, but she smiled anyway and unwrapped a gift from her mother. "Thanks." Abbie held up a cashmere cardigan twin set in bright pink. She folded the sweaters and put them back in the box. The present she got from her father was better—private lessons with the art professor at the community college.

One by one they went in a circle. Her mother opened a present, the tennis bracelet. "Thank you," she said. Abbie could tell she hated it. *Now you know how I feel every time you give me something pink,* Abbie thought smugly.

Abbie had to use the bathroom. "Don't open any more until I get back." When she returned, she carried a present.

"Daddy, this one's for you. Mom left it in the hallway."

"Wait." Her mother reached for the present and upset her wine glass. "Now look what you made me do."

Abbie's father was on his feet. "It's just a sofa, Grace. It can be cleaned. Abbie, get a towel from the kitchen." By the time the stain was blotted, every ounce of Christmas spirit had left for the North Pole.

Abbie's father studied the unopened present as if afraid to open it.

"Go ahead," her grandfather said. "Let's see what all the fuss's about." Abbie's mother folded her arms tight, her lips a straight thin line.

Her father read the tag. "Always and forever, love Grace."

"Aw, that's nice," Abbie's grandfather said. Her grandmother grimaced.

"Always and forever." Her father annunciated the words. "I love you, too." He unwrapped the gift, looked at the cover, and turned it face down.

"What'd you get, Daddy? Let's see."

Her mother reached for the book, but her father held onto it. The emotion on his face was impossible to read. His face was splotchy, red. He flushed when her grandfather laughed.

"Hey, Maxine. Maybe we should borrow that book after Rob's had a chance to read it." Abbie looked at her mother. Her face was pinched and pale.

"Where's that pie?" Abbie's grandfather interrupted the awkward silence, and Abbie's mother escaped into the kitchen. There was a rattle of plates and the whir of a mixer. As soon as they had eaten pecan pie, Christmas was over.

Merry Christmas, Abbie thought as she hugged her grandparents goodbye. If she ever married—maybe someone like Jeremy—she'd have better Christmases. There would be singing and laughing and hot buttered rums. They'd string popcorn and play games. People would beg to stay instead of hurrying away at the first convenient minute. Abbie stood at the door and waved. She'd never give presents like mandolin slicers. She'd never give anything pink or make someone turn red.

*   *   *

Christmas morning, Herb and Maxine made no effort to open their gifts. The present Herb bought Maxine was under the tree, a box of cherry cordials he didn't bother to wrap.

"Here are your presents." Maxine tossed the packages of socks and underwear at her husband, already drunk before noon on Christmas day. "Happy crappy Christmas." While he opened his gifts, Maxine threw the box of candy in the garbage and made a decision. The house was cold. She thought she heard a breeze, the sound the wind makes when it rattles the aspen trees. But it was only the filter in her fish tank where Elvis and Priscilla swam—round and round and round.

CHAPTER TWELVE

THE DAY AFTER CHRISTMAS, instead of the living room being scattered with opened boxes and presents, Grace had the tree all but undecorated by the time Rob came down the stairs for breakfast. She was standing on a stepladder, reaching for the tree-topper when he entered the living room.

"Grace, what are you doing?"

"Taking down Christmas."

"Already? You usually leave it up through New Year's." He held the ladder while she stepped down. "What's the hurry?"

"I'm tired of looking at it."

He picked up an ornament and turned it over in his hand. "The house will feel empty without it. I wish you'd waited."

"Don't you have to work today?" Grace put the topper into a box.

He waited for her to close the lid before he put his hand on her elbow. "We need to talk. Please sit down."

"Don't," Grace said. "I'm busy."

"That can wait. Sit down." He didn't release her elbow until she was seated on the sofa. He sat across from her and moved his chair close enough he could take her hands in his. "What's going on?"

She pulled her hands away and tried to stand, but he was too close; she couldn't move without pushing him out of the way. Seeing he was determined, she gave a heavy sigh and leaned back into the sofa. "Nothing."

"Is it your job?"

Grace laughed. "No."

"Abbie?"

Grace glanced around the room. She wasn't having this conversation. "No."

"Look at me. What's wrong?"

She looked at him—more like glared at him—and let her eyes meet his. Brown, there was no desire in them, not like in Michael's when he smiled at her. If Rob really loved her, he would be able to look into her eyes and know exactly what was wrong. But he was so busy with his work and his mystery writing, he couldn't see what was right in front of him.

They looked at each other, but they didn't connect. Grace stood. "Please, Rob. I'd like to get this done today. Since you don't have to work, maybe you can help."

When he realized she wasn't going to talk, he stood up and backed out of her way. But not without adding, "What about our New Year's party? It won't be festive without the tree."

They always threw a party on New Year's Eve, but this year, Grace didn't have the energy or inclination. She usually loved to entertain and took pride in her hors d'oeuvres, but with Michael away, she didn't feel like doing anything. She couldn't wait for the holidays to be over and for everything to get back to normal. "What if we skipped the party this year?" she said. "I think I'm coming down with a cold."

"We can't do that," Rob said. "I've already invited most of our friends. Tradition, you know. They look forward to it every year."

Grace sighed. She'd have the stupid party, but she'd have it without Christmas decorations. Or Michael.

The days following Christmas, Grace carried her cell phone everywhere she went, expecting Michael to text or call. Each day grew longer as she checked her phone a dozen times and wondered what was so important he couldn't pick up the phone and say I love you? Before long she started to panic. What if he'd had an accident? What if he was lying in a hospital somewhere with amnesia? Frantic with worry, she called his cell every hour and left a message. She sent him numerous texts. But he didn't respond.

She searched the Internet and Kansas City newspapers for information, but found nothing. It was as if he had simply gone to Kansas and disappeared. She was so worried she seriously considered buying a plane ticket to find him. But she wasn't ready to tell Rob, not yet, and waiting was one of the hardest things she had to do.

Beside herself, she called his cell and left a message. "Michael, if you don't call me back, I'm going to file a missing person's report. Please let me know you're okay."

The fear in her voice must have worked because he did call her, later that afternoon. She was fixing stuffed mushrooms and garlic escargot for the party. Her hands were wet, and she was tempted to let the call go to voice mail, but something in her gut told her to pick up. Her spirits lifted the minute she saw his number. "Michael!"

"Hi, Grace," he said. "I can't talk, but I wanted to let you know I'm fine. You don't have to worry. Happy New Year." He clicked off before she had a chance to say a word.

For several minutes, she stood staring at the phone. She started to call him back, but her oven timer buzzed. He was alive. He was getting her messages. Grace smiled. He'd be back soon. Everything would be perfect.

That old saying "absence makes the heart grow fonder" really was true. Three weeks felt like three years. It was just enough time for Grace to make up her mind. When Michael came back, she'd tell him. In the meantime, she tried to embrace a festive mood as she dressed for the party. Most of the guests were Rob's friends from work, people they had entertained for years. Nothing new here. Nothing to get excited about.

In a silver blouse and black slacks, Grace served stuffed mushrooms and filled champagne glasses. She discussed summer vacations on the coast and even kissed her husband at the stroke of midnight. But even as she kissed him, her heart wasn't anywhere near Aspen Grove. It was somewhere in Kansas City welcoming in the New Year with Michael.

*   *   *

Because her parents had joint custody, Heather spent most of Christmas vacation with her father and his new girlfriend in Cedarbrook. Texting was better than nothing, but it wasn't the same as hanging out at the mall with your best friend, or going to a movie and talking about boys. The days after Christmas drug on slower than a drought in summer, and Abbie couldn't wait for school to start again.

She tried to fill the long days taking walks and drawing. Her portfolio was almost complete. She couldn't wait to show Jeremy. She took her time, paying special attention to the lines and details. The portrait she was working on was proving to be the most difficult, probably because it was headshots of her family; more specifically, her grandmother and mother. She started it as a silhouette with her grandmother's face in the background and her mother's in the foreground like a ripple, but it didn't look right. She drew another composition, this time much better, more like a reflection. She worked from photos she'd taken over the holidays. The sketches looked striking in red ink.

The likeness of her grandmother was the easiest, maybe because Abbie's heart felt pride when she drew the broad forehead and thinning hair. Her grandmother's eyebrows were bushier than her mothers, who plucked her own into a thin arched line. As Abbie drew her grandmother, she sang some of her grandmother's favorite songs like "Don't Be Cruel," and "Are You Lonesome Tonight." As far back as Abbie could remember, her grandmother had always loved Elvis. She sang Elvis songs to Abbie at bedtime instead of reading stories.

Abbie's mother's portrait proved to be more difficult to capture. Where Abbie's grandmother's uneven teeth showed with her smile, her mother's smile was pinched shut. Her mother's pictures never revealed teeth even though they were perfectly whitened every month, every week if the dentist would let her.

"A-an-gel," Abbie hummed as she drew the noses, both small like her own. But that's where the resemblance ended. Her mother didn't have her grandmother's eyes or high cheekbones.

As Abbie labored over the drawings, she tried to see the similarities and the things that made them different. Her grandmother's face was kinder, tired looking, filled with resignation, while her mother's face looked determined, focused on more, focused on the future. It was also filled with longing.

As she drew, Abbie wondered what Jeremy was doing in Montana. With his mother. Given the little she knew about his father, she was happy for him. Hopefully, he was having a good time. Abbie tried to picture him on the ranch, or riding a horse. She flipped to a clean page in her sketchbook and soon her pen was flying. Jeremy on a horse. Jeremy in a pair of snowshoes. To each picture she added a signature in the right-hand corner, but instead of signing her name, she used the signature he had shown her by the river, the elongated S lying on its side with the words *forever and always* connecting the two sides making the sign of infinity.

Satisfied with her work, Abbie put the sketchpad away. Tomorrow would be New Year's Eve. Tomorrow she'd be one day closer to Jeremy.

*   *   *

Maxine looked at her Christmas tree and sighed. Once upon a time she loved Christmas. Once upon a time she loved everything, but time and loss had a way of wearing the edges of love thin until they dissolved into nothing. Each new Christmas made her sadder. Each new Christmas reminded her that she was wasting her life and for what? She no longer knew.

Grateful Herb was sleeping, Maxine sat on the sofa, smoked her cigarette and let her mind settle on her upcoming trip to Graceland. In a perfect world she would be going with her one true love Larry who walked and talked so much like Elvis they could have been brothers. She smiled at the thought, Larry and Graceland, what could be better?

The Elvis ornament Helen gave her for Christmas hung proudly on Maxine's tree along with Abbie's reindeer. Maxine wasn't one to wallow or to play make-believe like Grace, but seeing the ornament reminded her of Larry, and she sat back against the sofa and closed her eyes. If Larry were still alive, she wouldn't be riding a bus to Memphis. They'd be flying in a plane or taking the car. If Larry were still alive, she wouldn't be spending New Year's Eve alone. Herb wouldn't be down the hall snoring, and she wouldn't be watching the ball drop at Times Square by herself. Larry would be sitting beside her counting: 10 - 9 - 8 - 7 - 6. When the ball reached one, he would look into her eyes and say, "Happy New Year, Maxy," and she would kiss him with all her heart the way she did so many years ago.

But Larry was dead, and on the inside, she was, too.

Maxine yawned and stretched and went over to the fish tank. "Happy New Year, Elvis," she said. "Happy New Year, Priscilla."

Returning from the kitchen with a glass of water, Maxine sat on the sofa and watched the ball drop at Times Square and counted with the New York crowd: 3 - 2 - 1.

"Happy Crappy New Year," she said to the empty house. Long after midnight, she watched the lights flicker on her Christmas tree. *Happy New Year, Larry. Wherever you are.*

CHAPTER THIRTEEN

JANUARY WAS SUPPOSED to be a month for looking forward and new beginnings. But as Grace hit the buzzer on her alarm and snuggled into her pillow, she didn't feel like looking forward, or starting anything new. She was so tired, she wanted to sleep until next December.

"Grace?" Drying his back with a towel, Rob said, "aren't you going to work?"

Grace groaned. Everything hurt, even her hair. Shivering, she pulled the covers over her head, and then shoved them aside as she flew into the bathroom.

When she returned to bed, Rob said, "You look awful. You'd better stay home." She lay back on her pillow. All she wanted to do was sleep.

"Can I get you anything before I leave?"

She held her head. "No."

Fixing his tie as he left the room, Rob returned with a cup of tea, which he put on the bedside table. He kissed her forehead. "I'll call on my way home to see if you need anything."

"Thanks," Grace mumbled.

He stopped at the bedroom door. "I called your office and told them you wouldn't be in today. Get some rest."

Grace buried her head in the covers. She was exhausted. When she woke four hours later, she felt better. Yawning, Grace turned on her side and looked out at the snow-covered trees. What an awful way to start the New Year. Outside, the snow glistened in sunshine. She watched as a sparrow pecked at something in the tree. Too early to build a nest, she thought, reaching for her cold cup of tea.

She let the water from the shower wash away the lingering fatigue. She no longer felt sick, but she still felt wobbly and fat. She stepped on the scale, 125. She'd gained two pounds over the holidays. As soon as she felt better, she'd head to the gym and shed those extra pounds. A good workout always did wonders.

The afternoon dragged, pulling Grace down with it. She thought about calling Michael, but didn't have the energy. She checked her phone for messages. None. He was probably on a plane flying back to her. Too tired to fix dinner, she snuggled with a blanket on the sofa, where she promptly fell asleep. It was after eight when she woke. Disoriented, she looked around the room. She heard someone in the kitchen. "Rob?"

"Hey, there, sleepyhead." Wiping his hands on a dish towel, he entered the living room. "Feeling better? I brought home your favorite chicken soup from Rudy's."

The thought of chicken brought Grace to her feet, and she was in the bathroom emptying her stomach.

*   *   *

The last two weeks of December dragged like a funeral, and Abbie welcomed January because January promised to bring Jeremy back to Aspen Grove. Without Heather to distract and entertain her, Abbie rambled around the house. Sometimes, she'd scribble in her sketchpad or wander outside to sketch a bird. She even watched a documentary on pointillism thinking that would cheer her. But nothing helped. She couldn't wait to get back to school.

The halls buzzed with students returning from Christmas vacation. Half an hour early, Abbie had already collected her books and stood by Jeremy's locker. She wondered what he'd say about her new look: dark smoky eyes and a black turtleneck.

Where was he?

Many of the students passed her in the hall and stared at Abbie's face, as if by just changing her makeup, Abbie had changed who she was. One of the boys in Abbie's English class saw her and turned away as if she were contagious, or selling Avon door to door. Charles Kennedy laughed and said, "Nice. Wait till Jeremy sees this."

Abbie did wait. She waited until the warning bell rang, and then ran to first period where her teacher was already calling roll.

"Miss Buchanan," her history teacher said. "Glad you could join us. Please, sit down." Abbie lowered her eyes and slid into her seat. Great. Perfect way to start the New Year.

She tried to listen as Mrs. O'Dell droned on about what they would be studying—events in U. S. history from the Pre-Columbian period through the mid-nineteenth century, which meant everything about the Civil War—but all Abbie could think about was Jeremy. *Why wasn't he at school?*

She looked for him at lunch. What if he was still in Montana? What if he was never coming back? Too upset to eat, Abbie ran into the bathroom, slammed the door to the stall, and cried. She was standing over the sink, drying her eyes when Jessica entered.

"Holy shit. If it isn't Drabigail Buchanan a la vamp. What did you do to your face?" She didn't wait for Abbie's response, but started laughing. "If you think that's the way to attract Jeremy, you have another think coming. That's a good way to scare him away."

Abbie blew her nose. "You would know."

Jessica started to say something, and then flipped her hair over her shoulder. "You're so not worth my time." She walked out of the bathroom leaving Abbie glaring at the door.

The rest of the day was worse than the morning. Staring at Jeremy's empty chair, Abbie hadn't heard a word the art teacher said. She forgot to write down her math assignment. In P.E., she did pushups until the muscles in her arms shook with fatigue. In the shower, she let the water run until her skin was numb and class was over.

After school, Abbie went to her bedroom and locked the door. She glared at the mirror and made a face. "Abbie Buchanan. You're hideous and fat. You should have never been born." In the bathroom, she scrubbed her face clean. All it got her was a bunch of sarcastic remarks, and who needed that.

Waiting for Jeremy turned her inside out and upside down, into someone she no longer knew. She lay on her bed and turned on her TV. Loud. *Where was he? Why didn't he call?*

"Abbie?"

She sat up at a knock on the door.

"Open up." Her father was standing in the hall when she unlocked the door. "Your mother is trying to sleep."

"Sorry."

"Bad day?"

"No."

"Hungry?"

"No."

"I'll be in my office if you want to talk."

"K. " She huddled on her bed.

"Abigail?"

"Yeah, Dad?"

"Keep the noise down."

"Got it."

She turned off the TV and glared at the blank screen. This was the worst day ever. She wrote Jeremy's name on a piece of paper, over and over. If it weren't so late, she'd drive over to his house, just to make sure he was there. She knew she should be doing something constructive, like finishing her portfolio due at the end of the week. But she couldn't stop obsessing. She flipped off her light and tried to sleep. But when she closed her eyes, all she could see was Jeremy's face, that wisp of hair that wouldn't stay out of his eyes. His lips. The way he smelled like hope and sunshine. The way he made every day matter.

*   *   *

January brought with it more than snow. For the first time in a long time, January filled Maxine's house with excitement as she planned her trip to Graceland. She waited until the last possible moment to tell her family that she was going. She was settled at Grace's kitchen table the night before, sharing a rare cup of coffee with her daughter and granddaughter.

"Graceland?" Grace said, her mouth hanging open. "By yourself? Mother, that's not like you."

"I know," Maxine said. "And don't try and talk me out of it. This is something I've wanted to do all my life. And now I'm going to."

"Does Daddy know?"

"No, and I don't want you to tell him. He'll ruin it. I haven't had a vacation in years. I think it's about time I got to do something I wanted."

"Don't worry about Grampa," Abbie said. "I'll check on him every day."

Maxine patted her granddaughter's hand. "You don't have to do that, Abbie. He can take care of himself."

"Sounds like fun," Abbie said. "If I didn't have school, I'd go along to keep you company."

Maxine smiled at Abbie. "It's a bus full of old people, honey; you'd be bored right out of your head."

"Maybe." Abbie shrugged. "But at least you wouldn't have to go alone."

"Don't you worry about me. I'll be just fine." Maxine stood and put her empty cup in the sink. "Thanks for the coffee. I need to get home and start packing."

"I can't believe you're not going to tell Daddy," Grace said.

Maxine bristled. "The only reason I'm telling you is so you won't worry if you call the house and get no answer. I'll be back in a week."

"You should tell him," Grace said, "so *he* doesn't worry."

Maxine pulled on her coat. "Grace. I rarely ask you for anything, and now I'm asking you to keep your mouth shut. If your father finds out, he'll play sick and keep me from going."

"How are you getting to the bus?" Abbie asked. "Maybe I can take you. Does it stop by your house and pick you up?"

"No," Maxine said. "Shirley and Helen are going to drop me off."

"So you've already told them," Grace said.

"Yes," Maxine said. "They know."

"Well, then." Grace folded her arms across her chest. "Have a nice time."

Maxine gave Abbie a hug. "I intend to."

Once home, Maxine began to pack. In a perfect world, she would still be size twelve, and the clothes in her closet would fit. But her world was far from perfect, her body far from slim, so she settled on the few nice clothes she owned, most of them the hand-me-downs that Helen had given her before Christmas. Maxine would be gone a total of seven days, which meant she'd have to wear several things more than once. She was tempted to toss in her comfortable sweats, but they were stained dingy gray, no longer their original pretty forget-me-not blue. If she were going to toss them anywhere, it should be the garbage.

"Look at the bright side, Maxine." She unzipped a pair of pants and let them fall to the floor. "While others lug heavy suitcases, you can travel light."

The thought of traveling at all made her giddy, and she laughed. "Look at you, Maxine, you're finally getting some balls."

Maxine didn't tell Herb she was going. Nor did she leave him a note, but locked the door behind her, then handed the key to Shirley, who promised to look after the fish.

"All set?" Shirley asked as she placed Maxine's suitcase in the trunk of her car.

"You bet." Maxine waved at Helen, who was already in the car, a new purple hat on her head to celebrate the occasion.

"Don't forget to take lots of pictures," Shirley prompted as she backed out of the driveway. "You did remember your camera, didn't you?"

"Right here." Maxine patted the free canvas bag she got at the grocery store.

"Where's your umbrella?" Helen asked.

"She doesn't need an umbrella." Shirley turned the corner. "I saw on The Weather Channel Memphis is having a heat wave."

Helen wasn't convinced. "Maxine, you need an umbrella. Shirley, for God's sake, watch where you're going. You almost ran that light."

"Maxine," Shirley said, "did you get extra batteries for your camera?"

By the time they reached the bus, Maxine had enough dos and don'ts to fill a freezer. Take lots of pictures. Eat something decadent every day. Don't forget to send postcards. Don't forget to have lunch at The Rendezvous Restaurant.

When they arrived at the station, people were already climbing into the bus. Maxine's hands shook as she grabbed her suitcase, blanket, and pillow. "Goodbye," she hugged Helen and Shirley.

Helen pushed a small sack at Maxine. "There's juice and snacks in there so you won't get hungry."

"And don't forget these." Shirley gave Maxine three of her newest Harlequin romances. Maxine blushed at the titles. She couldn't remember feeling hot in someone's arms, or making love on a mountain. "So you don't get bored." Shirley gave Maxine a squeeze. Maxine dropped the books into the bag. Like that was going to happen.

"There's stamps in there," Helen said. "Keep us posted. Now go and have fun."

"See you in a week." Maxine waved and approached the bus.

"Hi." A woman in her mid-thirties with big blond hair and red lipstick stood by the side of the bus with a clipboard. "I'm your tour guide, Sunny Greene. And you are?" She held her clipboard expectantly.

"Maxine Foster." Maxine watched as Sunny put a checkmark by her name.

Sunny beamed. "Welcome, Maxine. Step aboard and find a seat."

With a timid smile, Maxine passed others already seated as she made her way down the aisle. About halfway in, she found a seat by the window. She could see Helen and Shirley waving. Shirley was jumping up and down, a smiling clown doing jumping jacks.

The last bus Maxine rode took her to school and back home again. This bus was nicer than a school bus. She didn't have to sit on a bench seat, and if she got tired all she had to do was push a button to recline her seat and go to sleep.

One week, a blessed vacation away from Herb. She glanced at the people filling the bus and waved at a woman she'd met at the Senior Center. The rest were strangers, mostly women like her: crazy in love with Elvis Presley, or who just wanted to get away. The gray heads and dyed hair reminded her of salt and pepper. *We are the salt and pepper group on our way to see the King.* A smile filled her face. The engine lurched to a low hum. Maxine waved until she could no longer see Helen and Shirley. She sat back in her seat. This was going to be the best trip ever.

Less than five miles out of town, a tiny Asian woman slid into the empty seat beside Maxine. The woman shoved her purse into the overhead bin and plopped next to Maxine with her pillow and blanket. "I was stuck behind an old man snoring so loud I couldn't think." She pushed the button on her seat and tilted back. There was an odd smell about her Maxine couldn't place. Not incense. Not perfume.

Maxine looked out the window, undecided. Should she talk to the woman, ask her about her children or husband? Should she encourage friendship? She didn't want to be rude, but she didn't want to share this adventure with a stranger, either. She turned toward the woman, who was sound asleep.

Hello to you, too. Maxine watched the scenery wondering how anyone could sleep on such an adventure. The excited chatter inside the bus reminded her of fieldtrips she used to take as a student, like to the state capital. That was a day trip; this would last for a week. They rode for miles until the snow-topped mountains turned to desert, until Maxine's butt was numb. She was glad when the bus finally pulled into a truck stop and slowed. Her legs wobbled when she stood and stretched. The Asian woman, Su Linn, was already out of her seat, standing by the door, waiting for it to open.

Sunny was standing at the front of the bus and spoke into a microphone. "We have an hour to eat folks, then we have to be moving along." The bus driver opened the doors, and everyone bolted, eager to stretch their legs and use the bathrooms.

There was a small café at the truck stop. Maxine ordered a grilled cheese sandwich and a cup of coffee. After eating, Maxine took a cigarette break behind the diner. She knew she should quit and had hoped to use this trip to do so. With all the distractions, she wouldn't have time to think about her pack of Pall Malls, but she'd been smoking longer than Herb had been abusing alcohol, and habits were hard to break. Taking longer than usual, she was last to board the bus.

As the driver started the engine, Sunny clicked on her microphone. "Folks," she looked straight at Maxine. "We have a tight schedule. We can't wait for you. If you're late, we may have to leave you, and you'll have to find another way home."

"She's talking to you," Su Linn accused.

"How do you know?" Maxine wished the old bitty would mind her own business. The afternoon passed much like the morning, with people chatting, sleeping and singing Elvis songs. Afraid to draw more attention, Maxine didn't sing but listened while Su Linn belted out the words to every song. *Show off.* Maxine frowned. That woman was proving to be a pain in the ass.

After stopping for gas and a quick dinner, they were on the road again with an added bonus, a showing of *King Creole* on the overhead screens. Pulling shades to block the setting sun, most of the passengers settled back to watch. Maxine glared at Su Linn when she started singing, "Farewell, Royal High School, we'll remember you." Her Asian accent made the words sound funny, almost a mockery.

Maxine twisted in her seat. That woman was ruining the movie, which reminded Maxine of her teen years and Larry Fisher. Maxine put her fingers in her ears when Su Linn sang "steadfast, loyal, and true." Tomorrow, she'd find another seat, even if it meant sitting beside the man who snored. Anything would be better than this.

CHAPTER FOURTEEN

MAXINE WASN'T MODEST OR PRUDISH. She could go camping and pee in the woods. She could even use a door-less toilet stall if she had to. What she couldn't do, she discovered, was walk down the aisle of a bus and stand in line to pee while forty-five people watched. So she waited—for nightfall, and all the passengers to fall asleep. While she waited, her stomach cramped, and her temper festered. She should have been smart about dinner and foregone the extra glass of water, but the fries had made her thirsty. Now she sat with her legs crossed, her stomach muscles clenched, and a tight grimace on her face.

She tried to focus on something besides her bladder, like what she'd see in Memphis. That worked until it started to rain. Then she had to move fast. Uncrossing her legs to stand almost created a crisis. She could feel the warmth leaking between the legs of her best pair of pants. She squeezed by Su Linn and moved quickly down the aisle.

The bathroom was unoccupied, and she pushed the door open. The room was small. If her butt were any bigger, she wouldn't be able to squeeze in. She turned in a circle and pulled the door shut not a moment too soon. She dropped to the seat and emptied her bladder.

Maxine sat back and relaxed her muscles. In spite of the sweet antiseptic smell overpowering her, it was nice to have a moment alone, even if it meant hiding in the bathroom. She rested her head against the wall and closed her eyes. She woke to someone pounding on the door.

"You all right in there?" Maxine opened her eyes, disoriented.

"Do you need help?" The door opened, and Maxine stared into the concerned face of the tour guide. "Are you okay?"

"Yes." Maxine scrambled to pull up her pants. Keeping her head down, she returned to her seat, avoiding the eyes of the curious passengers, whispering.

"What happened?" "Is she alright?"

A snicker. Another.

Su Linn stood to let Maxine by. "I send someone to check on you. You gone too long."

Busybody. Maxine dropped into her seat.

"Okay?" Su Linn asked.

"I'm fine."

"Good." Su Linn pulled her blanket over her head and went back to sleep.

Disgusted and humiliated, Maxine smacked her pillow into a ball. She'd slept on a sofa before. She'd even slept on the floor. But sleeping on a bus that swerved all night long was like sleeping on a fishing boat. She'd promised herself that everything about this trip would be wonderful. Now she wasn't so sure.

As Maxine waited for her eyes to grow heavy, Su Linn snored with a soft nasal lisp. Maxine wrinkled her nose at the sweet musky odor covering Su Linn like a second skin. Adjusting her pillow, Maxine kicked off her shoes and tried to get comfortable. She turned left. She turned right. She sat up straight. She slouched and rested her head on the window. The dark pane felt cool. She could smell rain. She looked at the stars, the moon and willed herself to sleep.

Maxine woke the next morning when the bus jarred to a stop. Her neck was stiff, her back sore, and she had a crease across her cheek where her face had rested against the window frame. Most of the other passengers were awake and chattering as they exited the bus. She followed them into a ma-and-pa café that smelled of bacon, toast and coffee. She headed for the bathroom where she waited her turn. As she stood in line, Maxine saw a woman who reminded her of Grace. Same dark hair. Same heart-shaped face. Here she was on her way to Graceland, the reason she had named her daughter Grace in the first place, and she was traveling alone. Grace should have been beside her. But they were as different as red and yellow, as far apart as black and white. It would have been nice if they could have shared this trip, if they had learned to laugh together instead of scowl and bicker, and even though Grace tolerated Maxine's love for Elvis, Grace would never be caught riding a crowded bus with a bunch of old people.

At the basin, Maxine washed her hands, then reached into her bag and took out her toothbrush. She'd never brushed her teeth at a public sink before. But, then, there were a lot of things she'd never done.

Back on the bus, still seated next to Su Linn because there were no extra seats, Maxine thumbed through one of Shirley's books. She read a few paragraphs and set it aside. Who needed a steamy romance when this time tomorrow she'd be in Memphis. The heater hummed as she looked out the window. Waiting to pee. Waiting to see Graceland. She was headed into another state, enjoying her new adventure, but one thing hadn't changed. She was still Maxine Foster, and she was still waiting.

*   *   *

Sitting at her desk, Grace flipped her calendar to January. Michael was supposed to be back before school started, but she hadn't heard a word since New Year's Eve. She'd driven by his house several times expecting, hoping, to run in to him. But his car was never there, and he hadn't returned her calls.

That wasn't exactly true. He'd left a brief message saying he'd run into some complications, and that he didn't know when he'd be able to call her. That only made her more curious. Surely he wasn't rethinking his decision to relocate, not after buying the house and becoming the new high school principal.

Impatient and eager for news, Grace dialed his number again, glad to be feeling less queasy this morning. This time, instead of going to voice mail, the phone rang, rang and rang. She wasn't good at waiting, but she didn't want to doubt him, or his love. He was on his way to school. He would call her later. Maybe they'd even have lunch. She sorted the mail and rubbed her neck. She'd missed two days at the gym and felt awful. Her back hurt, she had a headache, and her breasts were swollen from the toxins building in her system. Always meticulous about her appearance, this morning Grace had opted for a loose sweater instead of her usual fitted woolen suit. She didn't want anything touching her skin.

She distributed the mail and stopped in the break room for something to drink. The smell of coffee made her nauseous, so she settled for a cup of tea, which she took to her desk where the phone was ringing.

"Aspen Grove Realty," Grace smiled into the phone. "How can I help you?" She was entering an appointment to the calendar when it hit her.

She counted the weeks backward and had a fleeting sense of panic. Her cycle was just irregular, confused with all the stress and commotion of the holidays. She pushed the calendar away. She'd stop at the gym on the way home, have a good workout and reregulate her body.

Instead of going to the gym, Grace drove by his house. Her heart beat faster, skittered even when she saw his car in the driveway. Lights shone from the kitchen. If he didn't have a fire in the fireplace, they could build one. Talk and make love in front of the fire. She would tell him she was leaving her husband. Grace smiled as she approached his front door. Her heart beat so fast she felt light-headed.

She could hear the television from the living room as she rang the doorbell. "I'll get it," a woman called. Expecting the cleaning lady, Grace was surprised by the petite brunette at the door. Grace took in the delicate hands and the dishtowel, the aroma of tomato sauce and basil. This was no cleaning lady. Grace stepped backwards, almost falling off the step.

"You must be Lisa. Come in. Please. Michael said you might stop by."

Grace stepped into the foyer. Her tongue stuck to the roof of her mouth, so dry she couldn't swallow. The table was covered with a red lacey tablecloth. There were candles, wine glasses, and an etched pitcher of water. Family pictures hung on the once bare walls and a large-leafed philodendron filled the once empty corner along with a stack of boxes. There was even a fire in the fireplace. Grace moved closer to the door. Michael was on the floor in front of the television with two young girls; twins, if Grace could believe what she was seeing.

"Hi," one of the girls said shyly. "We're watching TV with our dad."

Her mouth wouldn't open. Her lips wouldn't move. He stood the minute he saw her. His look of surprise changed to one of caution. "Marci, this is Grace. From Aspen Grove Realty." He moved closer and put his arm around his wife. "This is my wife Marci."

"Nice to meet you." Marci offered her hand. "This house is perfect. We love it."

Everything stopped, even Grace's heart. She had trouble speaking. "So glad. Happy New Year." She rushed to her car, stumbling as she moved. Fumbling with the keys, Grace started the engine, but not before Michael rapped and pointed.

"Roll down the window."

She couldn't move her arms.

"Grace, roll down the window."

Her voice broke. "Why?"

"I'm sorry. I didn't know how to tell you. We reconciled. For the children." He was trying to whisper. She could see him shivering in the cold air. He wasn't wearing shoes. He wasn't . . .

Married?

"Move," she said, backing out of the driveway. She wasn't a fool. She wasn't stupid. She was still shaking when she dropped her purse on her kitchen counter. Stunned, she opened a bottle of wine. "You're lucky," she told herself as she filled a glass, "that you found out before you ruined everything with Rob." She stifled a sob. *Married?*

Grace sat at the kitchen table and stared blankly at the walls. On the outside she appeared quiet and controlled, but on the inside she was chaos. Well, she was married, too. Things didn't have to change, did they? *Children? Twins?*

She felt dirty in need of a bath. She took the Merlot to the bathroom, lowered her naked body into the water and started to cry. *Children, how had she missed that?* She put her head in her hands and sobbed, sending the water into ripples around her. *Stupid. Her life was stupid.* She stopped crying when she felt a cramp in her stomach. At least something was going right. She'd have her period by morning.

But when Grace woke the next morning, nothing had changed. She was still tired and achy. Her breasts were swollen, and the cramps hadn't brought on her menses. To make matters worse, she'd finished the entire bottle of wine. She had the headache to prove it.

*   *   *

Abbie grew up listening to Elvis because her grandmother had all of his records. If he were still alive, Elvis would be older than her grandfather, and that made Abbie laugh—the idea of someone her grandfather's age crooning to her about endless and forever love. Not that her grandfather hadn't tried to impersonate Elvis on more than one occasion, much to her grandmother's irritation. But maybe singers like Elvis knew something Abbie didn't. Being in love was supposed to be wonderful, but love was hard. It had you walking in circles singing, "Angel," or "Can't Help Falling in Love." Even this morning while she prepped for school, Abbie caught herself singing, "I'll Remember You."

She wondered if that was how her father felt, always wondering where he stood with her mother. In the Buchanan house, there was no way to please Mrs. Perfect. If everything wasn't absolutely ideal, there was hell to pay. Especially when her mother was in one of her moods, like the mood she'd been in since Christmas. There was no other way to say it. Since Christmas, her mother was nothing but a bitch.

Abbie put on her backpack and headed toward the door. If she had a nice husband like her father, she wouldn't be snappy or sharp. She'd show him her love, every minute of the day.

But first she had to find a nice husband, and she couldn't even find Jeremy without asking a lot of questions that made her sound pathetically love-struck or like the loser Jessica claimed she was.

Well, today she wouldn't be a loser. Today she'd focus on something besides Jeremy. She wouldn't watch for his car, or stop at his locker. She'd concentrate on her studies. Work on her portfolio. She didn't need to spend her time waiting around for some guy who was too busy to call. Her resolve lasted until after second period, when she saw Jeremy hobbling down the hall, trying to navigate. His left foot was in a cast. He tried to wave when he saw her and almost lost his balance.

"What happened?" Abbie raced to his side.

"Had an accident." He gave an embarrassed chuckle.

"What did you do?"

"Got careless. It's not broken." He looked happy to see her, which made Abbie love him even more. She walked him to class knowing she'd be late for English.

The warning bell rang. She had more questions, but they'd have to wait. She was coming out of English when she heard two students talking. Normally she wouldn't have eavesdropped, but she couldn't stop herself, not when she overheard Jeremy's name. "What do you think happened this time?" one of them said.

"Don't know, but I'm sure it has something to do with his father. He's always knocking Jeremy around."

Not true, Abbie thought. If it were, she'd know. He would tell her.

But when she asked him after school, he just shrugged and said, "Want to go for a ride?" He motioned to his Camaro.

"You drove?"

"It was that or walk." He winked. "It's only a sprain. See." He pulled off the temporary cast without flinching. Convinced he was okay, and because she was over the stars happy to be near him again, Abbie got into his car.

"I've missed you," Abbie said as he drove to their place in The Grove. From there, they could see the town below. A few of the houses were still decorated for Christmas, and the lights shining against the snow made the valley seem frosted with glitter. This was the Christmas feeling Abbie had missed. He kept the engine running, not that Abbie needed the heater to stay warm. She wanted to ask him about the rumor and his father again, but she didn't know how to begin. "How was your Christmas vacation?" she said instead.

"Nice. How was yours?"

"Boring. Lame without you or Heather."

They held hands tightly until he kissed her. When he touched her, it was like her skin was a canvas. Inch by inch, he repainted her heart. She would have continued, but he was the one to pull away.

"Need to get home before my old man calls the cops."

She held his hand all the way home and wondered what it would be like to fear your own father. She intended to go to her room and call Heather, but her mother stopped her on the stairs.

"Abbie, can you come in here?" Her mother was staring at the saltshaker on the kitchen table as if it threatened to run away.

"Mrs. Winters dropped off Heather's portfolio. She'd like you to turn it in for Heather on Friday."

Abbie took the folder and looked at the drawings. They were good enough to win one of the scholarships. "What's wrong with Heather?"

"She's still with her father and will be back next week. They're on some kind of vacation. Maybe a cruise."

Heather hadn't said anything about a cruise. Abbie took the portfolio to her room and laid it on the floor beside her. She spent the next hour working on her own drawings and wondering why she and Heather were no longer talking. Between weekends with her dad and hanging out with Tyler, Heather was always busy. If Abbie tried to text her, Heather would always reply, CAN'T TALK NOW. HAVE 2 GO.

Abbie crumpled her drawing and began again. Her fingers flew across the canvas, but when she stopped to examine her work, she was embarrassed. It wasn't a tree with an eagle's nest at all. It wasn't a drawing of her family, but she and Jeremy, twisted together in a knot.

There was a tap at her door. "Abbie?"

She picked up the drawings scattered on the floor, which included Heather's portfolio and shoved them into her bottom drawer, making sure they were safely hidden.

"Yes?"

Her father stepped into her room. "How's everything going?"

"Fine."

"Brad's ready to start your art lessons whenever you are."

"Cool," Abbie said.

"Dinner's on the table."

He looked at her, and Abbie wondered if he could see that she was changing. "Be right there." He was fairly perceptive. She'd have to tell her parents about Jeremy before they discovered Abbie wasn't at the library or hanging with Heather like she claimed. Aspen Grove was a small town, small enough for her parents to know what she was doing before she did. And even though she didn't want to introduce Jeremy to her mother because her mother always had something negative to say, she couldn't put it off much longer.

It helped, she supposed, that her mother had her own agenda and problems. But that wasn't news. Her mother was always conjuring up something, a new diet, or curtains for the bedroom. New exercises at the gym. Abbie might be able to lie to her mother—her mother might never notice—but sooner or later, her father would ask. She decided to tell them that night during dinner.

Passing the garlic bread her father said, "I hear the art department is planning a trip in the spring. They're talking about seeing ---"

Her mother interrupted. "Did you know Kent's wife had a facelift? Trudy said it makes her look ten years younger."

Abbie glanced at her father, who stared at the refrigerator while his wife carried on about sagging eyelids and puffy lips. When he caught Abbie watching him, he winked and said, "Maybe you should consider it." Abbie coughed and grabbed her glass of water.

To which Grace replied, "Are you saying I need a facelift? Already, at my age?"

"No, I was just saying---"

"There's this boy at school." Abbie's parents stopped talking and looked at her.

"What boy at school?" her mother asked.

"Jeremy."

"Does Jeremy have a last name?" her father said.

"Um. Blackburn. Jeremy Blackburn."

"Like in Blackburn Electric?" her father said.

"Yeah, I think so?"

"You don't know who his parents are?" Her mother reached for her glass of wine. She turned to her husband. "Didn't Blackburn get in some trouble with the college? Faulty wiring or something?"

"How well do you know this boy?" her father said.

"I see him at school. Or the library. He's in my art class. He's a very good artist."

"You're not dating." Her mother's voice rose, a little pitchy. "I would know if you were."

"No. Yes. Ummm." Abbie didn't know what to say. *Yeah, Mom, we're dating. We're doing more than dating.*

"We'd like to meet him," her father said.

Abbie looked from one parent to the other. Her stomach rolled as if she had just eaten a bowl of cold okra, which her mother insisted was good for Abbie's complexion.

"We should invite him for dinner. Soon," her father said. "Friday night? Right, Grace?"

Her mother prickled. "We have dinner plans with the Forrester's."

"Then I guess we'll have to change them."

The air around Abbie frizzled; first hot, then so cold she could almost see her breath. She didn't dare look at her mother, who declared, "I'm not cooking."

"No one said you had to." Abbie's father took his plate to the sink. "Abbie and I can manage, right, Pumpkin?"

"Sure." Avoiding her mother's polar glare, Abbie rinsed her plate and put it in the dishwasher. She was probably doing the wrong thing, introducing her boyfriend to her mother who would have so many objections Jeremy was sure to join the Army. But Abbie loved him. They'd have to meet him someday, and Friday seemed as good a day as any.

CHAPTER FIFTEEN

MAXINE WAITED HER ENTIRE LIFE for something exciting to happen. And now that it was, she couldn't quite believe her luck. The trip to Graceland would have been better with Larry or Grace by her side, but they weren't there, and no amount of wishing would change that. She could have had a poor pity party as Helen would say, but Maxine was determined to focus on what she had, and right now she was having a great time. She even stopped being angry with Su Linn for being so irritating.

"Look at that," Maxine said.

Coughing over Maxine's shoulder, Su Linn leaned toward the window.

"A pyramid right in the middle of Memphis. Can you believe that?" Maxine had read about the Mississippi, and now here she was, staring at the river from a bus window. Parts of Memphis were beautiful with tall buildings and tree-lined streets. Other areas were rundown, dirty and jumbled with vacant buildings.

"What's Egypt doing in the middle of Memphis?" She fished through her canvas bag, but by the time she located her camera, the bus had turned the corner, and all she could see was the top of the pyramid. "Crap." She would have loved to see the look on Helen's face when she showed her that picture.

The sun through the window was warm, a much needed spring tonic. Excitement grew as the bus moved toward Graceland. Two days was a long time to sit. They were all tired of riding, impatient to experience what they had traveled so far to see.

"Look." The woman in front of Maxine pointed to a man on the corner. "It's Elvis."

"Hi, Elvis!" Half the passengers stood and waved. The Elvis impersonator waved and swished his hips.

Sunny said, "Shall we ask Elvis to join us?"

"Yes!" The passengers cheered. The bus stopped long enough for the look-alike Elvis to step aboard.

"Hello, hello, hello," he sang. "Welcome to Memphis."

If Maxine hadn't watched the numerous programs about Elvis's death on television, she might have believed she was looking at the real King. Thinking how much he looked like Larry, Maxine's heart hammered faster when he smiled. Where were all these sexy feelings coming from? She thought she'd lost them years ago.

"Ladies and gentlemen," he pointed, "Welcome to the Memphis City tour. There on your right is Jefferson Davis Park. Now y'all know that Davis was an American statesman and leader of the Confederacy during the Civil War, right? He was one of the finest gentlemen officers the South has ever known."

Maxine hadn't thought about the Civil War since she studied history in high school. There weren't any black people in Aspen Grove. But here in Memphis, they were everywhere. Maxine pushed her nose against the window and gawked.

Riding through Memphis and hearing its history made Maxine contemplate her own ancestors. If one of her great-grandfathers had fought in a civil war, maybe he'd be special like Jefferson Davis. Then she'd be important too, a celebrity instead of stuck in Aspen Grove married to a drunk.

"Up ahead," the Elvis impersonator pointed, "just a couple a blocks is Beale Street. And just over there not too far away is the Peabody Place and the famous Peabody ducks."

Unlike many of the passengers who stood and tried to see the landmarks, Maxine didn't move. The street she was interested in was Elvis Presley Boulevard. She could see all kinds of ducks at home. Besides, she was too busy watching the Elvis look-a-like. He was gorgeous; what Shirley would call eye candy. About Grace's age, if Maxine had to guess. And more energy than a classroom of kindergarteners. Watching him perform made her smile, not to mention flush.

They turned a corner and the bus slowed. "Here on your right is the famous Sun Studio where I recorded my first record," the impersonator said. "That song, as y'all know, was 'That's Alright, Mama.'" A huge guitar hung over the entrance to the building, and Maxine wondered what kept it from falling on everybody's heads.

As they neared Graceland, the noise inside the bus buzzed like a hive. *Graceland is the honey*, Maxine thought, *and we're hungry little bees.*

The Elvis impersonator continued. "Now, I know y'all've heard about my Heartbreak Hotel. We're almost there, so I'm giving the mic back to Sunny here so she can tell y'all about it." Before he handed over the microphone, he hitched his hip and sang, "Well, since my baby left me..." Maxine wasn't too old to swoon, and she did along with the rest of the gray-haired ladies on board.

"Thank you, Elvis." Sunny waved a handful of envelopes in the air. "These contain your room assignments. If you didn't request a roommate, I've assigned you one." As she walked down the aisle with the envelopes, the bus turned into the entrance to the Heartbreak Hotel.

Everyone cheered. This time Maxine stood, eager to see the hotel.

"When we go inside," Sunny said, "wait in the lobby while I get your keys. Feel free to take pictures. Any questions?" A hand went up and a pink-haired woman in a fashionable red suit said she didn't want to share a room.

"Unless you can talk someone into switching with you," Sunny said, "I'm afraid I can't help you. The hotel is booked months in advance. We were lucky to get a block of rooms on the first floor."

"This is unacceptable," the woman complained.

A thin woman sitting behind Maxine said, "Two nights. Surely you can manage," to which the pink-haired woman turned her nose and sniffed.

Maxine opened her envelope. She hadn't marked a preference, assuming she'd be given a single room since she was traveling solo. Her mouth fell open. Room 118, and she wasn't alone. Her roommate was Su Linn.

She wanted to protest, but Maxine was no stranger to anger and frustration. She could endure two days. That was nothing compared to a lifetime with Herb.

Elvis helped them off the bus, and Maxine asked Sunny to take their picture. He put his arm around her, and Maxine rested her head on his shoulder. That would be something to show Helen and Shirley when she got home.

"Say cheese." Sunny snapped the picture.

"Thank you," Maxine said to the impersonator.

"My pleasure, ma'am," he said. "My pleasure." She watched him saunter away, her heart pounding like a hammer. His aftershave was strong enough to make her wish that she was younger than forty again.

The interior of the Heartbreak Hotel was nothing like its simple plain exterior. The colorful lobby boasted bold yellow and blue walls and a sitting area with plush purple chairs. An old-fashioned cabinet TV played in a corner where several guests gathered to watch Elvis perform on a rerun of The Ed Sullivan show. Maxine noticed a large sofa. If she grew tired of Su Linn, she would just come out here and sleep in the lobby.

Because she didn't travel, Maxine wasn't familiar with hotel keys. She'd never used a credit card to open a door. As she fumbled in the hallway, Su Linn pushed her aside.

"Move." Su Linn slipped her card into the slot, waited for the small light to turn green, and opened the door.

It was a simple room with two beds. Pictures of Elvis hung on the wall and the blond nightstand reminded Maxine of furniture her mother had in the 50s. She couldn't tell if the music came from the television or the radio, but she could hear Elvis singing "Heartbreak Hotel." A sign on the door said, "This hotel is a smoke-free facility." So much for smoking.

Maxine claimed the bed next to the window. While she waited to use the bathroom, Maxine fluffed her pillow and closed her eyes. Groggy, she woke several hours later as Su Linn shook her.

"Stop it." Maxine pushed Su Linn's hand away and sat up.

"Dinner time." Su Linn said.

"Stop acting like my mother." Maxine stumbled to the bathroom, irritated, but not with Su Linn as much as with herself. Here she was in Memphis, sleeping the day away. This wasn't the place for sleeping. She could sleep in Aspen Grove.

After dinner at a barbeque buffet, Sunny had arranged for an evening tour of Memphis. Maxine was surprised how different the city looked at night. She felt better after eating and had lost most of her irritation with Su Linn. But tonight, Su Linn was quiet, keeping to herself. In the evening light, Su Linn's face looked tired, even haggard, and Maxine felt sorry for her. She held open her canvas bag and said, "Want a cookie?"

"No thanks." Su Linn grimaced and seemed to shrink into her seat.

"Suit yourself." Maxine closed her bag and chomped on one of Helen's cookies. By the time the bus returned to the Heartbreak Hotel, Su Linn was asleep, snoring that irritating nasal lisp. This time it was Maxine's turn to prod, and she did it with pleasure. "Wake up." She poked Su Linn. "We're here."

Su Linn coughed and stood on wobbly legs, which Maxine understood all too well. Her own back and legs ached, creaked even as she walked toward the door. She looked forward to a real bed and sleeping through the night. But her plans for a good night's rest dissolved once they were in their room. Su Linn took her suitcase into the bathroom and closed the door. While Maxine waited her turn, she changed into pajamas—blue with white flowers, brand new from Kmart—and brushed her teeth at the vanity sink. She sat on the edge of the bed. Thirty minutes later she was still waiting. Unable to hold her bladder any longer, Maxine knocked. "You done in there?"

Su Linn coughed again. This time the cough sounded less harsh, less restrictive. And there was that odd smell that followed Su Linn everywhere she went, only stronger.

Maxine knocked. "Hurry up."

Su Linn opened the door, and the odor of burning maple leaves hit Maxine in the face. That crazy woman was burning incense in the bathroom.

Maxine pushed past Su Linn and locked the door. The smell inside the bathroom was so strong it stung her eyes. Maxine closed her eyes and tried to hold her breath. By the time she finished peeing, she was light-headed. She opened the bathroom door. Su Linn was sitting on the edge of her bed, eating Maxine's cheese crackers.

"Hungry," Su Linn said, washing down the snack with a bottle of Maxine's water. Without a 'thank you' she slipped under the covers. She didn't brush her teeth. She didn't say good night, but drifted to sleep, snoring that irritating nasal lisp while Elvis sang "Don't Be Cruel" on the television.

Maxine clicked off the TV and pulled the blanket over her head. The window was open, but she could still smell the sweet pungent odor coming from Su Linn and the bathroom.

In spite of her irritating roommate, Maxine giggled. She was in Memphis. Sleeping in the Heartbreak Hotel, just across the street from Graceland. Unlike Su Linn, who fell asleep as soon as she closed her eyes, Maxine lay in bed listening to the sounds—people in the halls—the traffic outside her window—Elvis Presley singing "Heartbreak Hotel." When Maxine did fall asleep, she had the strangest dream. She was dancing with Elvis on The Ed Sullivan Show and eating crackers in the lobby.

*   *   *

Grace pulled into her parking spot at work thinking, there are just some things you shouldn't know. Like, if your husband's being unfaithful. Or why your father drinks to excess. Or if your daughter steals from the makeup counter at Macy's when your back is turned. Knowing carried consequences, and Grace tried to avoid consequences when they reflected badly on her or her family. That's why she found it so hard to believe she was pregnant. Here she was acting like a high school dropout, wondering what to tell her parents. She recalled the high school myths: you can't get pregnant your first time. Douching with Coke will kill any sperm it doesn't wash away. Sneezing right after sex prevents pregnancy. Grace unlocked the front door and turned on the office lights. She wasn't sixteen anymore. She was forty-three and knew how to make babies. What she didn't know was how to make this nightmare go away. It wasn't like she could make a wish and blow out the candles.

Good at believing only what she wanted, Grace could watch her father drink a Coors six-pack in less than an hour and claim he was just thirsty. She could welcome an extra workout if her husband said he had to work late. She could believe Michael when he said he loved her. But she couldn't believe, didn't want to believe, what was right in front of her. That's why, while everyone else was eating ham and rye or sourdough and turkey for lunch, Grace searched the aisles in the nearby drug store, discretely selecting a white box with the letters e.p.t. splayed across the front like a banner. Just to be sure. Hoping she was wrong.

Waiting in line to pay, Grace felt like everyone in the store knew. She played with her bangs, as if pulling them over her eyes would keep her safe and hide her secret.

After work, Grace hung her dress in the closet and slipped into a loose pair of slacks. Her bra pulled across her chest so she unsnapped it and left it on the bed. Then she went into the bathroom and locked the door.

With her first pregnancy, Grace had been naïve, or rather in denial. Rob was the one who insisted she was pregnant. He said he could tell by her radiant skin. She had laughed and said she wasn't ready to have a baby. It was all a mistake, he'd see. She'd have her period in the morning. Grace didn't have another period until nine months later.

She opened the box and read the instructions. If she didn't take the test, she wouldn't have to know. Not really. At least not yet. She plodded down the stairs to the kitchen and brewed a pot of tea. While she waited for the kettle to whistle, she studied her face. Her skin didn't glow. Red patches and worry lines furrowed her brows. Crow's feet etched the corners of her eyes, which looked dark and dejected.

Carrying her cup into the living room, Grace settled on the sofa. She didn't pick up a magazine or turn on the television. She didn't call her husband or her mother. She hadn't run to her father for comfort in years. Letting the peppermint settle her stomach, she studied the museum-like room, the Queen Anne furniture and Monet print she had purchased, vowing one day to own an original. The mauve walls with their decorative crown moldings. Everything looked tired, shabby, forgotten, and unloved. Grace pulled the sofa blanket closer. She didn't want another baby. She could have an abortion. No one would have to know.

Grace stared at the Monet. An abortion at her age was common. Even legal. Could she do it? *Would* she do it? Find a magic potion and flush everything down the toilet?

No. This was Michael's child, perhaps the only thing left between them. This baby would bring them back together. She could still feel his hands caressing her body, his kiss in her hair. A boy. Maybe he'd secretly wanted a boy instead of girls. She'd have to tell him. And she would, as soon as she decided what to do.

But he was married.

She was, too.

Thinking the smart thing to do was to have an abortion and give her marriage another try, Grace walked down the hall to Rob's office and knocked. "Busy?" She opened the door and poked her head in.

He looked up briefly. "Hang on." He went back to work, his fingers flying over the keyboard. Watching him, Grace couldn't understand his passion for words. It was the same passion Abbie expressed over her drawings. Father and daughter were so alike. She often teased them about their "hobbies," but truth was, she knew they weren't hobbies. Some day Rob would be a published author. Some day Abbie's pictures would hang in a gallery. Grace wasn't passionate about anything, unless it was spending money and decorating. While she waited for him to finish, Grace looked around the room. Maybe she'd order new curtains for his birthday. New carpet and pictures for the walls.

"Okay, then." Rob leaned back in his chair. "What's up?"

"Nothing. I just thought we could spend some time together. Go out to dinner or maybe a movie."

"Tonight?" He didn't look a bit interested, not like Michael did when he brushed back her hair and kissed her. "I really need to finish this."

"Can't it wait?"

"Grace, it's been waiting for weeks. I haven't had a minute to---"

"Fine." Grace stood. "You care more about that damn book than you do me."

He gave a frustrated sigh. "Okay, sure. Let's go to a movie. What do you want to see?"

"Nothing." She walked toward the door.

He stood up and followed. "Let's go to Rudy's. I'll see if Abbie wants to go along."

Grace turned in the doorway. "Abbie isn't home, and you'd know that if you weren't so buried in your work." She said work like it was something bad, something to scorn.

His stance was steady. "Then it's just the two of us. I'll change my shirt."

Their dinner at Rudy's was a disaster. Already in a sour disposition when she walked in the door, Grace's heart twinged when they passed the booth she and Michael shared the day he fed her fondue and ravioli. Her vegetable lasagna tasted flat; the company was boring.

"You're not drinking your wine." Rob pulled a piece from the small loaf of fresh bread and dipped it into the olive oil and garlic, reminding her how Michael dipped bread in the cheese and brought it to her lips.

"Anything interesting going on at work?" he said.

"No. It's slow."

"Wish we were." Then he laughed. "No, I guess I don't. No business, no paycheck."

She watched him chew the bread, then tackle his spaghetti. Starting to gray around the temples, he was no longer the man she married.

The waiter returned and asked if they wanted dessert. "Grace?" Rob said. She shook her head. "Not even tiramisu?"

"No." When the waiter left, Rob put his fork down. "What you do want?"

She didn't know, but it certainly wasn't this.

He leaned forward. "Grace, I don't know what's making you so unhappy. What can I do to help?"

She almost laughed.

"You don't have to work, you know. You can quit your job if that's what's making you so miserable." He paused. "Maybe, when it slows down, we can take that vacation you've been wanting." He tried to hold her hand, but she pulled away.

He leaned back, his gaze turned grim. "Are we in trouble here?"

Grace grabbed her napkin to suppress her cough.

His hand shook. "Do you want to go to counseling?"

"And tell them what, that you love your job more than you love your family?" Grace stood. "I'm tired, I want to go home." The whole evening had been a huge mistake.

Later, as she brushed her teeth, she looked in the mirror. A new mother? At forty-three? She supposed there were worse things, but at that moment, she couldn't name one.

*   *   *

"Tomorrow night," Abbie told her parents before she left for school. "Jeremy is coming for dinner. Can we order pizza?"

"I'd like that," her father said. "Ride?"

Abbie shook her head. "Mom, did you hear me?"

"We can't have guests tomorrow night. The house is filthy."

"Is not," Abbie said. There wasn't a pillow out of place, a speck of dust on the furniture.

"I can't be expected to entertain guests on a moment's notice."

"Grace," Rob said. "This isn't a guest; this is Jeremy. And I'd like to meet him." He turned to his daughter. "Sounds good, Pumpkin. I'll pick up pizza on my way home."

"Thanks." Abbie hugged her father and tried to ignore her mother's bad mood.

"Don't worry, Grace," her father said. "You won't have to do anything. Abbie and I'll take care of everything, right?" Her mother answered by putting the milk back in the refrigerator, slamming the door, and leaving the room.

"Is she okay?" Abbie said.

"She'll be fine."

"I wouldn't want to be working with her today," Abbie said. "Feel sorry for Trudy." Abbie grabbed her backpack and kissed her father goodbye. "Later."

That decided, Abbie was more nervous than if she were having her first showing in the San Francisco Museum of Modern Art. She looked for Jeremy the minute she hit the high school parking lot, but he wasn't standing in his usual place beside his car. When she found him, he was near the front door, talking with Charles and Sheila Browning.

"Hey, Abbie."

She moved closer. He put his arm around her shoulder but kept talking. "I'll go if I can get my old man to agree."

Charles started to walk. "One more tardy, and I get detention."

They followed Charles into the building. "Jeremy," Abbie said. "Can you come to dinner tomorrow night? We're having pizza." They stood in front of his locker while he collected his books.

"I might have to work."

"Please? I told them you were coming."

The final bell rang. Abbie begged. "Please, Jeremy."

He banged his locker shut. "I'll try." He kissed her and ran to class.

She waited for him after school. After a few quick kisses in the parking lot, he said he had to help his father install a water heater.

"See you," she waved. "Don't forget dinner at my house tomorrow night."

It took discipline, but Abbie spent the rest of the evening working on her portfolio. Of the five pictures, she liked the eagle's nest best. But the picture of her mother and grandmother wasn't bad. It just might be the piece that helped her win. She included the sketch of the teeter-totter she drew down by the river. Jeremy's work was better, but she was good, she had a chance. She filled out the application and put it in her backpack. Then she set about planning dinner for Jeremy.

She'd stayed up too late and had trouble waking the next morning. Skipping her shower, Abbie rushed to school. When Mr. Young asked for the scholarship applications, she pulled hers from her backpack, glad she'd remembered to pack it the night before. When she handed it in, she froze. Heather's was still in Abbie's bottom dresser drawer. A better friend would have dropped everything she was doing, ran straight home and got that portfolio. But even if she did, Abbie might not make it in time. She only had an hour, and she still had a lot of things to do before Jeremy came to dinner.

Everything had to be perfect. Her parents had to love Jeremy as much as she did. Abbie hurried home from school and took a shower. She had the table set before her mother walked through the front door.

"Pizza," her mother said with disgust. No, "Hello, how was your day?" Abbie watched her mother rearrange the silverware on the table and replace the linen napkins Abbie had set beside each plate with paper towels. Then she said, "I'm tired. I need to lie down."

Abbie waited until her mother's door slammed shut. Then she replaced the linen napkins and tossed the salad. Everything was ready. Her father would be home any minute with the pizza.

Abbie ran upstairs and changed into her favorite purple sweater. She pulled it tight, wishing she had breasts like Jessica's. But she didn't, so she focused on her hair instead, fluffing it around her face. Then she ran back to the dining room, eager to open the door the minute Jeremy arrived. She jumped up when she heard a noise outside, but it was only her father, trying to open the door.

"An Idiot's Delight and a Meat Lover's Special." He took the boxes to the kitchen. "And vegetable lasagna for your mother."

She kissed her father. "Daddy, you're the best."

He hugged her back. "So, when's this Jeremy fella supposed to be here?"

"Any time." Abbie looked at the clock.

"Tell you what," her father said. "We'll put the pizzas in the oven to keep them warm."

"Guess what I got for dessert." He held up a box. "Tiramisu."

Abbie smiled at her father on her way to the door. She hadn't heard Jeremy knock, but he must be out there, parking his car. She stepped onto the front step and shivered. The street was quiet. *Come on, Jeremy. Where are you?* She stood as long as she could, until the cold chased her inside.

"Is he here?" her father called from the kitchen.

"Not yet." Abbie looked at the clock, now a quarter to eight.

Her mother appeared in the doorway. She had changed into a loose blouse and a gray pair of slacks. Her hair was neat, her makeup perfect. She pulled Abbie's salad from the refrigerator and put it on the table along with the salad dressings. "What?" she said when Abbie's father gave her a reproachful frown.

"We're waiting for Abbie's boyfriend."

"Well." Her mother glanced at the clock. "It's almost eight-thirty. How much longer do we have to wait?"

Her father looked at Abbie, who said, "Five more minutes?"

Ten minutes later, they were still waiting. Angry and embarrassed, Abbie said, "Let's eat." She grabbed the pizzas from the oven and took them to the table while Grace filled plates with salad.

"He must have had to help his father." Abbie picked at her pizza. "His father is an electrician."

"We know," her mother said. Then she looked at Abbie's father, a righteous smirk on her face.

Abbie pushed her plate away and dialed Jeremy's home phone. "Hello?" she said. "Is Jeremy there?"

"No." A husky voice answered.

"Do you know where he is?"

"Who cares?" Jeremy's father sounded mean and drunk.

Abbie clicked the phone off without saying goodbye. She ran up the stairs and slammed her bedroom door. When she was done crying, she rested her chin on her knees and watched the snow fall outside her window. She adored Jeremy. She didn't ignore him, not like her mother ignored her father. Maybe her mother deserved to be forgotten, to have to hold dinner, and then put the uneaten food in plastic boxes and stuff it into the fridge. "It isn't his fault," her mother always said. "He just got busy." Abbie sniffed. She couldn't believe this was happening to her.

It didn't take long for her tears to turn to anger. She wasn't a doormat, something he could take for granted. She went back downstairs. The least she could do was pick up the kitchen. But the lights were out in the kitchen, the food put away. Abbie walked down the hall to her father's office and knocked on the door. "Daddy?"

"It's open."

"I'm sorry you went to so much trouble."

He stopped typing and looked up at her. "I'm sorry he didn't show up."

Abbie nodded. She was sorry, too.

"Sit down." He motioned to the loveseat. "You can keep me company." He shuffled the papers on his desk and started to type again. Then he stopped. "You know, Abbie, with boys like Jeremy, it's better to take things slow. Don't get in a hurry to fall in love."

"I won't," she said, which, of course was the only thing she could tell her father.

Abbie moped around the house all weekend, didn't wash her hair, and wore a faded pair of sweats. She was in her room when the doorbell rang, but she was no longer interested in visitors. When her father called, "Abbie?" she sulked down the stairs.

"What? Oh." Her hand went to her face, her tangled hair. More than mortified, it was too late to run.

"Hi," Jeremy said. "I guess I'm late for dinner."

"Yes, you are." Abbie's father motioned to the living room. "Come in and sit down."

Abbie knew that tone. This wasn't going to be a friendly chat.

Jeremy looked uncomfortable in his black turtleneck. His eyes were red, and there were tiny spots on his face, a breakout of acne, if Abbie had to guess. He also had a black eye and a bruise on his cheek.

"Something came up." Jeremy sat on the sofa. "I'm sorry I couldn't make it."

Remembering Jeremy's father's voice on the phone, Abbie didn't doubt it. She knew all too well how things came up when her mother's drinking got out of control. Even that very minute, something had come up that had her mother resting upstairs.

"You should have called," Abbie's father reprimanded.

"Yes," Jeremy said. "I should have." His face, though bruised, looked sincere. "We had some trouble at home."

"I want you to know," her father said, his hands folded and thumbs tapping, "that Abbie went to a lot of work and---"

"I know, sir. Abbie, I'm truly sorry."

The silence was awkward. It was Jeremy who stood and said, "I know this is short notice." He turned to her father. "And I wouldn't blame you if you said no, but I'd like to take Abbie to a movie."

"I don't think that's a good idea." Her father's arms were crossed.

"Probably not, but I'd like to make up for yesterday. I promise to have her home early."

Standing in front of her father, Jeremy looked like he'd just run into a wall instead of being the coolest guy in school. Certain he wouldn't forget her on purpose, she wanted to know what had gone wrong.

"Daddy?" She held her breath. "Please?"

He scrutinized Jeremy. "Why should I trust you with my daughter?"

"I know I messed up. Give me a chance to prove I can do better."

Her father wasn't making this easy. "If I say yes, what time would you have her home?"

"Right after the movie, sir."

"Daddy?"

Her father looked from Jeremy to Abbie. It took a while for him to say, "All right."

Abbie raced up the stairs two at a time. She kicked off her sweats and shrugged out of her T-shirt. In the bathroom, she pulled her hair into a ponytail. Face clean and teeth brushed, she slipped into her jeans and purple sweater and was downstairs in less than six minutes. Long enough for her father to ask all his questions.

As Abbie zipped her coat, her father said, "Be home by nine. School tomorrow."

Abbie hugged her father. "Thank you. Thank you, Daddy."

"Thank you, Mr. Buchanan." Jeremy offered his hand. Her father gave Jeremy a stern look before he shook it.

As soon as they turned the corner, Jeremy stopped the car and pulled her close. "I'm sorry," he said, and kissed her.

"What happened to your eye?"

He shrugged. "I got careless."

She wondered if it had anything to do with his father, but didn't know how to ask.

Instead of going to a movie, he drove to their special place in The Grove where they held hands, kissed and steamed up the windows. Abbie traced the bruise around his eye, kissing it gently. "Did your father do this?" Abbie asked.

Jeremy shrugged. "I had it coming."

"I wish there was something I could do," Abbie said.

"There is." He pulled her closer. "Just love me."

She kissed him until she could no longer breathe. They held hands, made plans and promises, and even though it was hard to say goodnight, he had her home on time.

Standing beside her father, waving goodbye, Abbie hoped one day he'd love her enough to trust her with his secrets.

The next week, when Heather finally returned to school, she said, "Thanks for turning my portfolio in on time. I really appreciate it." They were eating lunch at Frosty Burger. Abbie choked on a fry. Heather thumped her on the back. "You okay?"

"Yeah." Abbie took a couple swallows of Coke. Her face pinched.

"What?" Heather said.

"I—um."

Heather looked at her so intently, Abbie was tempted to lie. They weren't as close as they once were, but she'd have to tell her sometime. "About that," Abbie said. "I forgot."

"You forgot what?" Heather stared at Abbie as if she had suddenly turned yellow.

"Your portfolio."

"You forgot to turn it in?" Heather stood.

"There was a lot going on."

"Let me guess. Like Jeremy Blackburn."

Abbie should have seen this coming, but at the time, all she could think about was Jeremy. "Maybe it's not too late."

Heather challenged. "You did that on purpose. You were afraid I was going to win."

Abbie stood. "Did not."

Heather slung her purse over her shoulder. "That's the last time I ask you for anything. Thanks for nothing."

Abbie's tongue wouldn't move. Her stomach was hollow. She had nothing to say. Not even goodbye.

CHAPTER SIXTEEN

IN LESS THAN AN HOUR, Maxine would see Graceland. She dressed quickly and threw an irritated glance at Su Linn, still sitting on the side of her bed in green floral pajamas. The small woman's eyes were swollen, as if she'd been crying all night. Besides smelling peculiar, she took forever to get up and moving.

Just because they shared a room didn't mean they were joined at the hip. As soon as Maxine was dressed—in her very best clothes, because it was Elvis's birthday—she was out the door and in the hospitality room drinking coffee and eating a Danish with other Graceland tourists. When Su Linn didn't show for breakfast, Maxine wondered if she'd miss the tour. But Su Linn straggled onto the bus at the last minute, stinking worse than a wet dog. As she took her seat, Maxine put her hand over her nose.

Her heart catapulted into an uneven rhythm as they entered the Music Gates to Graceland. She'd seen pictures of the gates on TV, but never expected to see them in person. She pressed her nose against the glass and stared. Counting the notes and staffs, Maxine tried to memorize every detail so she could tell Helen and Shirley.

As soon as the bus stopped, Maxine stood. She waited impatiently while Su Linn waddled down the aisle. Once outside, Maxine pushed past Su Linn and gawked at the old colonial house.

"Please take my picture." She handed her camera to Sunny and posed beside the stone lions near the entrance. Then she joined the rest of the group by the front door where a young man was telling the history of Graceland.

Shut up, Maxine wanted to say to Su Linn, who stood off to one side, speaking with a tour guide who looked so much like Su Linn they could have been sisters. If Su Linn was going to be disruptive and disrespectful, she should have stayed in bed. Better yet, she should have stayed home.

Maxine turned her attention to the guide who was talking about Grace Toof, the daughter of a prosperous Memphis businessman. Maxine always assumed Elvis named his mansion in honor of his mother who he claimed was full of grace, instead of a woman buried more than sixty years ago. Her own daughter, named in honor of Graceland, was full of lots of things, but none of them was grace.

Mostly, she'd been full of disappointment. When Maxine discovered she was pregnant, she was secretly elated. Her plans to further her education dissolved in her desire to be a good mother. It ran like a movie in her head. Pink dresses edged with white daises, hats and mittens, all crocheted by Maxine while she waited for her baby to arrive. A loving husband and father. The perfect marriage.

What she got instead was a rushed wedding and a change in plans.

After the baby arrived, she discussed naming her Grace with Herb. "I like it. She'll be my little Gracie." And she was, right from the start. It was Herb who bonded with the baby, while Maxine sat on the sideline and watched him spoil the child rotten. Any hope of capturing her daughter's heart gave way to watching them grow closer every day.

Too bad, Grace, Maxine thought as she listened to the guide. *Just look at what you're missing.*

The door opened. Maxine pushed to the front of the line and entered the house as if entering St. Paul's Cathedral. Her eyes went to the mirrored staircase leading to the second floor, corded off. She would never see the bathroom where he died, or his bedroom for that matter, clearly off limits, but she was luckier than many. She was inside his house, even if guardrails kept her from touching his piano or sitting on his fifteen-foot sofa.

She followed the guide into the dining room where the table was set and tried to imagine sitting next to Elvis as he ate peanut butter and bananas. Oh, if Shirley and Helen could see this. She took a picture of the chandelier, another of the kitchen, and posed for Sunny at the entrance of the Jungle Room with its garish green shag carpet.

After a tour of Elvis's media room, the guide led them outside. When she saw Lisa Marie's childhood swing set, Maxine remembered the one

Herb put up for Grace. But Grace, a prissy prima donna by the time she was five, never liked to swing. Herb hauled it off a few years ago when Maxine insisted she needed the space to plant vegetables. She reflected—nothing was ever good enough for Grace, especially Maxine's love, which festered into bitterness and resentment from all the trying. It didn't help that Herb took Grace's side, every single time.

Inside the Trophy Room, Maxine gawked, her mouth wide open. Herb gave her a bad time about the shrine to Elvis she kept in the spare bedroom. Well, he should see this—walls covered with records. Movie posters. Old time memorabilia.

Outside, she took a picture of Elvis's jet the "Lisa Marie" and lingered by the Meditation Garden where Elvis and his parents were buried. The small stone memorializing Elvis's stillborn twin brother Jesse made her melancholy. As much as she and Grace disagreed, she wouldn't want to bury a child. She felt empathy for Elvis's mother. Being a mother was harder than it looked. She stood a long time in front of Elvis's grave. She never believed the rumors that he faked his own death. And as she watched the eternal flame at his grave, she was sure. He was no longer on this earth, but he'd live forever in the heart of his fans. She didn't have to close her eyes to hear him singing.

Life was a mysterious game, she thought, as she stood in front of his grave. Filled with expectations and disappointments. Through all his ups and downs, Elvis always loved Priscilla. Just like she'd always loved Larry. How different her life could have been had she married Larry.

She was sitting on a bench resting her feet when Su Linn walked by, deep in conversation with that other tour guide. When Su Linn saw Maxine, she motioned.

Great, Maxine thought.

"This is Maxine," Su Linn said. She put her hand on the tour guide's arm. "This is my cousin, Annie."

Maxine smiled. "Hello." That explained the resemblance. Maxine shifted her body and attention to the people entering the gift shop. She'd have to find some nice souvenirs ...

"Are you coming?"

"Who?" Maxine said.

"You."

Maxine shook her head.

But Su Linn said, "You don't want to see those stairs?"

Maxine wasn't sure what stairs Su Linn was talking about, but on the slightest chance she meant *those stairs*, Maxine stood, her heart beating so fast she might fall over. She stayed close, trying to interpret their broken conversation. She caught bits and pieces about aunts, mothers and pictures. She followed Annie and Su Linn straight back into Elvis's house.

"This way," Annie unclipped the heavy cord and waved them up the stairs toward Elvis's bedroom. Maxine stood and stared, unable to believe her luck.

"Hurry," Annie prompted. She unlocked the padded doors to his bedroom. Maxine gawked from the doorway with wide-eyed wonder. In her excitement, she grabbed Su Linn's hand, as if they were best friends waiting at Baskin-Robbins for their favorite chocolate sundaes.

They couldn't enter, but Maxine could see the bed—big enough for four people to sleep on with room to spare. The red drapes made the room dark and heavy. The door to the bathroom stood open and Maxine strained to see where they found him on the floor. She shivered knowing this was the last thing he saw and she tried to memorize every detail.

"We have to go." Annie swooshed them down the stairs and out the back door before a new group appeared. She left them at the gift shop. "Write soon." She gave Su Linn a hug. "And let me know how you're doing."

"Thank you." Maxine pumped Annie's hand. "Thank you so much."

"You're welcome," Annie said. "Keep an eye on Su Linn for me."

"I will," Maxine promised. But Su Linn was tired and wanted to go back to the bus. While Su Linn rested, Maxine shopped, settling on a big hat for Helen, purple with the word "Graceland" embroidered on the large brim in bright yellow. For Shirley, she found a charm bracelet with a guitar, a record, a pair of shoes and a hound dog. She bought a pastel print of Graceland for herself and a bear that sang "Love Me Tender" for Abbie. That left Grace. She had no idea what to get her daughter, who seemed to be going through some sort of mid-life crisis.

She looked at a purse.

Wrong color.

A poster.

Too tacky.

A cookbook of Elvis's favorite recipes.

Too much fat and sugar.

Nothing seemed appropriate until Maxine saw the display of miniature pewter houses. Grace loved houses. Maxine picked up several, setting them down again when she saw the prices. She walked away from the display and wandered through the store. A scarf. A wooden bowl shaped like a guitar. No matter what she looked at, she kept returning to the pewter houses. Grace liked to collect things, especially if they were expensive. Maxine picked up a small replica of Graceland and hesitated. She'd never visit Memphis again. This was her daughter. She put the house in her shopping basket and added a red rose at checkout. She also bought a postcard of Elvis, planning to add it to her collection at home. As a last thought, she purchased a box of cough drops for Su Linn.

Outside, at the Meditation Garden, Maxine kissed the rose and pushed it through the fence until it rested on Elvis's grave. "Happy Birthday, Elvis." She stood there a long time—ten minutes, twenty—trying to feel his presence, trying to burn this moment into her head so she'd never forget. She could hear him singing, "I once was lost, but know I'm found." The words brought tears to her eyes. She was still wiping them away as she boarded the bus.

Later, when it was time for dinner, Su Linn was too tired to eat, preferring to remain in bed. Maxine was too hungry to stay behind. She ate with the rest of her group in a diner on Beale Street specializing in southern food where Maxine asked Sunny to take her picture next to a life-sized cutout of Elvis. Walking back to her room, Maxine smiled. What a wonderful glorious day. She pushed open the door to her room, and her good mood vanished.

Su Linn was sitting up in bed smoking something Maxine recognized from antidrug commercials as marijuana.

"What are you doing?" Maxine slapped her hand against the No Smoking sign. "Can't you read?"

Su Linn doubled over in a series of coughs, dropping the joint.

"What's wrong with you?" Maxine picked the joint up before it burned a hole in the carpet. "What's this crap you're smoking? It stinks." She stomped into the bathroom and flushed it down the toilet.

"Marijuana." Su Linn said. "For my cancer."

"Cancer?" Maxine took a hard look a Su Linn. Other than her swollen eyes, she looked fine. "Where?"

Su Linn held her hand to her stomach and coughed. Maxine gave her the bag of cough drops. "Here."

"Thanks," Su Linn said.

"You need some water." By the time Maxine filled a glass and handed it to Su Linn, Su Linn had picked up another joint and was smoking again. "Are you supposed to do that?" Maxine said.

"Helps with the pain," Su Linn said. "Not going to kill me."

Not funny. Not if Su Linn was dying.

Su Linn offered Maxine the small cigarette. "Help with your legs and back pain."

Pot? Maxine had never smoked pot in her life. Never had any desire. It made people do strange things, act dumb and stupid. That's what she'd heard.

"You try," Su Linn insisted. "You be surprised."

She'd be more than surprised; she'd be higher than a kite. That's what Shirley said about her grandson. He smoked pot and was always higher than a kite.

She watched Su Linn inhale. It looked easy enough. And that strange odor wasn't so bad once you got used to it.

Maxine kicked off her shoes and changed into pajamas. She rubbed her legs and grimaced. It wasn't that Maxine didn't know how to smoke. She did. And she enjoyed her cigarettes. But pot?

Su Linn lit another and showed Maxine how to hold the smoke in her mouth before slowly releasing.

What if it made her dizzy? What if it made her sick? They were going to Tupelo in the morning, and she didn't want to be heaving her guts out in the bathroom of the bus.

But what if it made her feel better?

The first puff brought tears to her eyes. Maxine coughed and tried to catch her breath. Now *she* was breaking the rules. She turned her back to the door and the No Smoking Sign. Some rules were meant to be broken.

Maxine studied the joint, turned it this way, then that before putting it to her lips and inhaling.

"Pull it straight into you," Su Linn said. "Deeper."

It wasn't long before Maxine felt lighter and more relaxed. The red bedspread looked beautiful, so bright. And the way Elvis sang on the television, why, he could have been right there beside her, singing in her ear. "I will love you longer than foreverrrrr . . ." She gave a small bounce on her bed. "Su Linn, no one is ever going to believe we saw his bedroom." She giggled and moved closer to Su Linn. "We should have gone in there. We should have laid right down on that bed and took a nap." She giggled again. *That* would have been something to tell Helen and Shirley.

Maxine took another puff. Elvis's airplane in the picture hanging on the wall was ready to fly. Why, it was going to zoom right out the window. This made her laugh even harder. She took another puff. Every sound, every movement was hilarious. She laughed so hard, she was howling and had to pee.

Coming out of the bathroom, Maxine was ravenous. "Where are those cookies?" She dug in her canvas bag until she found Helen's oatmeal crisps, which she shared with Su Linn. Maxine moved toward the door. "Want something to drink?" Su Linn nodded.

Chomping a cookie, Maxine searched the halls for a pop machine. She ended up in the lounge and returned with two Elvis Presley specials. Fried peanut butter and banana sandwiches with a large order of sweet potato fries.

"'Lady,'" she recapped her encounter for Su Linn. "'Do you know you're wearing your pajamas?' Stupid bartender. Told him to be glad I was wearing something." Maxine rolled on her bed, holding her sides as they laughed to tears.

They gobbled sandwiches and fries while watching *Blue Hawaii.* When Elvis sang, they sang, too. Maxine forgot all about the rules, her aching legs, and fell asleep in a drug-induced haze. When she woke the next morning, she discovered she could move without wincing.

"Good morning." Su Linn said, combing her hair.

"'Morning." Maxine stumbled into the bathroom and closed the door. They had a long day in front of them. A three-hour bus ride to Tupelo, then the long trip home. She brushed her teeth and grinned at the mirror. *You dope head. You pot smoker, you.* She giggled, dressed and packed her suitcase. But her mood changed when she watched Su Linn run a comb through her hair. "What about this cancer? How bad is it?"

Su Linn shrugged. "One month. Maybe more." She smiled. "Annie nice girl. Make an old woman's wish come true."

Maxine's throat was so tight she couldn't speak. It was time to go home, to make her own wish come true. But, before boarding the bus, she stopped to speak with Sunny. Then she took her seat beside Su Linn.

"On the road again," Sunny sang into the mic as the bus drove away from the hotel. But instead of moving past Graceland, the bus pulled up to one side and stopped at the Music Gates.

"We'll just be a moment, folks," Sunny said into the mic. "Su Linn, come up here. Maxine wants to take your picture." Su Linn gave Maxine a puzzled glance.

"Go," Maxine said. "Get moving."

Su Linn waddled down the aisle, and Maxine followed. Sunny snapped their picture standing beside the outline in the iron gates of Elvis playing his guitar. "Smile," Sunny said, and both women grinned at the camera. A warm breeze brushed the air. It was a perfect day for making dreams come true, and a perfect day for taking pictures.

Su Linn disembarked in Las Vegas. Before she left the bus, Maxine handed Su Linn the postcard she bought of Elvis. On the back, she had written her address. "Write to me," Maxine said. "And I'll write to you. I'll send you some of the pictures I took once I learn how to work that stupid camera."

Su Linn smiled. "That would be nice. You a good friend."

Maxine gave Su Linn a hug. She hadn't been much of a friend, not in the beginning. But she wasn't too old to change.

She waved goodbye to Su Linn and settled back into her seat. "On the road again," she sang along with Sunny, secretly surprised that she was glad to be heading home.

*   *   *

With her period six weeks late, Grace could no longer pretend there was nothing sprouting inside her belly. Womb, Rob would correct the way he always did whenever she was too tired to think of the right noun or verb. Today, it felt like a *belly*, big and hard and achy. Womb sounded like something dead, and the baby growing inside was anything but dead. She could already feel the flutter, the uncontrollable craving for salt. Which of course, created another problem. She couldn't go to Dr. Johnson. Their regular physician would congratulate Rob at the country club or on the golf course. Grace needed her own doctor, one who would keep her secret until she was ready to tell Michael. In spite of all her thoughts about abortion, she was keeping this baby.

She flipped through the Yellow Pages. She wasn't ready to be a mother when she'd had Abbie. This time she was going to do everything right. She would take her vitamins, drink her milk, avoid stress and get plenty of rest. This time, she would worry more about her baby's health than her expanding stomach, or the acne erupting on her face.

Thinking it would be best to drive to a town where no one knew her husband, Grace settled on a clinic two hours away. Once in the doctor's office, Grace was sure she had made the right decision. The building was new; the inside of the waiting room painted in Grace's favorite mauve. The hunter green loveseat gave the room a homey feeling, as did the brass lamp and English ivy on the end table.

While she waited for the nurse to call her name, Grace paged through the latest issue of *House Beautiful*. When she and Michael married—and they would marry as soon as she told him about the baby—they'd have dishes like those in the ads. Elegant white plates so beautiful they reflected the light from the chandelier. She turned a page. And a big brass bed with a down comforter and millions of posh pillows. She lingered over a picture of a two-story house, complete with rose bushes, lilacs, and a white picket fence. They'd live in a house like that.

"Mrs. Lancaster?" Grace looked up from her magazine and smiled. She rose and swaggered after the nurse, modeling her new name like a new dress.

Her blood pressure was normal, as was her temperature. While she waited for the doctor, Grace thumbed through a copy of *Parents*. She tore out an article, "Ten Easy Ways to Ensure a Healthy Baby." She laid her hand on her stomach. She would carry this baby low. She would eat garlic every day and sleep on her left side. When she dreamed, she would dream of a girl, insuring that the child she carried was a boy. By the time the doctor came in to examine her, Grace had already picked out the perfect crib and layette, Mickey Mouse driving a sports car on a carpet of royal blue fabric, bordered with red and white sailboats. There was even a red, white and blue mobile with cars and boats to hang over the crib and curtains to match.

"Let's take a look." The doctor placed her stethoscope on Grace's chest. "Deep inhale." The doctor was thorough, asking about Grace's health while she looked in Grace's ears and mouth. "Any surgeries?"

"No," Grace said. "Oh, wait. I had a mole removed here on my face."

The doctor checked Grace's reflexes and asked, "Do you take any medications?"

"I do," Grace said. "I take a multivitamin every morning before I run."

"Good. You're a runner. That explains your great muscle tone."

Grace smiled. "I try to stay in shape. I don't know what I'll do now that I'm pregnant. I don't want to stress this baby."

"Exercise is good for you and the baby," the doctor said. "We offer some wonderful baby yoga classes here at the clinic."

"That's nice," Grace said. But she wouldn't be able to attend unless the classes were held on weekends. Already she had had to ask for an extra day off.

She wondered how long she would have to work. She liked her job, but it interfered with so many things, like this appointment, for example. Surely, Michael would want her to stay home with the baby.

"Mrs. Lancaster?" The doctor looked concerned, even a bit irritated.

"What?"

"I was asking, is this your first pregnancy?"

"No. My first was a girl. Sixteen years ago. This time I'm having a boy."

"I see," the doctor said. "Lie back. Let's take a look."

Grace had never liked the feel of the white paper under her bare skin, or the sterile sheet the nurse had left to cover her naked body, but she lay back on the table and put her feet in the stirrups. *I'm doing this for us, Michael. To make sure we have a fine baby boy.*

While the doctor checked Grace's uterus, Grace looked at the walls, the ceiling. She liked the color of the walls. She'd read that robin's egg blue created a calming atmosphere, perfect for the nursery. The doctor said something, but Grace was too caught up in her own thoughts to listen.

"Mrs. Lancaster?"

"Uh-huh?"

"Did you understand what I just said?" She finished the pelvic exam and helped Grace sit.

"I, um."

"Even though you're in perfect health, there are certain risks you should be aware of."

"I love the color of these walls. I'm looking for something like this for my baby's room."

"When you're dressed," the doctor said, "we can talk."

Grace hummed while she slipped into her clothes. "What do you think, little one. Do you like this color?" If she painted the nursery robin's egg blue, it could clash with the royal blue blanket. Maybe she should paint the walls red or yellow. Wait. She couldn't paint the walls at all, that might harm the baby. Michael would have to do it. She was dressed when the doctor returned.

"As I was saying, everything looks good, but we need to keep a close eye on you and this pregnancy. Down syndrome is more prevalent with older mothers. Also, your chance for chronic diseases increases, not to mention gestational diabetes." The doctor made a note in her file and said, "I see you don't have insurance."

Afraid she'd been caught lying, Grace chose to ignore the remark. "I'll be fine. I'm already taking natal vitamins."

"You mean prenatal?" the doctor said.

"Yes. Yes, that's what I meant."

The doctor scribbled on her prescription pad and handed the note to Grace. "We want to make sure you're getting enough folic acid and calcium. We'll also want to watch your blood pressure. If you get dizzy or things seem blurry, let us know immediately."

"Thank you." Grace stood and extended her hand. "We're so excited. Michael has always wanted a boy."

"We'll settle for a healthy baby," the doctor smiled. "I'm sure your husband will be just as happy with a girl."

"Boy," Grace said. "We're having a healthy baby boy." The last thing she wanted was another daughter like Abbie.

With the exam out of the way, Grace drove to Aspen Grove singing lullabies to the baby. She couldn't remember all the words to "Day is Done," so she sang what she remembered of "Itsy Bitsy Spider," recalling how Abbie used to squeal the minute Rob drew an imaginary sun in the air and readied to pounce on Abbie as a spider. Whenever Grace tried to sing "Itsy Bitsy Spider," Abbie cried and reached for her father.

This time would be different. She would buy a baby book that had all the lullabies. And a rocking chair and sing Michael's baby to sleep.

"Itsy Bitsy Spider," Grace sang as she entered The Three Monkeys, Aspen Grove's independent book store. The trip to the new doctor took longer than expected, so she skimmed over the baby titles, selecting a book on what to expect when you're pregnant, a book of lullabies, and *The House at Pooh Corner*, which her father read to her when she was little. When Abbie was little, Grace had tried to read the same book to Abbie. But Abbie had always cried, "I want my daddy," and Grace had stopped trying. *Well,* Grace thought as she paid for the books. *A lot has changed in sixteen years.* This baby wouldn't flinch at the sound of her voice. This baby would coo and grin and squeal.

Grace looked at her watch, glad she asked for the whole day off. She still had so much more to accomplish. Stopping at Rudy's for a late lunch, she asked to be seated in Michael's favorite booth. While she dined on ravioli she looked through the classified ads, circling three houses she thought might work. She needed at least two bedrooms. Three would be better. She wanted a fenced backyard so Michael Jr. could play outdoors without wandering into the street. She also wanted a place close to the high school, so Michael could come home for lunch everyday. They hadn't spoken since that awkward day she learned he was married, but everything would change when she told him. He didn't have to stay in a loveless marriage just to save the kids. They would create a warm and inviting home where his girls were always welcome on weekends. She'd even make room for Abbie.

As soon as she finished eating, Grace went home and started dialing numbers. The first house she had circled—the one three blocks from the high school—was already taken. She moved on to her second choice. This place was still available, but it was nine hundred dollars a month. Grace put her hand on her stomach and said, "What do you think, baby? Can we afford it?" Grace calculated. She'd need at least two thousand dollars for first and last month's rent, not to mention extra money to hook up utilities. That meant she'd have to ask Rob for the money, or ask Kent for a raise.

The next morning, Grace was the first one to work. The coffee was made, and all the lights turned on before Kent entered the office. She had even stopped by the bakery and bought a dozen glazed doughnuts. Before he even had a chance to hang up his coat, Grace said, "I need to talk to you."

He motioned to a chair. "What is it?"

Grace sat on the edge of her seat. "I, um." She hated asking for money. It felt unnatural, like she was begging. She straightened her shoulders; she was worth it. "Well, I've been here for a while now, and I was thinking it was time to discuss a raise."

Kent cocked an eyebrow. "A raise?"

"Yes," Grace beamed. The Christmas bonus had been nice, but she'd already spent that.

"Well." Kent tapped his pencil against the edge of his desk. "Things are slow right now. Maybe we can talk about it again when sales pick up."

"What if I helped type the listing agreements? I could even help with the billing." Grace crossed her legs. One of the bad things about being pregnant was that she always had to use the bathroom.

Kent laid down his pencil. "You'd be interested in that?"

"I would love to give it a try," Grace encouraged. "I'm not the fastest typist in the world, but I can learn."

Kent said. "Let me think about it."

Grace stood, her knees pressed close together. "Thank you." She dashed to the bathroom, just in time to avoid an accident.

That night, Grace drove by the apartment that cost nine hundred dollars a month. She called the owner and made an appointment to see the rental the next day. It wasn't the big two-story house with a picket fence, but it would do. For now. She wrote a check for the first and last month's rent, knowing she would have to explain the large amount to Rob. But he wouldn't know for another month, and by then, she'd be settled in with Michael.

"You can move in the first of February," the landlord said when Grace signed the lease. That gave her plenty of time to decorate before she showed the place to Michael. On her way home, she stopped at the mall and bought new sheets and a set of dishes, not as pretty as those in *House Beautiful*, but pretty enough to begin her new life. She also bought a blanket for the baby, robin's egg blue.

Now that Grace had signed a lease, she could no longer put off telling her husband. She would ask for a separation, maybe even a divorce, depending on Rob's reaction. He'd have to admit this was *his* fault. He was never home.

She stopped at the market and bought the choicest prime rib she could find, as well as butter and sour cream, things she never kept in the refrigerator unless it was a holiday. While the roast and carrots baked, Grace set the table for three, even though she suspected Abbie would have an excuse to avoid dinner.

As Grace tossed the salad, she pretended she was preparing the meal for Michael. "How was your day?" she would ask pouring him a glass of wine.

"Just another boring day," he would answer, then kiss her lips. "The best time of the day is when I'm here alone with you." After dinner, they would snuggle on the sofa and pick out names for the baby. She was fond of Michael Jr. but suspected he'd prefer Tiger or Ben, since he always talked about how great they were on the golf course. She was pulling the roast from the oven when Rob entered the kitchen.

"Mmmmmm, something smells good." He leaned in to kiss her. She turned her head and his kiss got lost in her hair. "What's the occasion?" Before she could answer he asked, "Where's Abbie?"

Grace's fingers curled hard around the edge of the serving platter. She set the roast on the table before speaking. "How would I know? She never tells me anything. Maybe she's with that new friend of hers, that Jeremy Blackburn. Maybe she ran off and got married."

"Grace." She turned away from the harshness in his voice. "Why would you say an awful thing like that?"

"Dinner's ready. Would you like to eat now, or wait for your daughter?"

Rob looked at his watch. "It's past seven. She'll probably grab something at Heather's." He poured the wine. "Where's your glass?"

"I have a headache." She held her hand over her eyes to prove it was true. "I just took two aspirin. Maybe later."

Now that Grace had him all to herself, she wasn't sure how to begin. Putting a slice of meat on each of their plates and sitting at the table, she asked, "How was your day?"

"Hectic. Everyone wants to buy a car but they have no money. If it wasn't for credit . . ."

Grace reached for her glass wishing it were filled with wine instead of water. She sprinkled salt on her prime rib. Should she tell him now, or wait? "Rob?" She stalled.

"This is good, Grace. You make the best prime rib in Aspen Grove."

"I'm thinking about getting my own place."

He stopped chewing. "What?"

"A place of my own. I think we need a separation."

Rob's mouth fell open. "What are you talking about?"

She stared at her food. Her hands shook as she took her plate to the sink and dumped her dinner down the disposal.

His fork clattered to the floor. "What's going on?"

She kept her back to him. She didn't want him looking into her eyes and realizing the truth. Not yet. "Well, you're always busy." She rinsed her plate and put it in the dishwasher. "I get lonesome in this big house. Now that I have a job, I'd like to have my own place." She turned and faced him, her heart a hammer. "For a while."

"How long's a while?" His brow furrowed. "I thought you loved this house."

Grace glanced around the kitchen. They had had numerous delays waiting for her to decide on the color of the granite. "It feels empty."

"You designed it. That's all you talked about for months." He was standing now, a thousand questions washing across his face. "It's not my fault it feels empty."

Grace squared her shoulders. "But people change."

He ran his hand through his hair as if that would solve the problem. "What's this really about?"

Why was he making this so hard? She stood taller. "A separation?"

"A separation? You want a separation because the house feels empty?"

"No. Yes. I need a place of my own." This wasn't as easy as she thought it would be.

"This is your own," his voice grew louder. "You picked out every color, every window. Every fucking tile." He waved his hands to encompass the room.

Grace trembled with anger, and also a little bit of fear that he wouldn't grant her wish. "This is your house. Yours and Abbie's. I'm an intruder here."

"Don't be ridiculous. You're just bored."

"I mean it, Rob. I want a place of my own." She'd ask for a divorce later, once she got away.

"I don't know what's going on with you. When I asked, you said we didn't need counseling."

Sit in front of a stranger and tell all her secrets. Not a chance. "No, I don't want counseling. I don't think it would help."

"Then what do you want?" He was yelling, his face red with frustration.

"A separation?" Her voice broke; it wasn't at all as confident as it needed to be.

He narrowed his eyes and gave a sarcastic chuckle. "Nothing I do pleases you anymore. If you want a separation, fine, you've got one."

He pulled his coat from the closet and opened the door, letting the cold air in. "Better find someone to help you move. Because it isn't going to be me." She grimaced when he slammed the door.

"That went well." She placed her hand on her stomach, "Don't you think?" She put the plastic containers of meat and vegetables in the refrigerator and wiped the table. She took the tiniest sip of his unfinished wine and headed to the shower. Her hand shook as she turned the faucet. The water splashed over her shoulders, hot enough to make her flinch. She did what she had to do. There was no taking it back. She wouldn't think about her past, or how happy she was the day they married. That was history. A whole other life. This was January, a time for something new.

*   *   *

"Jeremy. Jeremy. Jeremy." Abbie kissed the note Jeremy passed her on his way to class. It was wonderful being in love.

It was so wonderful, Abbie's grades started slipping because she skipped class every time Jeremy asked her to meet him. When they met, he'd drive to their place at The Grove where they'd kiss and grope and steam up the car windows.

Instead of listening to Mrs. O'Dell explain the Mason-Dixon line, Abbie opened the note again. *Meet me after school. We're having a bonfire out at the grove.*

Abbie frowned. *A bonfire? We're?* She hoped he meant *we're,* as in she and Jeremy, and not any others. She wanted him all to herself, just like last Sunday night when they drove out to The Grove and parked. But the minute she saw him waiting by his car, smiling that lopsided grin that turned her to butter, it didn't matter who was there as long as she was with him.

"Hey, lover," Jeremy said as he held the door for her. She loved the way his car smelled like his aftershave, even if the interior needed new upholstery. She couldn't wait for summer so she could help him fix it up.

"Ready?" He revved the engine, punched the car into drive, and reached for her hand, holding it while he shifted gears. That's all it took to make her happy. Jeremy sped over the slick roads, undeterred by the ice. Although Abbie trembled, afraid they would crash, she enjoyed the adrenaline rush each time they skidded around a corner. Every minute beside him was an adventure, absolutely thrilling.

She could see the bonfire before they reached the trees. The flames blazed bright in the January sky. Someone hunkered around the logs toasting fingers and toes in an effort to stay warm. She recognized Sheila from school. Charles sat on a wooden box close to the fire.

"Hey," Jeremy said, taking a seat by the fire. They talked about movies, sports and video games—things Abbie didn't care about so she leaned her head against his shoulder. He gave her a hug and kept talking. When the fire died down, Jeremy stretched. "We should go."

"Not yet," Charles said. "I thought we were playing the game."

"What game?" Abbie looked at Jeremy for an answer.

"Nothing. Come on." He stood and reached for her hand.

They were walking towards Jeremy's car when Charles called, "You'll have to tell her sometime."

Abbie stopped. "Tell me what?"

Jeremy shook his head.

"Tell me what?"

By now, Charles and Sheila had joined them. They stood in a semicircle looking expectantly at each other. Weird. She'd never noticed it before. They looked odd in their dark turtlenecks, as if they belonged to a cult.

"We have to go," Jeremy said.

"Not until you tell me what's going on."

"We could show her." Sheila shuffled from one foot to the other, Abbie supposed in an effort to keep warm.

Jeremy reached for her hand, and Abbie pushed his hand away. "Show me what?"

Charles walked over to his car and opened the trunk. It was getting dark, but not so dark Abbie didn't see the rope he carried. She stared. "What are you going to do with that?" she stammered.

"It's just a game," Jeremy said.

"To get high." Charles put the rope beside the box and tossed another log on the fire.

Jeremy looked at her and kicked at the snow. It took him a few tries before he said, "I don't do it to get high. I do it for inspiration."

"That's true," Sheila said. "Jeremy does get inspired."

Abbie studied their faces in the firelight. This wasn't a joke, or a scene from a horror movie. She shivered. Why did they need a rope in the middle of the forest? She looked at the darkening sky afraid of the answer.

Jeremy took her hand. "It's called 'pass out'. We choke ourselves until we pass out."

"What?" She'd never heard of such a stupid game.

"It enhances the senses," Jeremy said. "It helps me draw better."

Abbie looked at Charles and Sheila. "You do this? *Really?*"

Sheila nodded. "It helps me forget, and Charles just likes to get high. It doesn't cost anything, not like drugs or alcohol."

"Show me."

She followed them deeper into the grove until they reached the gnarled old willow tree. Charles tossed the rope over one of the limbs and tied a noose. He tugged. Abbie could almost feel it burn as he wrenched the rope tighter. The sun was setting, staining the hills and trees a smoky frozen gray. Lights below in the valley blinked on one by one. She had no business being here, but it was too late to run.

Jeremy must have sensed her apprehension because he put his arm around her shoulder and pulled her close. "We don't have to do this."

"Yes, we do," Abbie said. "Show me."

Charles dropped the box under the tree and stepped up. He stuck his head in the noose. "Ready."

"Okay." Jeremy picked up the end of the rope and Sheila counted. "One."

Jeremy tugged the slack from the rope.

"Two."

Jeremy braced his feet, the rope coiled around his wrists.

"Three."

Charles kicked the box, scudding it a few feet away while Jeremy held the rope slack enough it wouldn't break Charles's neck. Abbie tried not to watch as Charles swung from the tree, his eyes bulging, his body twitching. Sheila whispered, "Charles. Charles."

Charles's body jerked in circles, then slackened as he passed out. Jeremy immediately released the tension on the rope.

"Get him down," Abbie cried. "He's going to die."

"No, he isn't," Jeremy said. "He'll be fine. Watch." He took the rope from Charles' neck.

Crumpled on the ground like a bag of garbage, Charles gasped for air. When he opened his eyes, he seemed confused. Even in the dusk,

Abbie could see his bloodshot eyes, the red spots erupting on his face. But Charles was still alive; nothing bad had happened.

"Sheila?" Jeremy said.

"No. Maybe next time. I gotta go."

Good. They were leaving. As far as Abbie was concerned, there wouldn't be a next time, not if she could help it.

She was quiet all the way home. When he kissed her goodbye, she trembled. There was so much about him—maybe she didn't want to know.

CHAPTER SEVENTEEN

MAXINE HADN'T EXPECTED to feel glad to be home. When the bus pulled into the parking lot, Shirley and Helen were waiting. Maxine jumped up and waved. She had so much to tell them.

"How was it?" Shirley hugged her.

"Fun," Maxine said.

"We want to hear all about it." Helen linked her arm in Maxine's while Shirley put the suitcase in the trunk. "Coffee and pie at Norm's."

While they waited for their order, Maxine gave each of her friends a present.

"It's you, all right," Shirley said when Helen modeled the purple hat from Memphis. "All you need is a pair of those big sunglasses I saw on QVC."

"Knew I'd forget something," Maxine said. "I need to go back and get them." This made them snicker.

"Ouuuu." Shirley latched the charm bracelet around her wrist and held it out for them to see. "I ain't nothing but a hound dog," she sang, making the dog dance. "Next time I'm going with you."

"Maybe they'll hire us as maids," Maxine said.

"Bite your tongue." Shirley choked on her cheesecake.

"For sure," Helen added. "Seeing's how Joanna's been cleaning your house for years." She took a bite of her lemon cream pie. "You'd better get her to give you some cleaning lessons before you go."

Maxine laughed so hard she spilled her coffee. Memphis was great, but today, Aspen Grove was even better.

"Where's the camera?" Shirley said. "I want to see the pictures."

Maxine gave Shirley the camera and watched as Shirley hit the display and scrolled through the images. "These are great," Shirley said. "Look, Helen, Graceland."

"Who's the woman with you by the music gates?" Helen said, handing the camera back to Shirley.

"That's Su Linn," Maxine said. "She was my roommate in Memphis."

"How'd that go?" Helen said.

"Better than you'd think." Maxine looked at Shirley, then Helen and wondered if they'd ever smoked pot. She wondered if she should tell them. Maybe, she smiled. Someday.

"I can take this home and print your pictures on my computer," Shirley said.

"That would be great," Maxine said. "When it comes to these new gadgets, I have no clue."

"Well, then it's a good thing you have me," Shirley said.

"Yes, it is," Maxine said, grateful for all of her friends.

When they pulled into Maxine's driveway, her yard looked magical. While she enjoyed balmy weather in Memphis, snow covered Aspen Grove, making it look like a giant frosted cake. Someone had shoveled the walks to her doorway, as though saying, nice to see you, Maxine, welcome home.

Shirley handed Maxine her house key. "I could only feed them once before Herb locked the screen door. Hope everything's okay."

Exhausted from her trip, yet happy and warmed by Helen and Shirley's friendship, Maxine unlocked the back door and glanced around the room. *Good to be home.* She set her suitcase on the bed and wrinkled her nose. Something smelled odd. Foul. Moldy. She checked the bathroom, hoping Herb hadn't messed his pants again. She found the bathroom much the way she left it. A pair of dirty socks next to the toilet. A towel lying on the floor.

What she saw in the kitchen reminded her why she left in the first place. The sink was full of smashed cans. The room reeked of stale beer. Maxine pushed open the window. "Damn you, Herbert Foster. You're worthless."

She opened the cabinet where she kept the fish food and called, "Hey, Elvis and Priscilla. Did you miss me?" She lifted the top to the aquarium and faltered. Elvis floated upside down in the brackish water.

Several beer cans bobbed in the fish tank, bumping into the glass and displacing the fish. Maxine reached in and flung the cans at the floor. "Damn you, Herbert Foster."

Searching through the slimy green algae, she called. "Priscilla? Priscilla? Where are you?" She found the small shark sideways at the bottom of the tank.

Maxine ran to the kitchen and drew a bowl of fresh water. She added aquarium stabilizer the way the man at the pet store showed her. Fishnet in hand, she lifted Priscilla from the aquarium and slid her into the clean water. Then she went to retrieve Elvis. She didn't need a net to catch him. He was so weak she could fish him out with her fingers.

"Poor Elvis." Maxine guided the small shark into the clean water. She thought he flipped his tail in appreciation. Weak, he gave his last flip at life and floated to the top of the bowl.

"Damn you, Herb Foster. Damn you to hell." Maxine stormed through the house. Tears streaking her face, she dumped his unopened beer in the garbage. She didn't stop until she found every one of his hiding places. She didn't quit until she was exhausted and both of her fish were dead.

"Do you hear me? I'm done with you," she yelled at the top of her voice. "You think I'm a crazy old woman? I'll show you crazy." Shaking, she searched through the phonebook and called a locksmith.

"This is an emergency. Our house was broken into, and we've been robbed. Can someone come and change our locks?"

While Maxine waited for the locksmith, she pulled all of Herb's clothes from the closet, tossing them out the front door and into the snow. She tore through the house collecting everything that belonged to Herb, adding it to the pile in the front yard. Exhausted, she sat on the sofa and waited for the man to change her locks.

"Lady," he said when he saw the piles in the front yard. "You weren't kidding. What a mess."

"I know," Maxine cried. "It was just awful."

When Herb came home that night, he had to ring the doorbell. Maxine ignored him, turning the television louder.

"Maxine," he pounded. "Dammit. Open the door."

She pushed the curtain away from the window and yelled. "You don't live here anymore."

"Maxine." Herb rattled the door. "Let me in. It's freezing out here."

"Good." She sat on the sofa until she was afraid the neighbors would call the cops. Ripping a blanket from the sofa, she opened the door and threw it at him. He lost his balance and fell on top of his clothes, the blanket wrapped around his head.

"I'm done taking care of your sorry ass. I'm done. You hear me? I'm done." Maxine slammed the door and turned the lock. "Go sleep at the Green Lantern."

She waited until she heard his truck pull out of the driveway. Then she made a cup of hot chocolate and turned on "Jeopardy!" It wasn't ten minutes before the telephone rang. "Shut up," Maxine yelled. "Shut up."

The phone stopped, and then rang again. "Shut up," she said. "Shut up. Shut up. Shut up."

"I'll show you." Maxine unplugged the phone and sat down to watch television. After a while she went to the kitchen and made a bowl of tomato soup and a tuna fish sandwich, something easy. She didn't know what Herb was eating for supper, and she didn't care.

She found an old black and white movie on TV, lit a cigarette and wondered about Su Linn. She hoped she was feeling better. Maxine tried to keep her mind busy, but the movie was boring. Before long her head nodded, and she was snoring. She should have been dreaming of Graceland, Su Linn and peanut butter sandwiches. Instead, her head was full of distorted visions of Herb and dead fish.

*   *   *

Grace yawned and stretched. Rob's side of the bed was cold. Soon, she could move into her own place, and Abbie could quit complaining about her father sleeping on the sofa. Before guilt made her weepy or do something she'd regret, Grace headed to the shower. Nothing gained looking backwards besides discontent.

After her shower and in spite of her promise to come in before nine and take on added responsibility, Grace dialed the office and said she'd be late. Then, because she was hungry and didn't want to make a mess in the kitchen, she stopped at a diner and ordered an omelet with hash browns and a large glass of milk.

Grace drummed her fingers against the table. *Michael. Michael.* She buttered her toast and pondered. Everything tasted so good. If she wasn't careful, she'd weigh a hundred and fifty pounds before this baby was born.

Finished with breakfast, Grace used a pay phone to dial Michael's home. Placing her napkin over the receiver to disguise her voice, Grace smiled when she heard the woman answer. "You don't know me, but there's something I should tell you. Your husband is having an affair."

Before Michael's wife could say anything, Grace replaced the receiver. *There. That should do it.* She paid the bill and left the diner. By tonight, he'd be looking for a new home, and she'd be right there, ready to help.

She waited all night for his call. The next morning, instead of reporting to work at eight, Grace drove into the parking lot at Aspen High. She kept a close eye on the students. She didn't want Abbie to see her. She ducked when she saw Heather, surprised Abbie wasn't with her. She looked around. Down the block. Toward the bus stop. Ah, there she was, on the steps. Talking to that Jeremy boy. Except, they weren't talking. Their heads nodded together; their arms twisted around each other like knots.

Inside the building she told the secretary, "I'd like to speak with the principal about my daughter."

"I'm sorry," the secretary said. "He hasn't arrived yet. Would you care to wait?" She pointed to a row of empty seats.

The foyer was small with no door or privacy. "Can I wait in his office?"

The secretary rapped her pencil against the desk. "I don't think---" She reached for the telephone. "Aspen Grove High School. Doris speaking. How may I help you?"

Graced mouthed the words and pointed, "I'll wait in there." She walked into the principal's office and took a seat. By the time Michael hung his coat in the closet, Grace was already inside, waiting.

His face flamed as he closed the door. "What are you doing here?"

Grace turned in her chair. "We need to talk."

"You've done enough talking." He clenched his hands, and for a moment, she thought he would hit her. "I want you out of here. Now."

Steady. "I have something to tell you. Please sit down."

He towered over her so menacing, she had to lean out of his way. "What were you thinking, calling my house?"

"I never called your house." She had to look at the floor to cover her lie.

"Oh, you didn't, huh? And I suppose you didn't tell my wife I was having an affair."

"No I didn't. Would you please sit down?"

"Well," he tapped his index fingers together as if in thought. "Then who do you think did?" He crossed his arms and waited for her answer.

Grace fidgeted in her chair. "You left me no choice. "

"I tried to explain."

He was going to say he was sorry. It was all a mistake. He still loved her. Instead, he said, "You have a daughter, a family I assume you'd like to protect."

She looked at him, searching his face for any sign of love or forgiveness. His jaw was set, his lips a straight firm line, but his voice indicated something else. "Grace, you have to stop calling me."

Grace gripped her purse tighter and dug her feet into the carpet. "I'm pregnant."

"You're what?" His voice was so loud, she was sure the secretary heard. She'd never seen a man so upset. Not even her father when her mother threw away his best fishing lures.

"The doctor confirmed it last week."

She lowered her voice to a whisper. "You're going to be a father. You're going to have a son."

"You're crazy." He dropped into his chair, her declaration buckling his knees.

"No, I'm not," Grace assured. "Just pregnant."

His eyes darkened. "You're lying."

She tried to grab his hand and place it on her stomach, but he pulled away as if her hand were hot as iron.

"Michael," she said. "I love you. We can make a good home for this baby."

"You're crazy," he repeated and pointed to the door. "Leave."

"What about the baby?"

His hand gripped the arm of his chair. "If you are pregnant, which I doubt, Rob can claim the child. That baby has nothing to do with me."

"This baby has everything to do with you. It was conceived in love."

"It was a mistake." His voice broke.

He looked miserable, which prompted her to ask, "Why didn't you tell me you were married? You knew all about me." She wanted to reach across the desk and take his hand. She wanted to do anything to make this nightmare go away.

"We were in the middle of a divorce," he said. "There was nothing to tell."

"Well, yes, I think there was." Grace took control of the conversation. "I didn't know you were married and had two children."

His eyes were dark with accusation. "Would it have made any difference?"

"No." Her smile was weak. "I suppose not." She leaned forward. "We can make this work, Michael, we have a special bond. You're my soul mate."

He laughed so hard she thought he would upset the coffee cup on his desk. She could smell the mint in his mouthwash, his aftershave. "We're done here," he said.

"Michael." Her legs wavered, but she stood tall. He was in shock. He'd come around. He held the door open, his face twisted.

"I'll call you later," she smiled. "After you've had time to think things over."

"Doris, if Mrs. Buchanan isn't gone in three minutes, I want you to call Officer Blake." He turned and slammed the door.

Grace smiled at the secretary who had her eyebrows raised in a question. "Don't bother your pretty little head, Doris. I'm going."

Grace hummed as she walked to her car. "That was your daddy," she whispered. Smiling, she turned the key in the ignition. It could have been worse. But he'd come around. This was Rob's fault, after all. If she hadn't been married to Rob when she started her affair with Michael, she could have gone to Kansas with him, and he wouldn't have had to face his estranged wife alone. He wouldn't have had to make a choice, because he would have already picked her. Michael could protest all he wanted that their life together was over, but she knew better. This was just the beginning.

*   *   *

There'd been rumors about The Grove ever since townsfolk discovered a man named August Pearce hanging from a tree there more than a hundred years ago. It was a bad place, some said even haunted. One should stay away, be careful and not linger there. But that was before Jeremy took Abbie into the woods. Now the woods had a special meaning, or had, until they started playing that game.

Abbie and Jeremy were already at The Grove, snuggled in his car, enjoying each other's kisses when Charles and Sheila pulled up beside them.

"Hey," Charles said when Jeremy rolled down the window. Abbie didn't welcome the intrusion, but these were Jeremy's friends, and she made an effort to like them.

For a while they all sat in Jeremy's car. They passed around small talk like it was a bottle of beer until Sheila said, "It's my turn. I want to play."

Abbie held her breath and hoped it wasn't the game. But when Charles opened the trunk of his car and pulled out the rope, she knew. She looked to Jeremy, but he was already out of the car. Abbie hesitated. She could stay in the car, or she could follow.

Apparently, she hadn't made her feelings clear. He didn't know how much she hated this game, but she would tell him. When she stepped out of the car, he was waiting for her. When he offered his hand, she took it.

They walked into the grove and stopped at the hanging tree. This time Sheila put the rope around her neck and stepped onto the box. It looked easy enough, but Abbie's pulse quickened, imagining the danger there. Like before, Jeremy held the rope and like before, nothing bad happened.

"Who's next?" Charles said.

When it was Jeremy's turn, Abbie wanted to leave. Instead, they were standing under a tree holding a rope and playing a stupid dangerous game.

"Can we go?" Abbie said. "I need to study."

"What are you so afraid of?" Charles taunted.

"Nothing."

"Then stop bossing him around. You're not his mother."

Abbie looked at Jeremy expecting him to defend her, but he was silent. Was she really bossing him around? Did he really want to do this? She put her hands in her pockets and scrunched deeper into her coat.

"Ready?" Charles said as Jeremy tightened the noose around his neck.

"One." Sheila counted and Abbie kicked at the ground, looked back towards town, at anything except Jeremy and the tree.

Charles coiled the rope around his hands and tugged up the slack.

"Two."

Abbie inhaled.

"Three."

Abbie turned her back to the tree. She couldn't watch the rope tighten around Jeremy's neck. She wanted him down. Now.

"One."

"Two."

"Three."

"Four."

"Five."

Charles slackened the rope and Abbie ran forward as Jeremy fell to the ground. He twitched and moaned something Abbie couldn't understand. Trying not to panic, she bent over him until his eyes opened.

"Hey." Jeremy reached for her, and she kissed him with so much passion she thought they'd melt the snow.

"Abbie?" Charles held the rope.

"No."

"It makes you weightless," Sheila said. "It makes you see wonderful things."

Abbie grabbed Jeremy's hand. "Let's go."

"Nothing bad will happen," Sheila said. "We won't let it."

Her heart was pounding. This was the last thing she wanted to do. But Charles and Sheila kept pushing.

"Leave her alone," Jeremy said. "She doesn't have to if she doesn't want to."

"Well," Sheila said. "She doesn't know what she's missing. It's a supercharged high, and it doesn't cost a thing."

Abbie looked at Sheila. Other than the red marks on her face, Sheila seemed fine. Abbie turned to Jeremy. He looked okay. And there was Charles with that smug look on his face, as if she were afraid of her own shadow.

Maybe this would bring them closer. Instead of having a girlfriend so cautious she wouldn't cross a yellow line, he'd be proud of her willingness to try something new.

"Fine," she said. "Show me what I'm missing." Abbie stepped up on the box. She felt the rope tighten around her neck. She swallowed twice and tried not to freak out. She clutched Jeremy's hand but didn't feel any calmer when he squeezed back.

"One."

The rope was tighter.

"Two."

She inhaled.

"Three."

She kicked at the box and lost her balance. She flailed in the air, grabbing at the rope, trying to keep it from pressing so hard against her throat.

"Relax," Jeremy coaxed. "Abbie, relax. Don't fight it."

Abbie tried to stop twitching. She pretended she was swimming underwater. *Count, Abbie,* she said in her head. *One. Two. Three. You can do this.* Lightheaded. *Four.*

She woke in his arms, her head fuzzy from lack of oxygen.

"Hey, lover."

Tingly and dizzy, her throat burned. She reached up and touched his face, thankful to be alive. She let him kiss her, but made a promise. This was something she'd never do again, not even for him.

CHAPTER EIGHTEEN

MAXINE HAD A WAY OF surprising herself. She didn't think she'd miss Herb at all, but she did. Maybe it was the picking up after him she missed, or his loud snores that rattled the windows. She'd locked him out less than twenty-four hours ago and already the house felt different. She couldn't put her finger on it, but as she wandered through the silent house the next morning, something was off. And daydreaming about Larry only made her feel worse.

After her trip to Graceland, Maxine planned to sleep in. She planned to change a lot of things, but she was awake by six, standing in the kitchen waiting for the coffee to brew. Out of habit, she searched the refrigerator for something to put in Herb's lunch. She pulled out a loaf of bread and the package of bologna she'd left for him a week ago, still unopened. As she added mayonnaise to the bread, her hand stopped midair. She dropped the knife in the sink. *What was she doing?*

Before she put the bread away, Maxine popped two slices in the toaster. At the kitchen table with coffee and buttered toast, she began sorting the mail. As a rule, Herb never looked at the mail, even if she called something to his attention. But while she was gone, he littered the table with opened envelopes, leaving her to clean up another one of his messes. Everything was hodge-podged together. She couldn't tell bills from junk.

It took most of the morning to sort the papers. Bills paid, Maxine walked through the house trying to see it with new eyes. What a sorry collection of bric-a-brac. Even after removing most of Herb's things, the house still looked cluttered.

Following a lunch of potato chips and a grilled cheese sandwich, Maxine poked around the garage until she found a couple of boxes. Back inside, she started in the living room. Anything outdated was going to the yard sale at the Senior Center. Everything except the few heirlooms she had inherited from her mother, which didn't amount to much—an old coffee grinder that didn't work and a flower vase—Depression glass her mother called it—that always sat on her mother's dining room table filled with those awful plastic flowers turned gray with dust.

Even though Maxine hated the vase, once it became hers, she had a hard time parting with it. She threw the flowers out but shoved the vase to the back of the bookcase. Knowing it was there gave her a strange kind of comfort she couldn't explain. The grinder graced the top of the bookcase, partially hidden by variegated ivy and all but forgotten.

Maxine gathered the collection of salt and peppershakers she began years ago. Even the first pair that started the collection, a chicken and a rooster, a Christmas present from Herb. She was putting them into the box when the doorbell chimed. Halfway expecting Herb, Maxine opened the door with caution. "Oh, it's just you," she said when she saw Shirley. "Come in. Want some coffee?"

"No," Shirley said. "Can't stay. Running errands and wanted to drop these off." She handed Maxine a large envelope.

The pictures of Graceland turned out better than Maxine expected. "They look really good," don't they?" she said. "And you didn't even have to take them somewhere to have them developed."

"Nope," Shirley said. "Let me know if you want any duplicates or any different sizes. It's easy to do on my computer." She took the envelope from Maxine and pulled out a picture. "I liked this one so much I made it bigger."

"Modern technology." Maxine shook her head. She was looking at the picture of her and Su Linn by the music gates. "Thank you," she said.

"You're welcome. And once you're settled in, we expect you to join us for lunch again at the Center."

"Sounds good." Maxine smiled and waved goodbye to her friend.

She went to her bedroom and found a framed picture of Herb. She replaced the picture with the one of Su Linn and put it on the shelf where she could see it. "How you doing, Su Linn?" she said to the picture, then returned to her work.

It took Maxine most of the day to work her way through the living room. Every time she thought she was finished, she'd spot something else. An inlaid jewelry box she hadn't opened in years. The silver-plated teapot she found at a yard sale for Abbie so they could have afternoon tea. She put these items in the box. Then she took the Depression glass vase from the bookcase and added that, too.

Not bad, she thought as she glanced around the room. It was starting to look better. She went to the kitchen to refill her coffee cup and upon returning to the living room, went over to the box and retrieved the teapot. It didn't take that much space. She eyed her mother's vase and debated. Should she give it to Grace or Abbie, rather than throw it away? She knew for a fact the vase wasn't good enough for Grace. She'd toss it the minute Maxine shut the door.

Thinking about her daughter made Maxine flinch. She hadn't called Grace in a while, and she missed Abbie and wanted to give her the teddy bear she'd bought. But that meant a conversation with Grace, and every conversation with Grace grew into an argument. Today, she didn't have the energy.

Too tired to sort through any more clutter, Maxine sat on the sofa and turned on "Jeopardy!" While Alex Trebek read clues, Maxine pushed aside the pile of books she still had to look through, including a photo album containing pictures of when she and Herb were married. She opened the album to a picture of their wedding day. Instead of wearing a white gown with lace, Maxine wore her favorite dress, a simple pink sheath trimmed in white daisies. Instead of a veil, she wore a daisy chain. She drew her finger across her likeness, so thin, so pretty. In his father's suit, Herb was trim and fit, a real looker. No one, not even a psychic with a magnifying glass, could hold the lens over her image and detect that Maxine was three months pregnant.

She was on the way to the kitchen for another cup of coffee when she heard him pounding on the door. "Maxine, let me in."

"Go away."

He pounded harder. "I live here, too."

"Not anymore, you don't." She turned the television louder and went to the back of the house where she didn't have to listen. If he hadn't killed her fish, she might have let him in. If he hadn't destroyed her dreams, she might have relented. But she was tired of being taken for granted, so she waited. It took a while, and she thought the neighbors would call the police before he finally pulled out of the driveway.

"Good riddance," Maxine yelled at the door. "Go live with Grace. Maybe she's crazy enough to take you in."

*   *   *

Grace's stomach ached so she hit the button on the alarm and returned to her dream. She and Rob sat at the kitchen table. They had just finished a bottle of wine. He took a bite and said, "Grace, you make the best prime rib in Aspen Grove."

"That isn't true," she smiled.

He reached across the table and took her hand. "After dinner, I have something to show you." She loved his grin, the mischievous promise in his eyes. Warmth spread through her, a long slow burn.

He helped tidy the kitchen while she loaded the dishwasher. Then he poured two more glasses of wine and led her to the sofa where he gave her an envelope. She snuggled next to him, her head on his shoulder as she worked the flap open. His morning aftershave lingered, still heady, still strong enough to make her dizzy.

"What's this?"

"Open it and see," he smiled.

Inside, she found two plane tickets and a weekend package to Las Vegas.

"Oh, Rob." She could see a show. Order room service. Lie in bed all day long if she wanted. He carried her up the stairs to their bedroom where they made love. Afterwards, her head on his shoulder, she traced the hair on his arm with her fingers. They made love again. She ached between her legs and woke with the memory of their lovemaking.

Her eyes fluttered open. Hand on her stomach, Grace listened for the shower. The room was empty, the house quiet. She lay against the pillow, recalled her dream and felt guilty. She should have been dreaming about Michael and the baby.

Grace glanced at the clock. Late again. If she hadn't been working at Aspen Grove Realty, she wouldn't be pregnant. She wouldn't be moving. But, of course, it was too late for that. She'd already signed the lease; she'd already told Rob she wanted out. Grace dangled her feet over the edge of the bed. She'd have to press for a settlement large enough to support her until Michael came to his senses.

Calling in sick, Grace paced the silent house, fluffing pillows, adjusting pictures, and dusting windowsills. Sipping peppermint tea, she stood at the window and looked out onto the snowy street. Everything looked blue. Shivering, she closed the blinds and went to the kitchen. She hated this house. Abbie did, too, or she'd be home more watching TV or blaring that teeth-grinding music Grace hated.

Grace took her baby books to the living room and curled up on the sofa. "John," she said. "Jonathan Michael Lancaster. Christopher. Christopher Michael Lancaster." She closed the book and stared at the calendar. Six more months and they'd be a family.

She carried a fresh cup of tea from room to room, wondering what to take with her. She didn't want the pictures or the books. Nor the expensive porcelain collectibles. Settling on the silver candelabra, Grace went to her bedroom to pack. In a large suitcase, she put her perfume and her prettiest negligees. Added a winter sweater. The candelabra. No sense packing anything else. She'd be replacing her whole wardrobe soon. Except the shoes. Maybe she could pack some shoes. It could be months before her feet began to swell. Grace winced at a small cramp and sat down. She should have settled on a smaller suitcase and not one so heavy.

She sat on the bed and surveyed the room, her eyes stopping on the wedding picture and the copy of their marriage certificate Rob had so lovingly framed. She knew she should feel something—regret or relief—instead of the desperate need to run, to be finished with this disappointing marriage.

A hot shower made her more optimistic. "Hungry again?" she said to her baby. "You're making quite a fuss in there. Let's see what we can find." She stood with the door to the refrigerator open. Cheese. Milk. Bacon. She didn't want to cook and settled on an apple. She jumped when she heard her daughter's voice behind her.

"What's this?" Abbie said.

Grace turned, and the refrigerator door banged shut. "Where did you get that?"

"On the sofa."

Grace held out her hand. "Give it to me."

Abbie flipped through the book. "Baby names? Who's having a baby?"

Grace grabbed the book from Abbie's hands, tearing some of the pages. "Now look what you've done."

"Is this why you and Daddy are fighting? You want another baby?"

Abbie tapped her finger against her lip as if thinking. "Wait. Didn't Daddy have a vasectomy?"

Grace's hand went to her stomach, and Abbie's eyes grew wide. "You're pregnant?"

"No. I'm not." Grace grasped the back of the kitchen chair for support.

Abbie smirked. "Great job, Mom. I thought only teenage girls got pregnant."

"Abigail."

"What?"

Grace fumbled. "Please don't tell your father."

"Or what, you'll send me to my room without supper?" Abbie grabbed her backpack. "You discover the funniest things when you show up unexpected."

"Abigail. Wait. We have to talk."

"You don't have anything to say I want to hear."

Grace found herself screaming. "You're such an ungrateful child."

Abbie stopped and faced her mother. "Me? Dad gives you everything you want, and it's never enough. I hate the way you treat him. I hate you."

Grace slapped her daughter. "Not as much as I hate you." She put her hand over her mouth. What was she doing?

Abbie's eyes grew dark with anger. She held her hand to her cheek, an evil smile challenging. "Does Daddy know what you've been doing Mother, while he's working?"

Everything was out of control. Grace snapped back. "Does your father know what you're doing with that Jeremy boy?"

Abbie narrowed her eyes. "*What* am I doing with that Jeremy boy?"

"I've seen you. At school. The way you hold hands and kiss when you think no one is watching."

Abbie guffawed. "Are you stalking me?"

"If you keep it up, you're going to be sorry."

"Not as sorry as you're going to be when I tell Daddy about your new bundle of joy," Abbie said. "I feel sorry for that kid, having you for a mother."

"*This* child will love me, not criticize and bring grief the way you do."

"Good luck with that." Abbie left the house, slamming the door behind her.

Grace didn't fix dinner that night. Instead, she stopped at a Chinese restaurant for takeout and drove to her new apartment. She used the key her landlord gave her so she could measure the windows for drapes.

The smell of paint permeated the rooms, so strong it gave her a headache. But she was pleased to see that the living room and bedrooms were finished, the kitchen windows taped and prepped.

Grace opened her suitcase and took out the candelabra. Using a sealed five-gallon bucket of paint for a table, she sat on the floor and lit the candles. They threw a cozy glow onto the freshly painted walls. She tried to eat the fried rice, but the smell of paint was making her nauseous. Pushing aside her dinner, she read her fortune. *You will be embarking on a new adventure. Yes,* she smiled. She would.

She sat back and looked at the room, rubbing at an uncomfortable pain in her side. She'd put a sofa in the corner, a mirror by the door. It wouldn't be long now; in less than two weeks this would be her new home. And once the baby came, Michael would fall in love with her all over again.

Her bladder full, Grace stood. Her stomach twisted into cramps. By the time she reached the bathroom, Grace was crying.

*   *   *

Snow fell as Jeremy punched the car into second. Still upset over the fight with her mother, Abbie wished he would just keep driving clear to Canada, or even Mexico. He squeezed her hand, and she squeezed back. He never spoke about his own mother, but seemed to understand about hers. Sitting beside him, she felt safe, sheltered from the unhappiness floating around her like big black balloons. Here nothing could touch her, not even her thoughtless mother. Abbie moved closer to Jeremy, kissing the side of his face as he maneuvered the icy road that led to the foothills and The Grove. He bent his head and kissed her. When he stopped, she was going to show him how much she loved him.

He parked in their usual spot near the hanging tree and left the engine running. They kissed, and the windows fogged over, creating a snug cocoon. Coat unzipped, the heat from his body warmed hers. Her head on his shoulder, he stroked her hair. "Sorry about your mom."

Snow fell in huge fluffy flakes, creating a blanket around them. Time should stop, stay like this forever. "Jeremy?"

"What?" He kissed her neck, her mouth.

"I love you."

"I love you, too." This kiss was different, driving his words straight into her heart. She let him unfasten her bra, something he was getting good at doing with one hand. When he entered her, she was ready. He exploded, and she welcomed the closeness, the way he clung to her, the way she mattered. She lay beside him and held him tight. She'd waited all her life to feel this special and loved.

She was lying in his arms, her head against his shoulder. "What happened?" She touched a mark that ringed his neck. It was red, like a scratch, part of it healing, part of it a great black bruise.

His hand went to his neck. "Nothing." He reached for his shirt, pulling the turtleneck over his head to hide the abrasion. Her hand went to her own neck. Stupid question. She wore her own turtleneck for a week, waiting for the wound to heal.

The snow falling outside was deeper. If they didn't leave soon, they'd be stuck. And the thought of maneuvering five miles of snow in her boots, even if she was with Jeremy, was less than appealing. So even though they wanted to stay, Jeremy started the car and drove her home.

It had been a magical afternoon, one Abbie played over and over in her head like one of her grandmother's records. She tried to find a word for her feelings. Euphoric wasn't strong enough, and ecstatic sounded more like her mother. Enraptured, for sure. Passionately in love, totally, totally, totally. She would have called Heather, but she knew Heather was still mad at her, and she'd never understand.

Humming, Abbie pulled out her sketchpad. Thinking about the picture she drew of her mother and grandmother that never felt quite finished even though she'd turned it in with her portfolio, Abbie started over. This time she drew her grandmother in the foreground. Directly behind her, Abbie placed her mother. And then, in the empty space to the left, Abbie drew her own face, the small nose and wide-set eyes. She let her hair fall naturally instead of pulling it back in a ponytail, the way she did when she didn't want to fuss with it on weekends. She didn't do it consciously, but their smiles were all the same.

Abbie set her red pen down. In spite of their differences, they were connected. The picture proved it. In the drawing, Abbie could see everything good and everything bad. She had just given herself to a man, the way her mother did everyday in her search for love. And she had a temper, like her grandmother, strong-minded and strong-willed. But it was their eyes that completed the drawing and entwined them. There was no sadness there, no despair. Every set of eyes radiated happiness, hope and love.

Abbie put the sketch aside. Love set you on a precarious path unsure of each forward step. Unsure of anything except the hungry, hopeful craving inside your belly that never went away. She was starting to understand her mother better. It was a path she openly welcomed and looked forward to, every single day.

CHAPTER NINETEEN

JESSICA WAS STANDING NEXT TO Jeremy and Charles in front of Jeremy's locker. She moved closer to Jeremy as Abbie approached, touching him as if she owned him. "That works," she said. "Catch you later." She ignored Abbie as she tossed her hair and walked down the hall toward her friends.

"What was that all about?" Abbie could feel herself turn green.

"Nothing."

She raised an eyebrow, and Jeremy said, "Her water heater's broken. She wants my dad to fix it."

"Her parents don't have a phone?" Abbie recognized her mother's voice slipping over her tongue.

Jeremy shrugged. They held hands as they walked to class. She expected to feel different, more grown up after making love. But she didn't expect to feel like this. She looked over her shoulder, hating Jessica and grateful she was gone.

After school they drove out to The Grove, where they made love again, and talked about summer. They would win those art scholarships and go to San Francisco.

Her father would be proud.

His father might not let him.

As soon as he mentioned his father, Jeremy's mood changed. There was a determined look in his eyes she'd never seen before, and Abbie remembered the way he acted the night they tried to double date with Heather and Tyler. This was the other Jeremy, the one she didn't know.

He put on his coat and said, "Come on."

Reluctantly she opened her door. "Jeremy?"

"Back here." The trunk was open. He held a blanket, the wooden box, and a rope.

Abbie stopped short. "I---"

He handed her the rope. "Take this."

"No."

He picked it up and started to walk toward the tree.

"I'm not doing this," Abbie called. "And you wouldn't either. Not if you loved me."

He stared at her as if she were speaking Portuguese. "You're overreacting. Nothing happens but a good buzz."

She pulled his hand. "Let's go back to the car."

"I want to get high first," he said.

"You can't do that by yourself," Abbie yelled.

"Yes, I can."

No, you can't. Abbie waited in the car, sure he would follow. When he didn't, she waited a while longer, festering. How could he be so careless when he was so talented? He didn't need to get high to draw; that was just an excuse. Besides, she didn't think he could manage on his own. He'd need someone like Charles to hold the rope.

She searched for her cell to check the time. But her battery was dead. Fifteen minutes. Maybe twenty. She was cold and wanted to go home.

"Jeremy?" She stepped out of the car and called. When he didn't answer she walked toward the gnarled tree. *He'd better be ready to go.*

She screamed when she saw his body.

At the end of the rope.

It swayed as if a strong wind had picked that precise moment to stir the air and trees.

"Jeremy!" Abbie ran forward and grabbed his legs, thinking she could get him down. But he was too heavy. She couldn't lift him, or create enough slack in the rope so he could breath. She called his name as she tried to free him, but his weight put the rope in a bind, kinking it tighter.

"Stop it!" Abbie tried to loosen the knot he had tied around the tree trunk to secure the rope. Her fingers bled and burned.

Get him down.

NOW.

Abbie searched her pockets. Nothing sharp she could use. She looked toward Jeremy's car. *Too far.* Besides, she didn't want to leave him. He would die if she did.

"Jeremy! Help me!" Abbie kicked at the tree and tugged on the rope. She pulled the hemp with her teeth, spitting the course fiber away.

"JEREMY." She tried to lift his body to create enough slack in the rope so he could breathe. The muscles in her arms quivered.

Tired.

Arms burn. Fingers numb.

She lost her balance. Slipped, and fell headfirst into the snow.

Brushing ice from her mouth, Abbie screamed until her throat was raw. "SOMEONE. ANYONE. PLEASE." Her voice broke. "HELP ME."

Time stopped as she searched for the box. Placed it under his feet. Tried to get him to stand on the box. Didn't help. His body, slack now, had stopped swaying.

She stood on tiptoes. She stood on the box, gave a small hop, and fell. Up on the box and on tiptoes again, Abbie extended her arms over her head, trying to reach the rope around his neck.

Closer.

Closer.

Snap. Abbie tumbled to the ground.

The wind kicked up, cold and biting. "Breathe, Jeremy. Breathe." She couldn't stop screaming. Tears froze on her face as she searched his pockets. Finding nothing sharp, Abbie looked toward the car.

He would die if she left him.

He would die if she didn't get help.

She dropped the rope and ran.

*   *   *

Doubled over on the toilet, Grace winced at another cramp and recalled her dream. She and Rob. No baby. No separation, no divorce. Worried, she wished the cramping would stop. She could endure the pain, six months of bed rest if that's what it took. She wasn't religious, but closed her eyes anyway. "Please don't let me lose this baby."

When the pain subsided, Grace put her hand on her stomach. "Thank you." Throwing her uneaten meal away, she took one more walk through the apartment. The dresser would go here, the crib by that wall.

Back at home, Grace filled the bathtub and had just stepped out of her clothes when the telephone rang. She let it ring until the persistent noise made her angry. "Yes!" she shouted at the receiver, clutching the towel to her body. "This is Grace Buchanan. *What?*"

She didn't remember hanging up or getting dressed. She didn't remember grabbing her purse and keys, or driving to the hospital. She parked in a no parking area and ran into the building, grimacing at the slight catch in her side. "I'm Grace Buchanan. Foster," she said to anyone who would listen. "I'm looking for my father." She stopped every nurse she saw until she found one that could help.

"He's in surgery," the nurse said. "You can wait here."

Grace paced the small waiting room. Not her father. "Why is this happening to me?" she cried.

This was her mother's fault. Grace stopped crying and called her mother. "Pick up," she yelled. But the phone just rang, no matter how many times Grace redialed. In the waiting area, she sat alone and stared at the walls. There was no one else to call except Rob. He was there in less than ten minutes.

"How is he?" Rob dropped his coat on the chair beside her.

"I don't know," Grace said. "They won't tell me anything."

"Wait here," he said. "I'll see what's going on."

Grace watched him walk toward the nurse's station, too dazed and exhausted to follow. He returned with more information. "Drove into a telephone pole. They'll know more when he comes out of surgery. They think he may have had too much to drink."

She was crying again. Rob said, "Do you want me to call your mother?" She nodded and blew her nose.

"See," she said when her mother wouldn't pick up. "She threw him out. Now she won't answer the phone."

"Should I go get her?" His brow furrowed with concern.

"No. She doesn't care about him anyway." They stared at each other in silence.

"You know, Grace, you're more like your mother than you'd like to admit."

She raised a hand to slap him, but he intercepted the blow. "Maybe I made a mistake calling you," she said.

"Wouldn't be the first." He dropped her hand, and she wavered between anger and fear. She didn't want to fight with him, not now, but she hated his smug attitude. She didn't want to be alone, and she couldn't stop crying. In spite of everything, Rob held her as the minutes passed. Ten. Fifteen. An hour. She was feeling calmer when he said, "We should try your mother again. She needs to know."

"I'll do it." When her mother answered, all Grace could say was, "I hope you're proud of yourself. You finally got what you wanted."

*   *   *

Wondering why she hadn't heard from Helen or Shirley, Maxine picked up the phone and looked at the receiver. It was dead. Then she remembered. She'd unplugged the phone because it wouldn't stop ringing—Herb wouldn't stop begging to come home. She looked at the clock. It was late enough now, he'd be passed out somewhere. He wouldn't be calling anymore tonight. She plugged in the phone, turned out the light, and headed to bed. The phone rang as she walked down the hall. *Shit.* She picked it up.

"You don't live here," she yelled, "so stop calling." She paused when she recognized her daughter's voice. "Grace? Is that you?"

Grace sobbed, "I hope you're happy. You finally got what you wanted."

"Calm down. What are you blubbering about?"

"You, you stupid --- you killed Daddy."

"I did not." Grace was hysterical, but Grace always overreacted. Even as a toddler, she would fall and run for her father to kiss her boo-boos. Herb always obliged, tickling Grace until she rolled into a ball of laughter.

Kids.

Maxine glanced at the clock. Almost ten-thirty. Most nights, Grace was in bed before ten, getting her beauty sleep. Now she was incoherent, screaming on the other end of the phone.

"Grace, calm down and go to bed. Where's Rob?"

"Right here." Grace screamed in Maxine's ear.

Rob relayed the news. There was a wreck. "We don't know how bad it is," Rob said. "He's in surgery now. I can come and get you."

"No," Maxine said. It wasn't necessary. Grace was there. But later in the bedroom, when the shock started to register, Maxine sat on the bed and reconsidered. She didn't know if he was still alive, or dead. She could see Herb on a slab waiting for someone to claim his broken body.

This was something she couldn't put off on her daughter. Maxine reached for the telephone and dialed.

"Aspen Taxi," a raspy voice answered. One of these days, she was going to get her own car.

Herb. It was hard picturing him dead. She watched the traffic lights from the backseat of the taxi. He didn't have a will. They had no funeral plans, no money put aside for a service. Who would she get to serve as pallbearers? Befuddled, she rang her hands. She'd thought of this day many times, but not hard enough to envision the details.

It was close to eleven-thirty when Maxine arrived at the hospital. No pink lady met her to guide her to her dead husband, so Maxine searched the halls for help. At the end of the hall, she saw a nurse rolling a machine on wheels toward a patient's room.

"Excuse me," Maxine said. "I'm looking for my husband."

The nurse looked up. "What's his name?"

"Herb Foster. He was in an accident earlier tonight. My daughter called and said he was dead." Her voice faltered.

"I'm so sorry." The nurse pushed the machine against the wall and put her arm around Maxine. "Are you all right?"

Maxine nodded. Her head was full of cotton. She couldn't control her hands.

"Come with me. We have a room where we can talk." She led Maxine to a private sitting area where she asked again, "What was his name?"

"Herb Foster. Herbert Allen Foster," Maxine choked out his name, and her thoughts flashed to the day they married. *Do you, Herbert Allen Foster take Maxine Zelda Eklund to be your lawful wedded wife?* Squishing deeper into her chair, Maxine was a discouraged fraud. What began as a promising life, full of hopes and dreams, had turned into a huge disappointment. She swiped at the tears, angry, yet surprised she still cared so much about her husband.

"Wait here," the nurse said. "I'll see what I can find out."

Maxine looked around the room, at the picture of the white gazebo covered with wisteria hanging on the wall. At the *People* magazines scattered on the table. She settled on the goldfish in the aquarium, and her face puckered. Her fish were dead, just like her husband.

"Mrs. Foster?" the nurse said.

"Yes?"

"I found him. Please, come with me."

Maxine followed the nurse past two swinging doors into an area marked ICU. Inside the critical care unit the hospital felt more sterile. She could hear the whir of the machines and blanched. The last time she'd been in ICU was when Helen's husband suffered that fatal heart attack four years ago.

The nurse stopped in front of a room and opened the door. "He's in here. Stay as long as you like."

"Steady old girl," Maxine mumbled under her breath.

Inside the dimly lit room, she expected to find a body on a gurney, draped in a white sheet. She expected the smell of death to fill the room with grief and sadness. Instead, she found her husband hooked to an IV, his left arm in a sling. His bruised face was puffy. An oxygen tube stuck up his nose.

Wide-eyed, Maxine stared. The sonofabitch was still breathing.

CHAPTER TWENTY

MAXINE EXHALED AND APPROACHED the bed. She put her hand on Herb's chest to make sure she wasn't hallucinating. How long she stood like that, she didn't know. She didn't know where Grace was either, or why she'd left Herb all alone. The way Grace had called, crying and hysterical, Maxine expected to find her daughter stationed outside his room, making sure no one entered to steal his heart or kidneys.

Maxine glanced around the sterile room, wishing she were still in Graceland, dreaming of Elvis. But she wasn't in Graceland, and she was still his wife, so she plopped into the chair next to Herb's bed and watched him breathe, in and out like a baby drugged on mother's milk. He had a large bruise under his left eye where he hit the windshield or steering wheel. This wasn't his first accident, and it didn't look like it was going to be his last. The sounds of the machines lulled her to sleep. She woke the next morning when a nurse entered the room. Someone had covered her with a blanket.

"Good morning, Mrs. Foster," the nurse whispered. "Can I get you anything? Coffee? Juice?"

What she wanted, they didn't have. "Coffee."

Herb groaned and Maxine sat up. "What's wrong?"

"He's sedated," the nurse said.

"He almost died."

"Actually," the nurse said as she adjusted his IV, "his injuries aren't bad. I can have the doctor explain in more detail if you'd like."

What Maxine would have liked at that moment was to pull the pillow out from under Herb's head and hold it over his face. She'd push the pillow down tight until her anger drove every ounce of alcoholic breath from his body.

The nurse returned with coffee. "If you need anything else," she said, "I'll be at the nurse's station."

Maxine drank the coffee and watched her husband sleep. He hadn't always been a drunk. He didn't touch a single drop of alcohol when he was working for that football scholarship. He didn't start drinking until later, several years after they married.

Maxine sat in the chair and brooded over the past. She was still brooding when the doctor entered the room. He extended his hand. "Dr. Carver." He looked like he was twelve years old. How was she supposed to take anything he said seriously? But he was serious when he said, "His liver is enlarged. His labs suggest he's a heavy drinker."

"A little." Maxine waited outside the room while the doctor finished his examination. So this was how it was going to end. Instead of drinking himself to death, he'd keep having accidents until there was nothing left to destroy.

The doctor opened the door and patted her arm. "Your husband's going to be fine. He got lucky last night."

That's what you think, Maxine thought.

"We need to run more tests. His liver doesn't look good. We're going to keep him for a while."

Keep him forever, Maxine thought as she watched the doctor walk down the hall, turn the corner, and disappear. She jumped when Herb groaned.

"Hurts."

"Made a mess of things this time, didn't you?" she said.

"Need a drink."

"I need lots of things, but it looks like I'm not going to get them." Maxine waited a good amount of time before she poured a glass of water from the green plastic jug.

He waved it away. His body shook. "Want to go home."

She leaned in closer. "Don't always get what we want, do we?" Then she picked up her purse and moved away from the bed. "By the way, they're keeping you here until you dry out. I'm going home to finish cleaning up the mess you made while I was gone."

"Shouldn't have left." Herb winced.

Thirty years ago, Maxine might have felt sorry for him, banged up, black and blue, with his arm in a sling. But thirty years could wear you out. He could rot in that hospital bed for all she cared. "You think that's leaving?" She pushed on the door. "Watch this."

*   *   *

Grace and Rob stayed at the hospital until her father was stable. Sitting around the waiting room with worry wasn't doing any of them any good, least of all, Grace, who was so tired she was shaking.

"Go home," the doctor said. "If there's any change, we will call you."

Because Grace was so upset, Rob insisted on driving her home. Once there, he made sure she was steady before he went to bed. Things between them were still tense, but he had proved he was still her husband. He'd shown up as soon as she called. Unlike Michael, he at least answered his phone.

What promised to be a happy new year was deteriorating into chaos. First Michael, and now her father. Grace turned out the lights and slipped into bed. She was almost asleep when the pain started again. This time it didn't stop. Between the smell of paint and stress, the baby didn't have a chance. By the time Grace made it to the bathroom, she was passing blood.

Her periods were often painful, but never had she felt pain like this. Her whole stomach was on fire; all her expectations quickly gushed away.

When the pain subsided, Grace had to deal with the mess. She could have asked Rob to take her to the emergency room, but then she'd have to explain. Better to take care of it herself.

Shaking and light-headed, she mopped the floor with a towel. She used Lysol, even though it made her sick. She cried as she scrubbed, "I'm sorry, baby." *I'm sorry.* The last thing she wanted to do was clean, but she scrubbed at a spot on the floor until her face was dry. "It's not the end of the world," she said. "You can have another." But, of course, she knew that would never happen.

Naked and sticky, Grace stepped into the shower. She let the water run until she was numb. Hearing the water, Rob opened the door. "Grace," he said, "are you okay?"

She made her voice sound calm. "Just tired. Go back to bed." She didn't step out of the shower until she was certain she was alone. Then, exhausted and smelling of soap, Grace crawled into bed. Whenever a thought circled her head—what she should wear in the morning, what she would tell Michael and Rob, what she should do about her father—she pushed it away, unwilling to think about her dark and empty future. Her hand went to her stomach, now empty, too.

* * *

Abbie couldn't feel her fingers. She couldn't feel her toes, or her hammering heart either. Everything around her had stopped. The wind. The snowflakes. Her future. She put the key in the ignition. The engine wouldn't engage.

Abbie pounded on the steering wheel. "Start, damn it." Crying so hard she couldn't see the trees or the road, she lay on the horn. Panicked and shaking, she got out of the car, took a few steps and stopped. She was his only chance. She would drive that car, no matter what.

She tried again. This time she kept her foot down instead of jerking away every time the engine lurched. "Keep your foot on the clutch," she prompted in her father's voice, the way he did when he taught her to drive the riding lawnmower. "Steady. There you go." After a few false starts, Abbie shifted into first and inched down the hill toward town.

As the windshield wipers beat at the falling snow, Abbie stepped on the gas. The car fishtailed, pulling her toward a snow bank. Easing up on the pedal, Abbie overcorrected and the car slid toward a drop-off. She hit the gas again and the car spun in circles, almost hitting the guardrail.

The adrenaline rush triggered by fear stopped her tears. It took a steady hand and driving slower to keep the car on the road. She wanted to go faster, but she held back, guiding the car over the ice.

She could see the lights in the distance. Her first thought was to get her father. But that was clear across town on the other side of Aspen Grove. Her grandmother was closer, but that would be a waste of time.

Clutching the steering wheel, Abbie maneuvered another icy corner. Unable to see, she lowered the window. But that didn't help; the snow falling inside the car only made her shiver more. A hundred thoughts raced through her head. *Taking too long. Going too slow. Jeremy, hold on.*

The car slid again, but she was closer, nearing the bottom of the hill where the road straightened out into a long narrow ribbon. Now she'd make better time. Accelerating, the car fishtailed and stalled. She cranked the key in the ignition until she smelled gas.

Abbie stood by the side of the car and looked into the night. She'd have to walk, but wasn't sure which way to go—back to Jeremy, or on to Aspen Grove.

She walked a mile, maybe two, before she saw the lights again. A farmhouse, not far from the road. Running as fast as she could on the ice, Abbie fought her way toward the lights. She fell once, twice, even more, but got up and kept going. By the time she reached the porch, her hair froze in strings to her face.

"Help." She pounded on the door. "Help." She hammered until someone answered.

"What's wrong?" A gray-haired man in a plaid shirt and faded jeans held the door open. "Come in. Come in. Get out of the storm."

Abbie wouldn't budge. "My boyfriend." She pointed to the road, incoherent as she tried to pull the man outside and explain.

"Hold your horses, young lady. Just hold on."

"Henry?" A woman appeared behind him. "Who is it?

"Good, Lord," she said when she saw Abbie. "Get in here out of the weather."

"Please," Abbie sputtered. "He's in the tree."

"Ellen," the man grabbed his coat. "Call the sheriff. Tell him there's some trouble down at The Grove.

"Come on." He clutched his keys. "Show me where you left your friend."

They made better time in his truck. It didn't slip or slide on the road like Jeremy's Camaro.

"There," Abbie pointed. "Up there. Hurry." She was out of the truck before he killed the engine.

"Oh, my God." The man pointed his flashlight at the tree. He shoved the light at Abbie. "Hold this."

She tried to keep the light steady while he untied the knot and lowered Jeremy to the ground. He felt for a pulse. "What were you doing?" He took the flashlight from her and his voice softened. "Come, we can wait in the truck where it's warm."

"I'm not leaving." Abbie wrapped her arms around Jeremy's neck. She covered his face with kisses. "I'm sorry," she sobbed. "I'm so sorry."

"Miss." The man took her arm. "You'll freeze out here."

Abbie tried to hold onto Jeremy's neck, but the man was stronger. When the sheriff arrived she was sitting in the truck staring dumbly at the tree.

A female deputy wrapped a blanket around Abbie's shoulders and waited with her while the sheriff checked the scene. Cameras flashing. Sirens. Someone yelling. A lot of people moving around in the snow.

Returning to the truck, the sheriff said, "He's gone. How's the girl?"

"In shock," the deputy said.

"Who are you?" the sheriff asked the man.

"Les Brown. I live at the bottom of the hill."

After questioning the man, the sheriff turned his attention to Abbie. "What were you doing out here?"

She flinched at the sound of the siren, the flashing lights. A floodlight. Strangers talking. A flurry. A flash.

"Where are your friends?" the sheriff asked. Abbie's head was foggy. "What?"

"Your friends, where did they go? Looks like they left in a hurry."

What did he say? Was he there to help? She sat inside a strange vehicle, cold even though the heater rattled full blast.

"Your name. Can you tell us your name?" the female deputy prompted. "And where we can find your parents."

Abbie shook. She couldn't get warm.

"Who helped you put him in the tree?" the sheriff said.

"Nobody."

"Then how do you explain all those tracks?" He pointed to the road where she'd lost control of the car.

"What were you doing?"

"A game," she whispered.

"What kind of a game? Were you trying to kill him?"

Abbie looked at the sheriff. "What?" *Where was the nice man with the truck? Where was her father? Jeremy? Where was Jeremy?*

The coroner left, and the ambulance with Jeremy locked inside was pulling away. "No." Abbie screamed until she had no voice, until she was nothing.

She couldn't remember the ride to town in the patrol car. The flashing lights and siren had stopped. The one thing that hadn't stopped was her heart; it continued to beat while Jeremy's stayed silent.

They put her in a small room at the police station and asked more questions.

"Were you drinking?"

"No."

"Did you have a fight?"

"No."

"Why were his shoes lying in the snow?"

"Huh?"

Again and again.

"Who helped you put him in the tree? Where are your friends?"

Abbie stared at her hands, cut and bruised. She had no answers.

The sheriff pressed harder. "Did you let him die on purpose? Why didn't you help him?"

"I tried," Abbie whispered. *When had she entered this awful dimension?* She wanted to return to yesterday, to the first time he kissed her.

The sheriff left the room and the female deputy said, "We should call your parents. "What's your number?"

Abbie couldn't remember. She could barely remember her name.

They were still asking questions when her father appeared. When Abbie saw him, she cried. "Oh, Daddy. I killed Jeremy."

When her father tried to console her, the sheriff said. "Please have a seat, we have a few more questions." Then he asked Abbie, "Was this your idea?"

"No."

"Where did you get the rope?"

"It was Jeremy's."

"What were you---"

"Could you be a little kinder?" her father said.

"I know this is hard," the sheriff said. "She can answer my questions, or spend the night in Juvie." He laced his fingers together and put his hands behind his head and leaned back in his chair as he waited for an answer. Her father pulled his chair closer and held Abbie's hand. She did her best, but she couldn't remember.

What had happened?

The rope was too tight?

Did she place the rope around his neck? No.

What did she do when he passed out? Panicked. Screamed. Froze. Ran.

They questioned her for another hour and finally released her. Her father didn't scold. He didn't tell her she was a spoiled brat. "We'll get this figured out in the morning," he said. "Don't worry."

But Abbie did worry, all the way home. On top of everything that had happened, she kept hearing her mother's chiding voice. *You're going to be sorry.*

CHAPTER TWENTY-ONE

ABBIE'S HEAD WAS FUZZY from the sleeping pill her father insisted she take. Now he stood by her bed, concern etched in his face. She wanted to slip back into her dream and Jeremy's arms.

Jeremy?

Her eyelids flickered wide as she remembered. She started to shake and cry again.

"Come downstairs," her father said quietly. "We need to talk."

She wanted him to hug her and call her Pumpkin. To tell her everything would be all right. He did neither, but waited at her door, looking old for a man in his forties.

She swallowed her tears and followed him to the kitchen where her mother sat at the table, staring into her empty cup. Her mother's face was ashen, her hair unkempt. She looked up when Abbie entered the room.

Here it comes. Abbie wanted to bolt. "I can't do this."

Her father pointed to a chair. Abbie searched his face for his usual kindness, but his stance was stoic so she sat down.

"You ungrateful brat." Her mother stood and slapped Abbie's face. "While your grandfather lies in a hospital bed fighting for his life, what are you doing?"

Her father put his hand on her mother's shoulder. "Sit down."

"I will not sit down." Her mother shouted. "Things aren't bad enough? Our daughter puts a rope around a boy's neck?"

"Did not," Abbie said. Her voice cracked.

"Stop it, both of you." Her father raked his hand through his disheveled hair. "We have a lot to sort out. Casting blame isn't helping."

"Your daughter needs to know that actions have consequences." Her mother took a glass from the cupboard and opened a bottle of wine.

"Consequences?" Abbie said. "Consequences? Daddy, did you know—"

"Abigail Lynn." Her mother's face twisted, red and threatening.

Standing at the counter, his arms folded over his chest, her father looked defeated. "I know your mother spent her evening thinking her father was dead."

It took several seconds for his words to register. "Grampa's dead?" Abbie fell back in her chair.

"Like you care, you selfish, spoiled—"

"Grace, stop it." Abbie's father leaned against the cupboard, his arms crossed over his chest. "There was an accident. Your grandfather is in the hospital."

"He's critical." Her mother's voice broke.

Abbie whispered. "Gramma?"

"Your grandfather could be dead for all you care."

Abbie's father raised his voice. "Oh, for God's sake, Grace, shut up. Your father is a drunk, but he's still alive. Your daughter just watched her friend die."

Her mother opened her mouth, then closed it, biting back whatever she wanted to say.

Abbie was crying again. "Grampa?" Abbie looked at her father. "Is he going to be okay?"

Her father nodded. "I think so." There were dark circles under his eyes. "We can see him later. First we need to talk about what happened last night."

"What were you thinking?" her mother said. "Playing a stupid game like that." Her mother was so cold, so righteous, *so mean.* Abbie bit her lower lip to stop its quivering.

Still standing, her father said, "How many times have you played this game?"

He said 'game' as if it was forbidden, like sex or drugs.

Her voice shook as she tried to explain. Only once. It was stupid. She wasn't strong enough. Yes, it was a dangerous thing to do. They talked for more than two hours, her father acting as referee whenever her mother's voice rose or became demanding. He ended the conversation by saying, "Get dressed. They want us at the police station. When we finish there, we'll go see your grandfather."

"I'm not going to the police station," her mother said and pushed away from the table. "I'm going to the hospital to check on my father."

Good. The last thing Abbie wanted was her mother making another scene.

Abbie's father grabbed her car keys and dropped them into his pocket. "You're in no condition to drive."

"Then I'm going to take a shower." Her mother stomped up the stairs and slammed her bedroom door.

The next four hours blurred by, more miserable than a blizzard, more terrifying than a blazing hell. After extensive questioning, the police said there would be no charges. It wasn't a homicide, just an unlucky accident. As they were leaving the police station, the sheriff handed Abbie's father a card. "Be good if she talked to a professional. I can't mandate therapy, but I strongly recommend it."

"Thank you," her father said. Abbie grabbed the card and crumbled it into a ball. Talking wouldn't change the fact that Jeremy was dead.

Later, they stopped at the hospital. Abbie was all but catatonic. A plastic smile was frozen to her face. Her grandfather looked frail, dead even, lying in his bed hooked up to the thousands of tubes and wires curtaining him like a web. Still in ICU, he was allowed limited visitors, family, but only one at a time.

When it was Abbie's turn, she sat by his side and whispered. "Hi, Grampa. It's Abbie." She tried to hold his hand in spite of the IV. It was cold, like Jeremy's. Tears flooded her cheeks and her voice broke. "Get better soon."

Her parents were waiting outside the door. Her mother went in and closed the door. Her father put his arm around Abbie's shoulder. "Let's see if we can find something to drink."

When they returned, Abbie's mother was standing in the hallway. Unsteady on her feet, she looked like she could collapse any minute. Abbie's father put his arm around her and said, "Come on, Grace. We can come back later." She expected her mother to pull away, but she didn't. She let him lead her back to the car. Once home, Abbie fell into bed exhausted, her head full of accusations, her heart bruised and broken.

All she wanted to do was sleep because awake she had to remember. Denying didn't work in daylight, but under the covers, alone in her bed she could pretend Jeremy was still there, smiling and coaching her fingers across the paper. For days, she walked around too dazed to eat. Her parents didn't make her go to school. Her father even took time from work to help cook and clean. He fed her mother sleeping pills when she needed them and comforted Abbie when she cried. Whenever they needed anything, he was there to lend a hand or chase away the tears.

The day of Jeremy's funeral, Abbie's father stood at her side, strong and steady. Her mother refused to go, saying, "I'm not trudging through the snow so everyone can point and say, 'There goes the mother of a murderer.'" She made it known that *she* wasn't standing in the cold mourning someone she didn't know when her own father was dying. Even in shock, Abbie was relieved. It would be easier if her mother stayed away.

Bundled against the weather, Abbie hugged Charles at Jeremy's grave. "I should have been there," he said, which only made Abbie cry harder.

"I'm sorry." Sheila wrapped her arms around Abbie, but Abbie didn't return the embrace. If it hadn't been for friends like Charles and Sheila, Jeremy might still be alive.

She was surprised to see Heather and Tyler standing toward the back of the gathering, which was small. They didn't come forward to speak, and Abbie didn't approach them. She desperately wanted to hug Heather, to have her best friend's comfort once more.

A slight woman Abbie learned was Jeremy's mother stood near Jeremy's father. Her hair was dark like Jeremy's, and she looked as stunned as Abbie felt. Her glassy eyes met Abbie's briefly. She sobbed when they lowered the casket.

Another woman Abbie recognized as Jeremy's aunt stood next to Jeremy's father. When she saw Abbie, she looked right through her, as if Abbie were responsible for the loss of such a fine and gifted son and nephew. *How dare you show your face? How dare you mock our sorrow?*

Abbie and her father stood beside the grave long after Jeremy's family drove away. The white rose Abbie brought to put on his coffin was still in her hand. She glanced behind her. Heather and Tyler were no longer there.

"Abbie," her father urged, "we need to go."

She placed the flower on his grave. "I'm sorry," she whispered. "I will love you, always." Her voice broke when she added, "for forever."

On the way home, her father said, "Hungry?"

"No."

"You have to eat."

If she had her way, she'd never eat again.

That night alone in her room, Abbie changed into her pajamas and crawled into bed. She pulled the covers over her head and cried until her pillow was wet, until her face burned. She lay awake all night and looked at the ceiling. If only they hadn't gone to The Grove. If only she had stayed by his side. If only she had gotten help faster. She didn't want to live without Jeremy knowing that the rest of her life would be filled with "if onlys".

*　　*　　*

Grace's life was a pitiful shambles. No God in his right mind would make her suffer so much grief and humiliation. Or take away the baby she was starting to love. She would have come apart if it wasn't for Rob. He'd been a rock, dropping everything to sit with her while her father had surgery. Rob was the one who took her home and put her to bed, sitting beside her until she fell asleep. He fixed her breakfast and called her office to tell them she wouldn't be coming in for a while. She didn't know how she would have made it through the week without him at her side.

He was the one who took care of Abbie when Grace could barely get out of bed. Yes, Abbie was grieving. But Grace was grieving, too. She felt sorry for her daughter, but there was no way she could attend Jeremy's funeral without thinking about her own loss.

Without Rob, Abbie might have ended up in jail. Or worse. He went to the hospital every day to check on her father and returned with a full report. Then drove across town and made sure her mother had everything she needed.

Rob did all of this without knowing what Grace's body was doing. While he was checking on her father, her stomach was cramping. She was still passing blood. Emotionally, she knew the miscarriage was for the best, but physically, her body felt like she was riding a rollercoaster. If it didn't stop, she'd have to make a doctor's appointment, and that was the last thing she wanted to do. So she stayed in bed and took it easy. She slept so she didn't have to think or remember. Rob thought she was upset about her father. Little did he know. It took several days for Grace to feel better. Still queasy and unsteady, she finally felt strong enough to see her father.

She hated hospitals, the floral scent piped through the air vents to mask the smell of sickness and death. Stopping at the nurse's station, Grace learned he was still in ICU. The door to his room was closed. Grace pushed it open and whispered, "Daddy?"

He looked like he'd been run over by a semi, instead of just hitting a telephone pole. His arm was in a sling. His left leg elevated. His face was bruised and unshaven.

"Daddy?" She gave him a little shake, and then jumped when a nurse entered the room.

"He's sedated, but you can stay as long as you like." The nurse motioned to a chair. After the nurse left, Grace pulled her chair closer to the bed and held her father's hand.

He looked awful. His body quivered in short tiny spasms.

"Daddy. Please wake up. I need you." She cried and held his hand for an hour. "There's this man. Michael. I think I love him. But Daddy, he's married and has two kids. He doesn't love his wife, Daddy. He loves me. What am I going to do?" Grace blew her nose.

The outing helped, and the talk she had with her father cleared her head. But it wore her out. At home in front of a fire, Grace poured a glass of wine while she waited for Abbie and Rob to come home. She closed her eyes and savored the Merlot, knowing it could no longer hurt the baby.

The baby. She wanted to tell her father, but she was afraid of what he would say. God forbid she should tell her mother. Grace knew what *she* would have to say about that.

In the kitchen, Grace searched the cupboards and refrigerator. She returned to the living room with a slice of cheese. She poured another glass of wine, just enough to make her sleepy. She had another. And another, until she fell asleep and the bottle was empty.

*   *   *

"How is she doing?" Maxine's hand shook as she gripped the receiver. She remembered all too well the day Larry died. This was something Abbie would never get over.

"She's hanging in there." She heard Rob take a deep breath. "It isn't easy."

Tears streamed down her face. "I know. Is there anything I can do?"

"No," he said. "I don't think so."

"Well, give her my love. Tell her I'll be over tomorrow to see her."

"Thanks, Maxine. I will. How are you holding up?"

"I'm tough," she said. "Don't worry about me. You have your hands full." She blew her nose. "Is Grace feeling any better?"

"I think so. I'll tell her you called. Oh, and Maxine? If you need a ride to the hospital, just let me know."

"Thanks," she said. "I will." But she avoided the hospital for three more days. By then, the house was clean enough to put on the market, not that she was going to sell and move away. She'd always thought she'd enjoy being alone, but as she pushed the dust rag over the furniture, Maxine realized she missed Herb's whistle and the way he yelled at the television. Every time she passed Su Linn's picture, she sang, "Steadfast, loyal and true," remembering how Su Linn sang with the movie on the bus. She wondered how Su Linn was doing and hoped she'd get a letter soon.

When she could put it off no longer, Maxine asked Shirley to drive her to the hospital. Rob had enough to do. Her heart was conflicted: she truly wanted to hate Herb, but her conscience wouldn't let her. So, instead of going to his room, she stopped at the nurse's station. "I'm Maxine Foster," she said. "Checking on my husband."

The nurse at the desk said, "Who's your husband?" She chewed gum and reminded Maxine of Abbie. Hospital employees were sure getting young, or she was just getting old. "Herb Foster." She hoped the girl was old enough to read a chart.

"He's much better," the nurse said with a smile. "Your husband is remarkable."

Maxine fumbled with her purse. Herb was many things, but nothing she'd call remarkable.

Dr. Carver, who had stopped by the nurse's station, recognized her. "Mrs. Foster? Nice to see you again. How's your husband this morning?"

"Don't know," she said. "On my way to see him now."

"I'll walk with you," the doctor said. "He's a lucky man. There for a while it was touch and go. Temperature spikes. Rapid heartbeat.

Hallucinations. I think he's through the worst of it." He put his hand on Maxine's shoulder. "Your husband will need therapy for that leg. I think we can release him tomorrow. Are you ready to take him home?"

Hell, no. Missing him was one thing. Having him underfoot yelling, "Where's that beer, Maxine?" was something else. "What if I don't want to take care of him at home?" Maxine said.

"That's understandable. He's going to need a lot of help. We can move him into transitional care or a nursing home until he's more mobile," the doctor said.

"Send him to the nursing home," Maxine said. "If he falls, I can't lift him."

"I agree." They stopped in front of Herb's room. "We'll let Riverview know he's coming." The doctor left Maxine to break the news to her husband.

No longer in ICU, Herb now shared a room with a younger man hooked to oxygen. Herb was sitting up in bed watching television. His face was shaved, the bruise on his face almost gone. Maxine walked into the room and for a moment they stared at each other, neither sure of what to say.

"You can't come home," she blurted when she found her voice. "Until you can walk. Tomorrow they're sending you across the street to Riverview."

"I don't want to go to Riverview," Herb said.

"You should have thought about that before you tried to run up that pole." The man in the next bed gave her an unsympathetic glare. Maxine walked over and pulled the privacy curtain to block his gawk.

"Maxy?"

"What?" He never called her Maxy. That was Larry's nickname for her. His eyes met hers, pleading.

"No."

She held his gaze until he looked away. His nose tube was gone, the puffiness leaving his face. In that hospital bed, Herb looked like a broken old man in desperate need of some good old-fashioned home cooking. Backing away, Maxine whispered under her breath. "No." She hurried from the room before she changed her mind.

She didn't visit him again until they moved him into Riverview. He needed something to wear besides a drafty hospital gown, so Maxine stopped by to drop off his clothes. After getting his room number at the front desk, she lumbered down the hallway. Wasn't bad for a nursing home. At least it didn't smell like a hospital.

When she reached his room, she pushed the door open. The private room with one bed was empty. Instead of putting his clothes away, Maxine wandered into the hall and followed the aroma of cinnamon rolls and coffee. Walking the corridor, Maxine wondered where Herb was. Probably in the kitchen, drinking vanilla extract. Or rubbing alcohol, if an aide was stupid enough to leave it sitting around. She stopped when she heard his laughter.

Turning a corner, Maxine entered a large room. There she found bookcases filled with paperbacks, a television blaring in a corner, and her husband seated across the table from a blue-haired woman playing checkers, a game he used to play with Grace when she was little.

"You're so funny, you clever little devil." The woman slapped his hand and tittered as he tried to claim one of her red checkers. "Got me this time," she said. "But I'll get you next."

It had been a long time since Maxine had seen Herb with another woman. This one gazed at him, doe-eyed, a warm blush on her cheeks. She looked ridiculous with her blue hairdo and red lipstick, as if she was going out to a fancy dinner. Maxine hated the way her pink blouse flattered her small face. She'd like to rip it to pieces and wrap it around her pretty little neck.

Keep your hands to yourself, Maxine almost said when the woman touched his arm. *You wouldn't want him if you saw him passed out on the toilet.*

Self-conscious in her baggy sweats and old T-shirt, Maxine walked over and stood by the table where Herb played checkers. "Brought your clothes." She enjoyed the look of surprise on the blue-haired woman's face.

"Maxine," Herb said. "This is Lucy. She's beating me at checkers."

"No, I'm not," the woman tittered. "He's teaching me. He's so smart, he can do anything." Lucy blinked several times and giggled.

That's what you think, Maxine thought. She turned to her husband. "Where do you want these?"

"In my room." He studied the checkerboard. "We can take them there after Lucy beats me."

"I'll take them there myself." Maxine huffed her irritation. She wanted to drop his clothes on the floor and go home, but she wasn't about to leave him alone with that blue-haired floozy. She sank into a nearby sofa and picked up a magazine.

Thumbing through the articles, Maxine pretended to read, but she was watching Herb. He'd lost weight. His face was thin, clean-shaven, and he vaguely reminded her of the man she married.

"Stop that." Lucy slapped Herb's fingers and laughed.

Maxine dropped her magazine and walked over to the table. "I have to go."

"Excuse me, Miss Lucy. Duty calls." Herb tipped an imaginary hat to the woman and turned his wheelchair away from the table. His arm was still in a sling so he struggled. If she'd been a better wife, she would have helped him. Instead, she followed Herb down the lime-green halls as he rolled the wheelchair to his room. Using one arm, he didn't do bad considering his foot kept bumping into the wall. When they reached his room, he said, "You can put those in that dresser over there." He pointed to a small chest under the window.

"I can, can I?" Maxine dropped them on the bed and surveyed the room. One window. A small television. A bathroom with a shower. It wasn't home. She wouldn't want to live there. But she doubted Herb knew the difference. In fact, he seemed to like it, and why not? A staff to feed him and do his laundry. A lonely old floozy to laugh at his jokes.

Herb motioned to a chair near a small desk. "Open that drawer and bring out those chocolates."

He was giving orders again so he must be feeling better. She handed him the box. He opened the lid, took out a chocolate and gave the box to her. "Have one."

"Where did you get these?" Maxine looked over the assortment before she selected a chocolate square, hoping for caramel inside. She took a bite. It was.

"Lucy. Says I need fattening up."

"Humpf." Maxine started to spit out the candy, but swallowed it instead. She didn't have to deny herself just because the woman was love-struck.

"The doctor has some papers you need to sign." Herb opened the top drawer of the desk. "Insurance forms."

Maxine squeezed her eyes to read the tiny print. "Didn't bring my glasses. I'll have to take them home." Thumbing through the papers, Maxine stopped at a sketch of Abbie. Herb used to draw wonderful pictures. He had more patience than anyone she knew. When Abbie was small, he'd sit beside her and guide her tiny fingers for hours over the paper. Maxine smiled at the girl in the picture.

Wait. That wasn't Abbie. Maxine held the drawing closer. "I always liked that dress." She put the picture down because her hand was shaking.

"I always liked you in it."

She looked at her husband. He wasn't drunk. He wasn't joking. She felt a flutter in her stomach, remembering how hard he had worked to make her laugh when they were dating. There was a time when he would do anything for her, even gave up that football scholarship to provide for the baby she carried. Maxine stuffed the papers into her purse. "I have to go."

There was an awkward silence. "Maybe you can stay longer next time." Although it was hard for him to maneuver, Herb moved closer and tried to kiss her on the cheek. "I miss you, Maxy."

She gave him a brief hug. By the time she reached Shirley's car, Maxine's face was twisted tight with emotion.

CHAPTER TWENTY-TWO

WHEN THE FIRST WEEK of February arrived, Grace was no more ready to move into her new place than fly to Jupiter. What she hoped would be the best month ever, turned gloomy and cold. The refrigerator she had planned to fill with Michael's favorite foods was empty, as were the cupboards. To make matters worse, she no longer had a job at Aspen Grove Realty. Kent needed someone more reliable. Grace didn't care. She didn't want to work for someone who couldn't be flexible. In truth, she didn't want to work at all. So, instead of moving out, Grace refocused on her marriage.

She'd read in one of her women's magazines that she shouldn't make major decisions under stress, like the death of a spouse. Her spouse hadn't died, but he may as well have been dead for all the attention he paid her. Once the crisis with Grace's father passed, Rob was back to his old habits, working late hours and falling asleep at his desk. He didn't mention the fight or the separation. Believing fate had handed her a second chance, Grace determined to turn her life around.

After a visit to her hairdresser and a fresh manicure, Grace went shopping. She picked out a smart outfit, gray fitted slacks, and a lacy top that emphasized her bosom, which was no longer sore. In fact, she'd had her period and her body was returning to normal.

She had a facial to relax the lines around her eyes, hoping that would make her look younger. When the beautician handed her a mirror, Grace smiled. Not bad for forty-three.

On the way home, Grace stopped by the florist and selected a spring bouquet. The house was too dreary, needed more color. Before summer, she'd have the walls repainted and move the furniture. Pick out new carpet.

She spent the afternoon fixing Rob's favorite dishes. Disappointed to get his voice mail when she called the dealership, she left a message. "Don't be late. I'm planning something special for dinner."

She was even in a good mood when Abbie got home from school. "Hi, honey," she said. "How was your day?"

"Awful." Abbie clomped up the stairs. Grace heard the bedroom door slam. She should follow, but this was a special night. Dinner had to be perfect. So instead of chasing her daughter, Grace went back to the kitchen and her dinner preparations.

They were seated around the dining room table like in a Norman Rockwell painting. Prime rib instead of turkey. Carrots *and* celery. Scalloped potatoes instead of mashed. Her best china and linen napkins. *Nice*, Grace thought as she sipped the red wine.

"How was school today?" Rob asked as he passed the potatoes.

"Fine."

"Do you have a lot of homework to make up?"

"Not much."

"Are you drawing again?"

"No." Abbie pushed the carrots around on her plate.

Grace smiled. "You don't have to eat if you're not hungry."

Abbie looked up. "Can I be excused?"

"Of course," Grace said. "I'll save you a piece of cheesecake. Rob, another glass of wine?" She rose and took Abbie's plate to the kitchen.

Rob nodded. "Nice dinner, Grace. What's the occasion?"

She refilled their glasses. "Maybe I just wanted to spend some quality time with my family." She tugged at his hand, but he quietly pulled it away. "Come. Sit with me by the fire. I'll be glad when we're done with this dreary weather. I envy the Petersons. We should get a place in Yuma so we can go south for the winter.

"Rob?" In spite of all her hard work the evening wasn't going as planned. It was flat, unexciting. Strangers going through the motions. He worked on his book while she cleaned up the kitchen. "Come to bed?" Grace poked her head into his office when she was finished and the dishes were put away.

"In a minute." He shrugged her off and went back to work.

She took a shower and put on her prettiest negligee. Tonight would be a new start. They were done with sleeping apart; she'd make sure of it. When he didn't come to bed, she padded down the stairs. "Rob?" Grace opened the door to his office. He was curled up on the sofa, sound asleep.

So much for passion or red-hot desire. So much for a new beginning. Grace stood a long time watching him sleep. He didn't move, not even when she called his name. When she shut the door, her eyes were dry and her future decided. She was done trying to make him love her.

                    *   *   *

February was just another month without Jeremy. Another month to fight with her mother, worry about her grandfather, dodge odd looks from the kids at school and try to meet her father's expectations. Abbie didn't deserve his respect or adoration. She deserved to be hanging from a tree. Sitting on her bed holding Jeremy's picture, Abbie reflected over the last six months. Everything had gone wrong, beginning with the summer art scholarship.

Abbie opened her bottom dresser drawer. Under her sweats, she found the reason she and Heather were no longer friends.

The next day, Abbie waited for Heather after school. When Heather saw Abbie, she turned her head and kept walking.

Abbie ran after her. "Heather, wait."

Moving toward Tyler's car, Heather said, "What for?"

"These." Abbie held out the folder with Heather's drawings.

"Oh, you found them." Heather didn't stop or hold out her hand. She didn't smile.

"I'm sorry." Abbie was out of breath.

Heather took the file without looking at the pictures. "I don't get it. You have everything. A nice house. A father who loves you. What's wrong with you?"

"I forgot."

Heather turned away.

"What if I wrote a letter to the board and explained?"

"You've already done plenty," Heather said.

"I'm sorry," Abbie said. "I miss you." They were standing in front of Tyler's car, where he was waiting.

"What's going on?" he said.

Heather held up the folder. "Look what Abbie found."

"I said I'm sorry. I'd still like to be friends."

Heather's voice softened. "I'm sorry about Jeremy, but I don't want to be your friend." She looked at Tyler. "Let's go."

Abbie held up her hand to wave, but no one acknowledged her, not even the wind.

That night, Abbie tried to talk to her mother, who was in front of the fire, drinking wine and reading a book called *The New You.* Abbie wondered if it was a novel. She sat in the chair across from the sofa and said, "Mom, can we talk?"

Her mother looked up. "What is it?"

"I just wanted to say I'm sorry."

"For what?"

"Being so much trouble."

Her mother closed the book and tucked the blanket around her feet.

"How's the baby?" Abbie was almost afraid to ask, afraid they'd start fighting again.

"What baby?"

"You know. The baby."

"There is no baby."

The dull tone in her mother's voice scared Abbie. *What did you do?* Abbie almost blurted. But seeing the haggard look on her mother's face she said instead, "Always wanted a brother. Or a sister."

"You did?" her mother said. "I never knew that."

"Yeah. It sucks being an only child."

Her mother smiled. "I know what you mean."

The silence was uncomfortable while they both struggled to find something to say. Finally, her mother asked, "What happened between you and Heather?"

"Stuff," Abbie said. "I wasn't much of a friend."

"Well." Her mother kicked the blanket away. "Maybe she wasn't much of a friend, either." She stood. "Going to the kitchen. Want anything?"

"No."

Abbie followed her mother into the kitchen and watched her open another bottle of wine. Her mother took a sip and said, "Care to join me?"

"No." Abbie shook her head, then reconsidered. One glass wouldn't hurt. It might help her feel better.

Abbie took a sip. It tasted awful. She took another sip, then handed the glass to her mother. "I don't know how you can drink this stuff." She looked at her mother, really looked at her, and wondered what her mother was trying so hard to forget.

*   *   *

"How's Herb doing?" Helen asked as they waited in line at the Senior Center.

"Better. Suppose it won't be long before they release him." Maxine's first time back since Herb's accident, she was enjoying chatting with everyone, not to mention anticipating Dixie's carrot cake again.

"Bet you're looking forward to that," Shirley said.

"No," Maxine said, but maybe that was a lie. The few times she'd visited Herb at Riverview, he seemed changed, more like the promising man she'd married. And then there was that floozy Lucy.

"Are you going to let him back in the house?" Helen asked.

"Suppose I have to. All banged up like that, he can't sleep in his truck."

"What about the garage?" Shirley teased.

"Or the Green Lantern," Helen added.

They took their trays to a table and sat down. The sweet potato casserole and herbed pork tasted good, not to mention the buttery, homemade dinner rolls. It made Maxine think about baking something besides cookies.

"Don't envy you," Shirley said.

"Mmhm," Maxine said with her mouth full. Since her trip, she'd given her marriage a lot of thought. She couldn't just up and desert him, not while he was still hobbling around on one foot. But she couldn't stay in the house with him either. If she had to look at his face all day long, it wouldn't be long before he was as dead as her fish.

When she finished eating, she went into the kitchen to thank Dixie for the meal. "You did a great job again," Maxine said. "I love the casserole. Not to mention the cake."

"Thanks," Dixie said. The kitchen was a mess with pots and pans waiting to be washed. The sink was full of dishes. Dixie brushed a strand of hair from her face. "Don't know anyone who needs a job, do you?"

"No," Maxine said. "But I can help." She rolled up her sleeves and filled the sink with hot water. Then she plunged her hands in and started to scrub. While Helen and Shirley played bingo, Maxine helped Dixie.

When the kitchen was clean, Dixie cut two pieces of carrot cake and motioned to a table. "Sit down and join me."

Maxine didn't have to be asked twice. She sat next to Dixie and savored each bite. They were enjoying another cup of coffee when Dixie said, "I'm serious. Ada quit, and we're short handed. We need somebody like yesterday."

Maxine considered. Linda had already cornered her, asking her to resume her knitting and crochet classes. And they could use the money.

"What would I have to do?" Maxine said.

"Come in about ten and help me start the meal. Peel potatoes, make bread, stuff like that. And keep up with the dishes."

"Every day?"

"Would that be a problem?" Dixie said.

Maxine glanced around the kitchen. "No, probably not. When do you want me to start?"

Dixie laughed. "Honey, looks like you did all ready."

Before Maxine left the Center, she went into the office and filled out some papers. She'd have to take her chances. Maybe Herb wouldn't start drinking again. Maybe this is just what she needed. If he relapsed, she could always take away his house key.

By the time Shirley dropped her off, it was midafternoon, and Maxine felt like a nap. Right after she checked the mail. Junk mail, bills, the usual. Except for the envelope addressed to her.

Maxine's pulse quickened. She didn't recognize the handwriting or the address. Maybe it was good news. She hoped it was from Su Linn.

Sitting on the sofa, she eagerly opened the letter and started to read.

Dear Maxine,

I'm sorry to have to tell you that Su Linn passed away last night peacefully in her sleep. The last two weeks have been hard. She was heavily sedated to mitigate the pain. I want you to know that the time she spent with you in Memphis was one of her happiest events. She spoke of you often and made me promise to write you if she couldn't. Last week, at her insistence, we were

going through pictures, and I found this one of her as a little girl. It made me
smile. I hope it makes you smile, too.

   Sincerely, Annie.

   Maxine set the letter aside and looked at the picture. Su Linn was
eating an apple and grinning, her two front teeth missing. It was so cute,
so endearing. Maxine smiled until she started to cry.

CHAPTER TWENTY-THREE

JUST WHEN MAXINE THOUGHT she had everything figured out, Herb had to go and get sober. He was drawing her in again, the way he did all those years ago. Sober, he still had the power to make her laugh. Unlike Maxine, who turned abrasive when stressed, Herb had a way of putting everyone at ease. Way back in high school when he was working so hard for that football scholarship and a better future, he went out of his way to make people feel important. Like her. Who was she? Just a nobody who fell in love with the wrong boy. But Herb swept her up and carried her along just the same. Always made her feel special when she'd let him. She knew exactly why Lucy was drawn to her husband.

Now, instead of avoiding Riverview, Maxine found reasons to stop by on her way to work—a new shirt she found for him on sale. Paper and pencils so he could sketch. If Helen had asked her why she visited the nursing home every day, Maxine would have denied going. But her trips were becoming more than a habit. They were becoming one of the reasons she got out of bed every morning.

She bought some nicotine patches to help her quit smoking. She even got a haircut and changed the color. Not gaudy blue like that love-struck Lucy's, but a soft auburn reminiscent of when she was younger. Instead of baggy sweats, she wore a pair of slacks that fit and a new sweater. She found Herb where she expected, in the rec room playing checkers. He was looking better every day. "Hi," she said bashfully, approached the table and pulled out a chair.

"'Afternoon, Ms. Foster. You look lovely today." He contemplated his next move. Lucy seemed flustered and made so many mistakes she lost the game.

"Ready to go again?" he teased.

"No." Maxine collected the red checkers. "It's my turn, and I'm gonna beat your ass. Move over Lucy."

Lucy left the room as if she'd eaten something horribly disagreeable, but Maxine didn't care. This was *her* husband. Lucy could find one of her own. Maxine didn't win the game, but she'd made her point. Maybe now Lucy would keep her distance until Herb was well enough to come home.

While waiting for Herb to heal and finish therapy, and because she was ashamed to have to keep begging Helen and Shirley for rides, Maxine talked Shirley into teaching her to drive. They practiced in the high school parking lot.

"Maxine," Shirley said, "you don't need my help."

"Yes, I do." She'd picked up a driver's manual at the courthouse and memorized all the answers. She wasn't worried about the written test, but she stressed over the driving test where she was told a deputy would sit beside her and watch her every move.

She was lucky Rob worked for a car dealership. They fixed Herb's truck and had in running again in no time at all. Using the pickup instead of Shirley's automatic, Maxine practiced starting and stopping. When she felt comfortable enough running through the gears, Shirley made her drive out of town where Maxine could practice on the hills, which was tricky considering the truck always wanted to slip backwards instead of idle. She tried to parallel park, which was a disaster. She had a hard time judging when to turn the wheel and more times then not ended up crooked and too far out in the street. This made them laugh until they realized laughing wouldn't help Maxine get her license.

Three days later, Maxine was ready. Shirley drove her to the courthouse and waited while Maxine took the tests. In spite of her sweaty hands and nervous stomach, Maxine passed. With her temporary driver's license in hand Maxine said, "Let's celebrate. My treat."

They celebrated at Norm's diner with chocolate cheesecake and Maxine's favorite, carrot cake.

"Well," Shirley said. "You should be proud of yourself. You did it. Waiter?" She held up her cup. "Could we have some more coffee?"

"Don't know what took me so long." Maxine said. "Guess I didn't want to give that old goat the satisfaction."

Shirley raised her eyebrow. "What do you mean?"

"When that truck was new, he washed it every weekend. Waxed and shined it until it looked like a polished apple. Wasn't touching anything that meant that much to him."

"And now?" Shirley said.

Maxine ate the last bite of her cake and licked her fork. "Now I'm tired of depending on others. Now if I want to drive that damn truck, I'm gonna."

Shirley laughed. "Good for you, Maxine. Good for you."

"Damn right." Maxine paid the bill with some of the money she earned at the Center. In no time at all she was on her way to being less of a burden.

The day they released Herb from Riverview, Maxine was ready. She was almost as excited as the day she boarded the bus for Graceland. Planning to surprise Herb, Maxine pulled in front of the entrance and left Herb's truck there while she went to get him. She thought she'd find him hovering over the checkerboard and flirting with Lucy. Instead, he was near the front entrance, his meager belongings packed in a plastic sack dangling from his hand. "What's this?" he said upon seeing the truck. "I thought Grace was picking me up."

"She has stomach problems." Maxine waited for the aide to help Herb into the passenger seat. Then she pushed the vehicle into gear and pulled away from Riverview. "Don't forget your seatbelt," she said.

Herb fumbled with his left hand.

"Oh, for Pete's sake." Maxine stopped and fastened his seatbelt. She let her body linger too close to his, and for a moment she thought he would kiss her. "Humpf," she said, pulling out into traffic.

"Look at you, Maxy." Herb whistled. "I didn't know you could drive."

She glanced at him. "There's a lot you don't know about me." She flipped the signal and turned to the right as he tried to settle into his seat, his left foot in the way.

"I guess I have the rest of my life to find out, then, don't I?" Herb winked.

Maxine smirked and kept her eyes on the road, sneaking a peek at him when he wasn't looking.

Once home, he settled in front of the TV while she put his clothes away. She could hear him changing channels. *Here we go*, she thought, dreading the blaring music announcing "Wheel of Fortune."

"What do you want for supper?" she called from the kitchen.

"I'm not hungry," he said. "Come here and watch this."

Before long, he'd be yelling at the contestants. But she sat beside him anyway while he flipped the remote. At least he was sober.

There they were, those annoying horns blaring "Wheel of Fortune's" theme song. Her shoulders tensed when Pat Sajak introduced Vanna White. Maxine stood.

Herb pushed the remote. The tick tock music from "Jeopardy!" filled the room. "See," he said. "I didn't forget."

Her shoulders relaxed. She settled beside him. He reached for her hand, and she let him.

The next day, singing "Suspicious Minds" along with Elvis on the record player, Maxine was making a cake from scratch to celebrate her birthday when Herb wandered into the kitchen. "Happy Birthday, Maxy." He put his arms around her waist and kissed her neck.

"Stop calling me that." Maxine jerked away, splattering the counter with cake batter.

"Why?" he said, surprised. "You used to like it when I called you Maxy."

"Did not. That's what Larry called me."

He stood by the doorway, just looking at her. They stared at each other a long time before he said gently, with no argument in his voice, "Larry never called you Maxy."

Wooden spoon raised as if to strike, Maxine glared, daring him to call her a liar. "Yes, he did. All the time."

"No, Maxine," Herb said. "That was me." He limped over to the record player and turned up the volume. "I bought you this record, too, for your birthday, in case you forgot."

Maxine narrowed her eyes and bent over her bowl, beating the batter as hard as she could. When she turned to apologize, he was gone.

*　　　*　　　*

If Grace had liked problematic challenges, she would have stayed and fought for her marriage. But she knew she was just wasting time so she made an appointment with an attorney.

As she combed her hair and put on makeup, Grace felt like an imposter. A brand-new suit waited on the bed. New suits were for churches and weddings. What did you wear to end your marriage?

Grace equated failing with weakness and tried to mitigate her feelings by blaming Rob. If he was home more. If he'd been more attentive. By the time she applied lipstick, Grace had convinced herself that Rob left her no choice. If he had loved her more she would have never ended up in Michael's arms, or on her way to see an attorney.

"These are your options," the attorney said later as he explained what she needed to do to obtain a divorce. Yes, he'd represent her if she'd give him a retainer.

Grace pulled out her wallet and signed a check. She shook his hand and tried to smile. It wasn't all bad. Soon she'd be single again. Maybe this time she'd find someone who would really love her.

It had been a while since Grace had visited her father. She kept putting it off, wanting to avoid another confrontation with her mother. But she wanted him to tell her she was doing the right thing. That she wasn't a coward, or running away. Grace looked at her watch. If she was lucky, her mother would be eating lunch with Helen and Shirley at the Senior Center.

She parked in front of her parents' house and debated. She could see them through the large picture window, seated around the card table her mother used to work her jigsaw puzzles. Grace leaned in closer. *What were they doing?* She didn't knock, but opened the door and stuck her head in. "Hello?"

Without looking up, her mother said, "Hello, Grace."

Grace closed the door and took off her gloves. "I came to see how Daddy's doing."

"I'm doing just fine. See?"

Grace wrapped her arms around her father's shoulders and gave him a hug. Instead of working on her mother's jigsaw puzzles—border complete and uneven pieces sorted by colors into trays—they were playing bingo.

"B-3," Maxine said.

"Bingo." Herb pushed his card to the center of the table. "Pull up a chair, Gracie, and join us."

Grace hated games. They were a waste of time. Worse, she hated losing, so to keep things safe, Grace never played. She hadn't played board games in years.

"Yes," her mother said. "Sit down and join us. I don't have any wine, but I can get you some coffee."

Grace glared at her mother. She didn't need a glass of wine. Why was her mother always so judgmental?

"Thanks, but I can't stay." Grace kissed her father. "Daddy, you're looking well. Keep up the good work." She was out the door, buttoning her coat before her mother could say goodbye.

This town is too small, Grace thought as she drove around Aspen Grove. She avoided Cedar Lane, denying that she had ever wanted to live there. She drove by the gym and almost passed it, then turned around. A good workout always made her feel better. Besides, she needed to get back in shape.

Grace didn't have workout clothes with her, but that didn't matter. The rec center always had T-shirts and sweats for sale. She found a cute pink set and was signing in when the girl at the counter said, "Hi, Grace. Have you met our new trainer Ricky?"

"Ricky." Grace extended her hand. He had a strong grip. She liked his cologne. "Nice to meet you." He was younger than the last trainer. Much more muscular. Handsome.

"What are we working on today?" he asked.

Grace smiled and patted her hair. "My abs. I hope you can show me some new techniques."

"I can," he said. "Just follow me."

Her step was lighter, her mood instantly brighter. "Lead the way."

*   *   *

Abbie couldn't focus. She forgot to hand in her homework. She neglected her appearance, letting her hair hang limp, unwashed for days. She didn't brush her teeth and refused when her parents suggested counseling, again.

She wasn't crazy, she told them. Just heartsick. And she counted the weeks like birthdays. Six weeks. Six weeks ago her life with Jeremy ended.

Every day Abbie tried to find something worthy of her attention. Even today, the sun had started out high, promising a bright adventurous day. But it was quickly turning dark and gloomy. The snow was melting. It wouldn't be long before Abbie's grandmother patrolled her yard for crocus and daffodils. At school, talk focused on the upcoming prom, something Abbie didn't want to think about.

Hoping time with her grandparents would cheer her up, Abbie stopped by their house on the way home from school. Her grandmother was in the kitchen making meatloaf while her grandfather sketched at the kitchen table. "The hardest thing about being sober," he told Abbie, "is keeping busy."

Abbie understood the need to keep busy. She leaned over his shoulder. "What are you drawing?"

"A mess," he said. Three women. Abbie recognized their faces. She took his pencil, erased a few lines and redrew the noses.

"Noses and fingers," her grandfather said. "Always gave me fits. I think that's why I stopped drawing." He held up the picture. "What do you think, Maxy?"

Her grandmother looked at the sketch. "Nice."

"How's school?" her grandfather asked.

"The same." Abbie sat beside him and doodled.

"Those kids still giving you a hard time?"

"Not so much anymore. Mostly they ignore me." She crumpled up her drawing. "They're focused on senior prom."

"Ah," he nodded. "Senior prom and all that hullabaloo." He looked at her grandmother and said, "We missed our senior prom, didn't we Maxy?"

Her grandmother stuck her head in the refrigerator and pulled out a carton of eggs.

"She's getting hard of hearing," her grandfather said with a wink. "Won't admit she wanted to go to prom, but wouldn't let me take her. I would have, too. Would have bought her the prettiest corsage. I used to do a mean Texas Two Step."

Her grandmother hit the switch, filling the kitchen with the whir of the mixer.

Abbie reached up and hugged him. "I love you, Grampa."

"Love you, too, Squirt. Grab a couple of sodas from the fridge and stay for dinner."

Abbie opened the refrigerator and handed him a soda.

"How's your mother?" her grandmother asked.

Abbie shrugged. "Okay."

"Still going through with that divorce?" her grandmother scowled.

"Yeah."

"I'm sorry, honey." Her grandmother gave her a hug.

Abbie put her arms around her grandmother's waist and kissed her cheek. "I love you, Gramma."

"Love you, too."

Later, while her grandfather was napping, Abbie's grandmother said, "So, what are you doing now to fill your days?" They were sitting at the kitchen table eating banana bread and ruining their dinner.

"Nothing."

"Anything I can do to help?"

Abbie shook her head and wished it were this easy to talk with her mother. She took another bite of bread and said. "Gramma, do you ever get over your first love? I thought Jeremy and I would be forever."

Her grandmother smiled. "Can't say that I have an answer for that. Maybe your first love isn't the person you're supposed to be with. Maybe your first love is just there to help you find your way."

"Sucks."

"Yeah," her grandmother said. "It does."

Abbie put her plate in the sink. "Thanks for the banana bread. I gotta go."

"Sure you won't stay for dinner?"

"Can't. I have some things I have to do."

Her grandmother was still waving when Abbie pulled out of the driveway.

Abbie stopped at the mall, hoping to find something special for Heather. Something that said, "I'm Sorry." Then she went to the cemetery, something she'd been doing every day for the last week. She thought she would cry again, but her eyes stayed dry as she approached Jeremy's grave. Sitting cross-legged in the snow, Abbie leaned against the back of his marker. The stone was cold and sent chills through her body, deep into her bones, and she rubbed her hands to keep them warm.

"Charles and Sheila broke up. She's dating Robbie now. I think they're going to prom." Abbie brushed a couple of dead leaves from his grave. "Wish we were going." The wind shifted. The sun cast odd shadows on the tombstones. She stood. "Bye, Jeremy. See you soon."

She'd thought about the tree all week long. Out there in the grove. The last place he'd kissed her. The first place they'd made love.

She parked in a thicket. She took her time, making sure the sun was just right. She stood in the exact place Jeremy had six weeks ago. Holding a rope, she looked up at the sky, remembering that awful night. The weatherman had predicted snow. But the sun was still shining. No fluffy flakes clouded the sky like they did the night Jeremy died.

She took the rope and tied it around the tree limb. Tugged, pulled it tight. Stood back and assessed the tree. Nothing would ever be the same again. Nothing else would ever matter.

"Jeremy?" Abbie pulled on the rope. "Are you still here?" She tilted her head and listened. "Can you see me?"

"I love you."

She walked to her car and returned with an axe and her chainsaw. She picked up the ax and swung it as hard as she could.

One.

Two.

Three.

She felt the metal grab. She worked until her shoulders ached, and her fingers bled. She hacked and chopped, chopped and hacked, but no matter how many blows Abbie delivered, she couldn't bring the tree down. Even when she tugged at the rope with all her strength—tying the rope to the fender of her car and pulling—the tree still stood, silently mocking.

Desperate to destroy the gnarled old willow, Abbie used her chainsaw and cut a ring around the trunk. "There," she said, exhausted and panting, her hands covered with blisters and blood. She might not be strong enough to chop it down, but she was smart enough to know how to kill it.

CHAPTER TWENTY-FOUR

GRACE WALKED AROUND her small apartment, adjusting the pillows on the new loveseat. It wasn't what she wanted, but it would do. For now. She found it impossible to believe the attorneys couldn't work out the settlement when it was so easy. She should get half of everything and alimony. Abbie could live with her father—Abbie would insist on it anyway—so he wouldn't have to pay child support. How hard could it be? It wasn't like she had to sit home and be mother of the year. If Abbie visited her at all, Grace suspected the visits would be limited.

In the meantime, she needed a job. Things hadn't worked out at Aspen Grove Realty. Grace didn't like answering phones and she wasn't very good at typing. But she did think she'd be good at teaching Pilates at the rec center, so she decided to apply. They gave her a trial class with six students.

"Good morning class," she said with enthusiasm. Wearing a new pink outfit, she was ready to make them sweat. "We'll start out easy and work our way up. By the end of summer, every guy in town will be asking for your number."

She sipped from a bottle of water and waited for them to roll out their mats. Recapping the bottle, she said. "Let's get started. Reach for the sky, then reach for the floor." She demonstrated, stretching and turning to the music coming from her CD player. When she had them warmed up, she made them do crunches. Ten. Twenty. Thirty. Take a sip of water. Do it again. The hour passed quickly and Grace was just getting started.

"Thursday," she said as her students left the room, groaning. "See you all Thursday." This was so much fun. She loved exercising.

But teaching two classes a week didn't earn enough to pay the rent let alone the utilities. Being married did have its advantages. Maybe next time she'd marry someone more agreeable. Someone who wasn't married to his work.

Grace looked through the classified ads. Most of the clerical jobs called for experience, which she had, but didn't care to repeat. She'd heard waitresses made good tips, but she prided herself on never having had to wait tables, and she wasn't about to start now. Looking for jobs made her depressed so she picked up her purse and went shopping.

She was trying on fragrances at the perfume counter in Macy's when she overheard two clerks. "No, I can't go. I have to work."

"Have they found anyone to replace Laurie yet?" the clerk with long hair said.

"No, and I wish they would. I'm getting tired of working double shifts."

"Excuse me," Grace interrupted. "Where can I find your manager?"

"Over there," one of the clerks pointed.

"Thank you," Grace smiled. She'd love to demonstrate perfumes. How hard could it be?

*   *   *

Maxine drummed her fingers against the vinyl chair. Unable to sit still, she paced the small room and looked out the window. It seemed too early for cherry blossoms, but there they were, ready to explode. The door opened, and she searched the doctor's face.

"We can talk while Herb gets dressed." He laid his glasses on the desk and rubbed the bridge between his eyes. "I wish I had better news."

Maxine studied his face. Herb's health had deteriorated since his accident. She had her suspicions and braced herself, hoping she was wrong.

"The tumor is attached to his liver. Surgery will kill him."

Her mouth was dry. "How long?"

He gave her a comforting smile. "A month. Maybe two. But often the will to live is stronger than the cancer. I really can't say."

There it was making everything final. Funny how life had a way of giving you everything you wanted, but not necessarily in the right order.

When Herb returned, the doctor explained their options. "Best get your affairs in order," he urged. Herb's hands trembled, and his eyes watered while Maxine continued to drum her fingers on the vinyl chair. No. Not now. She couldn't help but think about Su Linn. How fast she was gone.

Later that evening, as Maxine fixed Herb's supper, it was all she could do to control her feelings. She slammed doors and dropped spoons. She boiled the potatoes dry. Once supper was on the table, she fussed around the kitchen, scrubbing at a pot, slamming dishes into a cupboard, anything to hold in the frustration.

"Maxine." Herb put his spoon down. "Sit down and eat."

"I'm not hungry."

"Neither am I. But we gotta eat."

"Why?"

They stared at each other until his face softened. "Because that's what we do."

She sat down and picked up her fork. If he could do this, so could she. One day at a time. The potatoes were bland. Maxine reached for the rooster saltshaker, the one she had rushed to the Senior Center just last week and rescued from the spring thrift sale. Even then, she'd sensed time was running out, and she'd wanted to save everything she could to help her remember.

The next day, Maxine woke at six. Out of habit, her feet hit the floor, and she headed to the kitchen before realizing what she was doing. Herb wasn't going to work ever again. She stood for a long time, staring at her husband snoring from his side of the bed. She could have gone back to bed but went into the kitchen and made a pot of coffee. While she waited for it to brew, she looked out the kitchen window at spring teasing from the backyard. The grass was already green in places. Just yesterday, she'd spotted a crocus. Any other year, she would have her seeds spread across the kitchen table, deciding what to plant. Maxine glanced at the empty table. She'd be deciding soon enough, but she wouldn't be planning a garden.

Later that afternoon while Herb napped, Maxine gathered more items for the spring thrift sale. Books she would never read. Knick-knacks that always needed dusting. While in the cleaning mode, Maxine opened the bottom drawer to the dresser that held her yarn and crochet thread.

There, shoved in the corner, was a gold-colored cardboard box. Years ago, the box had held a corsage Larry had given her. Now it held the few mementos she kept of Larry—a stub to a movie, a love letter, a photo of them taken in a booth at Woolworth's.

Maxine picked up the picture. They were so young, so crazy in love. He was so handsome. She loved those dark brown eyes. While Herb snored in the other room, Maxine took the box into the living room, ripped it into small bits and used it to start a fire. One by one she laid the items in the flames, ending with the photo. If she wanted to remember him, all she had to do was look into her granddaughter's eyes.

*   *   *

If rage and hate for the old willow tree had been enough to cure Abbie's depression, she wouldn't have had to sit across the desk from Dr. Howard, discussing feelings she'd rather not explore. She answered his questions in monosyllables. Yes. She knew why she was there. Yes. She was filled with rage. Yes. She hated trees. At least, that one.

She was also filled with hope, but she didn't bother to go into that with Dr. Howard. If he was so smart he could figure that out by himself. She'd be seeing him every week for the next six months. Maybe longer. That's what happened when you took an axe to trees on government property. She understood fully that destroying the tree wouldn't bring Jeremy back any more than saying I'm sorry would make everything right with Heather again.

Dr. Howard looked at the clock. "Well, Abbie, we accomplished a lot today. Good work. See you next week."

With school dismissing for spring break soon, there was something Abbie had to do. She waited until after school to talk with Mr. Young. She found him in the art room going over student drawings. He was holding one of Jeremy's when she approached him. "Mr. Young? I need to tell you something."

He smiled when he saw her. "Well, hi there, Abbie. How are you doing?" He laid the drawings on his desk. One of Jeremy's was on top.

Abbie's heart still broke every time she thought of Jeremy, every time she heard his name. She tried to steady her voice. "I need to talk to you about the summer art scholarships."

Her teacher nodded. "Soon we'll be announcing the winners. What a wonderful opportunity for two lucky artists." He wasn't making this easy. What she had dreamed of, studying with Jeremy in San Francisco, was never going to happen. But maybe it could happen for Heather.

"You know Heather Winters."

"Of course I do. She's very talented. I was surprised when she didn't apply."

"She intended to," Abbie said. "But she was gone and I was supposed to turn in her application."

He was leaning against his desk, arms crossed and eyebrows raised as if he wanted to say something, but he didn't.

Abbie took a deep breath so she wouldn't wimp out. She met his eyes. "She depended on me, and I forgot. If I withdraw my application, would the board consider Heather's? I have it right here." Abbie pulled the portfolio from her backpack along with Heather's application. It had taken hours to recreate the drawings so Heather wouldn't detect the difference. She handed him the originals.

"I'm sorry." He glanced over the drawings. "The deadline is passed."

"I know. I just thought I'd ask." She started to leave, but wavered. "Would it be okay?" Her hand hovered over Jeremy's drawing.

Mr. Young nodded. "Promising young man. Terrible loss."

The drawing was amazing. One of his best. She tried not to cry. He would never become another Andy Warhol or George Bellows. She handed the drawing back to her teacher. "He was very talented."

"Yes, he was," Mr. Young said. "But so are you."

He waved Heather's portfolio at her. "I'll see what I can do."

"Thanks," Abbie said.

She'd thought all the other students had left so she was surprised to see Jessica coming down the hall. Wanting to avoid another taunting, Abbie turned to walk the other way. Then she stopped and faced Jessica. *Bring it on.*

As Jessica approached, her face twisted into a smirk. "Well," Jessica said, 'if it isn't Drab--" Her words floated above their heads toward the ceiling until there was nothing left to hear but silence. The derision in Jessica's eyes flattened. Jessica pushed by Abbie without another word.

Back at the house Abbie heard her father shuffling things in the kitchen. "How's it going?" She stepped around the boxes cluttering the floor.

"Not bad." He smiled at her from the stepladder. "Can you take this for me?"

"Sure." Abbie grabbed the waffle iron her mother never used. How long had it been since they sat around the kitchen table eating her father's strawberry waffles? So long, she couldn't remember.

Her father checked the top cupboards, then stepped down from the ladder. "How was your session with Dr. Howard?"

Abbie shrugged. "Okay."

He kissed the top of her head. "It'll get better."

She leaned into him for a hug. "I know." Her eyes welled. She went to her room and started packing. In a way, it felt right to be moving and leaving behind the bad memories. It wasn't that she wanted to avoid them. She just didn't want to think about them every day.

A lot of her clothes were going to Goodwill, especially the pink sweaters. She packed shoes and books, and a separate box for her drawings and sketches. Taking a break, she settled on the bed with her drawings, wondering if the ones she'd selected for her portfolio would have been good enough. She looked at the calendar. By this time next week, she'd know if they'd accept Heather's application. It would be great to spend the summer studying art with Heather in San Francisco. But even if that couldn't happen, things would still work out. Heather wasn't talking to her now, but someday she'd forgive her. The cute teddy bear dressed like Tyler and the "I'm Sorry" card sat on the dresser waiting to be delivered.

Saturday, Abbie stopped by her grandparent's house to drop off a box for the spring thrift sale. The box held things her mother said she didn't want anymore; her grandmother could decide what to keep and what to donate.

"Hey, Squirt," her grandfather said when she opened the door. "How's it going?"

"Fine," Abbie said with a smile.

"Come here and give an old man a hug."

Abbie put the box on the kitchen table and went over to her grandfather. His hug was warm like a fleece blanket. "Love you Grampa." He never let on that he was dying. If he could be strong, so could she.

He gave her a squeeze. "Love you, too."

"What you got there?" Her grandmother's arms were full of wood for the fire.

"Stuff for the thrift sale."

Her grandmother stacked the wood near the fireplace. "Let's take a look."

There were a lot of new clothes, tags still attached. Shoes that had never been worn. Dishes and glasses never once used. The tennis bracelet from Christmas, which Abbie claimed, fastening it on her wrist. Her mother had no trouble getting rid of things she no longer wanted, like a used husband and daughter. Good thing Abbie had her grandparents.

They set aside the box, and her grandmother said, "Pick out a prom dress yet?"

Abbie reached into her pocket and pulled out a department store flyer. "Can you help me decide? I like this one." She pointed to a dress the color of a summer sky. "But I also like this."

Her grandfather tapped on the pale yellow dress edged with white daisies. "I like this one."

"What do you think Gramma?"

Her grandmother nodded. "It'll look nice with your pretty eyes. So, what's your mother up to these days?"

"Far as I know, she just sits by the phone waiting for Ricky to call."

"Ricky?" Her grandmother frowned.

"Yeah, that guy at the gym." She mocked in her mother's voice, "'He's helping me with my abs.' She's still teaching Pilates. Oh, and she signed up for an interior design class at the college. Wants to be an interior decorator."

"She'd be good at that," her grandmother said.

"I know, right?"

They both laughed.

"Okay, that's settled. I'm on my way to buy a dress. Saturday night, Grampa. Pick you up at eight."

"Sure you want to take a broken-down old man?"

"You'll be the coolest guy there. Besides, you promised to teach me the Texas Two Step."

He smiled. "I'll be waiting with bells on."

"A tie, Grampa. No bells." She kissed him goodbye, holding back the tears that so often flooded her eyes when he was near. It wouldn't be the same as going with Jeremy, but it would be more fun than going alone. With arms around each other's waists, her grandparents waved from the porch, proving love wasn't just a word in the dictionary.

Abbie stopped by her house and picked up the bear and card. Then she drove over to Heather's. Knowing Heather, she already had a dress and was fussing with her hair. But that wouldn't stop her from helping Abbie if she wanted to. Maybe they could double date. The thought was hilarious, and Abbie couldn't stop laughing. Maybe her grandfather could teach Heather the Texas Two Step. It would be more fun than they'd had in, like ever.

It wouldn't be easy.

Bear and card in hand, Abbie knocked on the door. Getting Heather to forgive her would be hard, but then, in many ways Abbie was just like her mother. She never ran away from a challenge.

ACKNOWLEDGMENTS

Thank you to Paula Marie Coomer and all creative writing teachers who give generously of their time and encouragement. Thank you also to Trevor Dodge, Patricia Santos Marcantonio and Dixie Thomas Reale who have been at my side every step of the way.

MORE GREAT READS FROM BOOKTROPE

Biking Uphill **by Arleen Williams** (Contemporary Fiction) Sometimes the best family is the one we build ourselves. A heartwarming story of enduring friendship.

One Day in Lubbock **by Daniel Lance Wright** (Fiction) William Dillinger despises how he spent his life and has one day to find out if rekindling love can change it.

Thank You For Flying Air Zoe **by Erik Atwell** (Contemporary Women's Fiction) Realizing she needs to awaken her life's tired refrains, Zoe vows to recapture the one chapter of her life that truly mattered—her days as drummer for an all-girl garage band. Will Zoe bring the band back together and give The Flip-Flops a second chance at stardom?

Grace Unexpected **by Gale Martin** (Contemporary Romance) When her longtime boyfriend dumps her instead of proposing, Grace avows the sexless Shaker ways. She appears to be on the fast track to a marriage proposal… until secrets revealed deliver a death rattle to the Shaker Plan.

Autumn Getaway **by Jennifer Gracen** (Contemporary Romance) Newly divorced mom meets a chivalrous and handsome man at a destination wedding. Can she overcome her fears for a second chance at love?

Dove Creek **by Paula Marie Coomer** (General Fiction) After a disastrous and abusive marriage, single mother Patricia draws on her Cherokee roots for courage. She finds her place as a Public Health nurse, but she must constantly prove herself—to patients, coworkers, and family members—in her quest to improve the lives of others.

Discover more books and learn about our new approach to publishing at www.booktrope.com

CPSIA information can be obtained at www.ICGtesting.com
Printed in the USA
BVOW05s1516090914

365754BV00002B/7/P